Franklin Horton

Cover by Deranged Doctor Design

Editing by Felicia Sullivan

ISBN: 9781703731323

ALSO BY FRANKLIN HORTON

The Borrowed World Series

The Borrowed World

Ashes of the Unspeakable

Legion of Despair

No Time For Mourning

Valley of Vengeance

Switched On

The Locker Nine Series

Locker Nine

Grace Under Fire

Compound Fracture

Blood Bought

The Mad Mick Series

The Mad Mick

Masters of Mayhem

Stand-Alone Novels

Random Acts

ABOUT THE AUTHOR

Franklin Horton lives and writes in the mountains of Southwestern Virginia. He is the author of several bestselling post-apocalyptic series. You can follow him on his website at franklinhorton.com.

While you're there please sign up for his mailing list for updates, event schedule, book recommendations, and discounts.

THE UNGOVERNABLE

1

The Power Plant

WHEN BOSS SAW his own hand dropping away from his body, severed at the wrist, he knew he had to act fast or he was a dead man. He was already groping for the tourniquet on his belt as he rolled from the icy steel decking. He plunged into the dark, icy water with a heart-seizing abruptness. In his multifaceted career, Boss had taken the Army's Combat Water Survival Training. He'd also taken cold weather training with the Norwegian Army, which had required jumping through a hole cut in a frozen lake. Unfortunately, none of the techniques he'd learned in those trainings would help him at this very moment. He would die quickly unless he stemmed the free flow of blood from his wrist.

At his back, he tugged at an orange nylon tab, opening the pouch containing his tourniquet. He got a firm grip on it, knowing he was screwed if he lost the precious lifesaving device in the current. He thrust the stump above water, looped the wide tourniquet around it, and tugged the device as tight as he could. When the Velcro end was fastened securely, he twisted the capstan and locked it down, gritting his teeth against the painful pressure.

There was too much blood and too little light to know if he'd been successful or not. He'd know shortly. If he passed out and died he'd have his answer.

Containing the bleeding alone did not guarantee his survival. He'd only dealt with one of the multitude of threats trying to kill him at the moment. He would die in the frigid water if he didn't get out and get warm. There was shock to contend with, and the possibility he'd lost too much blood to function effectively. Still, quitting was not in his vocabulary.

He scanned his surroundings for both threats and an escape route, but the limited light prevented a thorough visual assessment. In a small blessing, the swift water had carried him away from the scene of the fight. He saw no one in any of the pockets of light. Neither the men he'd been fighting nor his own men.

The entire scene was surreal. Steam rose in dense clouds as floodwaters hit fiery furnaces. Emergency floodlights sliced through that steam, creating sporadic pockets of glowing fog. The scene was eerie and nightmarish. In some areas the facility lighting faded and blinked out as water shorted electrical components.

Carried by the current, Boss was slammed against a steel beam protruding from an unlit platform. The bone-jarring impact rattled him and he grunted in pain. He managed to hook a leg around the beam and stop himself. The current pulled at him but he clung tightly to the beam like a bull rider, his legs wrapped around it, a single arm upraised and held out of the water.

He started to shiver. That was okay. When the shivering stopped his heart might not be too far behind. Time was running out. So was his strength.

In the shadows he could see the beam below him was attached to a steep structure that rose high above the roiling waters. There was a raised platform over him, attached to more catwalks and platforms. He spied a familiar vertical pattern in the darkness and prayed it was a ladder. He scooted along the beam, pulling himself toward it until he was close enough to grope for it. His single frozen hand banged against smooth rungs and he locked onto it with a death grip. He unwrapped his legs from the beam and floated toward the ladder, aware that losing his grip at this point would be a death sentence. He only had the strength for this one chance.

His feet banged against the submerged rungs of the ladder and he jammed a heavy boot onto it. Once he had a secure footing he wasted no time. He had to climb immediately but the shivering and stiff muscles made it difficult. His body was going numb and he was losing dexterity. He had to focus on every single movement. He could not rush. Any mistake at this point would be fatal and Boss refused to die of weakness, of his own inability to complete the mission.

He climbed a single step at a time, getting both feet on a step before sliding his hand upward and locking it in place. He did this repeatedly until eight feet of precarious climbing got him to the level of the raised platform. He rolled onto a deck of rusty steel grating, the texture rasping and grinding against his skin. He staggered to his feet. Stillness was death. There was no time to rest. No time for anything but getting his body temp back up to where it was supposed to be.

A gust of wind blasted him and passed right through his damp clothing. He wondered what the temperature was with the wind chill. Low thirties? High twenties? Either way, it was too cold for a wet man to survive much longer.

He forced himself in the direction of the nearest shelter, some type of structure on the catwalk. He wove back and forth between the yellow safety railings like a pinball. His target was thirty or forty meters away. He stumbled several times as his legs increasingly refused to cooperate. He commanded and they tried to ignore him.

Boss hit the steel door and groped for the knob. Thank God for lever handles. He pressed down and the lock opened. The door flew open and Boss fell inside, landing on the floor. He lashed out with his foot, catching the door, and kicking it shut.

The room was heated, or at least it had been. It was warmer than the temperature outside. Boss yanked a chemical lightstick from his vest and cracked it. He could see now that three walls of the structure were mostly glass but one was covered in dials and gauges. Boss got to his knees, then stood.

He scanned the room, trying to find the source of the heat and see if he could possibly ratchet it up. He saw no ductwork, no radiator, nothing that looked like a heat source. As he moved around the room he felt a pocket of warmth near the gauges. He put the lightstick in his mouth and felt around the wall. He found heat coming from an insulated pipe running to a gauge.

Boss pulled his knife from his belt and slashed the length of insulation, tearing it away with the tip of the knife. Below it was a stainless steel line about the size of a regular residential plumbing pipe. He stuck a finger to the line and found it hot to the touch. With a furious cry he began hacking at the pipe with the heavy knife. After several vicious slashes he heard a hiss and steam sprayed from the damaged pipe. Boss stepped back and delivered a firm kick to the pipe. It bent, the opening growing wider and releasing more steam into the room.

Boss backed away from the wall, moving to the farthest reach of the steam. He hesitated, then eased himself into the warm cloud. The steam was rapidly losing its heat and did not burn him, instead enveloping him in a lifesaving mist. He dropped his knife to the floor, then hit the buckle on his battle belt, which clattered to the deck.

He struggled to wrestle his way out of the thick fleece pullover he wore as outerwear. Beneath that was a heavy skintight Under Armor compression shirt. He tried to take the garment off but it was too tight. When he managed to get it over his head and off a single arm, he allowed the damp shirt to hang loose, trapped beneath a tourniquet he had no intention of releasing.

With further difficulty, the boots, pants, and thermal underwear followed. When he was as naked as he could manage to get, he felt better. The room was heating up around him. He hadn't succumbed to blood loss. He might survive this after all. He searched the room for anything that could be used as clothing but the stark, industrial space had little to offer. Finally his eyes settled on the coal-stained rugs at the two entrances into the room. He rolled one around the lower part of his body, then the second around his torso. If the steam quit, this might still be enough heat to keep him alive until morning.

He propped himself against the wall and studied the stump of his arm. That was a bad call. Once he did, he felt a devastating wave of pain and nausea. All the limb pain he'd ignored while nearly freezing to death came rushing toward him. He reached for his pants and fished a device from a cargo pocket—an emergency satellite beacon. Even in these conditions it would trigger a rescue. There were men on the other end who owed him. Men who wanted him alive. He pressed the SOS button.

He sagged to the floor, allowing the device to slip from his fingers. The skin beneath his short hair was pressed against the cold, gritty floor. His thoughts were a flurry. How could his operation have gone so wrong? Who had done this to him? To the country?

He would find out. When he did, they would pay. He would kill them one inch at a time. He would torture them, bring them back to life, and torture them some more. They would know his suffering and worse.

A wave of dizziness hit him and he reeled. His eyes fluttered and he started to slump over. Refusing to succumb to unconsciousness, he banged the stump of his missing hand against the ground. White hot pain exploded in his head. Every nerve in his body surged as if his wiring had been overloaded with a voltage it was incapable of handling. He threw his head back and roared with an animal rage.

2

An Army chopper crew was overnighting in Oak Ridge, TN, after delivering some human cargo. They'd ferried several utility engineers and a couple of bean counters there to provide an assessment of what might be required to provide full power restoration to the Tennessee Valley area. The Crew Chief, Gordon, was awakened at 3 AM by a persistent beep from the control panel.

The interior of the chopper was not much warmer than the winter air outside. Gordon could see his breath in the pale artificial light filtering through the windshield. He groaned and slithered out of his sleeping bag. He turned on a light, slid on a headset, and tried to focus on pushing the right buttons. After a brief discussion that mostly consisted of him making affirmative, one-word responses, he slid the headset off and sagged back in his seat. He wanted to get back in his sleeping bag but that would only delay the inevitable.

He spun in his seat to wake the other two men, both pilots, but found them already sitting up expectantly.

"What's up?" Davis asked.

"We need to get in the air," Gordon said. "We have to investigate a high-priority distress beacon in the southwest Virginia area. The distress signal happens to correspond with a power plant going offline at the same location around the same time. They can't raise anyone on the radio."

There was a groan and a string of curses from Stanley, the co-pilot. "Dude, when are we getting a day off? We're running missions all day, every day. Aren't there regs about this shit?"

"I'm sure you could get a transfer," Gordon said. "You want to pull guard duty at one of those comfort camps? Would you rather sit on your ass and guard a power plant all day, every day?"

No one replied. They knew they had better duty, and considerably better living conditions, than most people did right now. They had weapons, they were eating regularly, and their odds of survival were pretty darn good. It was best to choke down any dissatisfaction and keep their mouths shut.

Their biggest complaint was they were often short-handed. They'd have preferred a four-man crew but were stuck with three now. The desertion rate was high. Men were understandably worried about their families and were slipping off at the first chance that presented itself to them. No matter what role the military found itself in during this crisis, they always seemed to be a few men short of a full complement.

Someone flipped on a light in the back and the men crawled out of their sleeping bags, shivering from the cold. They fumbled for jackets. Everyone already slept in hats and gloves. They'd been offered accommodations inside one of the buildings but the crew slept on the chopper for most of these runs outside the wire. Even within secure facilities, this was the only way to be certain they wouldn't lose fuel, gear, or even the chopper itself. They all knew there were desperate men who'd love to steal their bird and fly home to their families. None of the crew wanted to be stranded at some distant hellhole just because they decided to take a warm bed over the cold deck of a Black Hawk.

"So, no word on who the beacon belongs to?" Stanley asked. "With all the shit going on now we're supposed to be jumping just because a beacon is triggered? Are there actually people out there worth this much effort?"

Gordon shrugged. "I guess somebody thinks so. All I can say is, if they want him brought in, then somebody in the government really has a soft spot for this guy."

The crew stowed their gear and jumped into preflight checks. Though they had gear for making coffee they didn't have time to make any. Everyone lamented that fact but readied themselves as fast as possible and powered up the engines.

"Whoever this VIP is, he owes me a hot cup of coffee," Stanley grumbled, slipping on his headset.

"Quit your griping," Gordon said, taking his station.

"Here we go!" Davis called into his headset, sounding more like a cowboy leaving the chute on the back of a bucking bronco. Davis didn't particularly care where they were going. It had to be more exciting than running a shuttle service for engineers. Those dudes weren't much for conversation.

They were soon up to a speed of over one hundred and sixty miles per hour, racing across the dark hills of eastern Tennessee. They sometimes had a hard time believing this was America, where lights were usually plentiful. Not anymore. Once they left Oak Ridge, there was nothing. No flashing cell towers, no bright parking lots, no rural porch lights, and no glowing cities reflecting off the cloud cover.

In about an hour the crew closed in on the coordinates they'd been given, a small community in southwest Virginia that didn't even qualify as a town.

"What the hell?" Davis muttered. "We've been here before. This place should be lit up like a Christmas tree. They make their own power. They can waste as much as they want."

There was no power now, only sporadic pockets of illumination that likely came from battery-powered emergency lighting. It was not nearly bright enough to conduct a search by.

"I remember this place," Stanley said. "It's a bit tricky. There are transmission wires and towers all over the damn place. It's like an obstacle course. We doing this by night vision or spotlight?"

The chopper had wire strike protection, mechanical cutting blades designed to slice through wires before they had a chance to crash their aircraft, but it was not a foolproof system in tight quarters, like the river valley below them.

"Stay in position," Gordon said. He unbuckled from his seat and clipped into the tether system that would prevent him from falling out when conducting open-door operations. He shoved the door back, filling the cabin with gusts of bitter cold air, folded his night vision goggles into position, and stared below him.

"What do you see?" Stanley asked.

"Lots of water. The damn place is flooded!" Gordon announced. "The landing pad we used last time is gone. The whole valley is full of water and there's debris everywhere. I even see a few bodies snagged down there."

"Oh shit," Stanley mumbled. "I wonder what happened."

"There's a lot of snow and ice right now," Davis said. "It's possible there was an ice dam beneath a bridge somewhere downstream. With no one to report it and no one to clear it, the water could have backed up into the plant."

"That's a huge loss," Gordon said. "They had this place up and running. I remember someone saying it was ready to start transmitting power."

"Well, I don't know what the hell's going on," said Stanley, "but I hope our guy is not one of the bobbers you see down there. If so, we just wasted a lot of fuel for nothing."

"Can you tell where the signal originates from?" Gordon asked.

"Sixty-five meters from our position," Davis said. "To my ten o'clock."

In the cabin of the chopper, Gordon worked to translate those coordinates onto the terrain visible through his night vision. "There! A catwalk with some type of structure along it."

Davis activated a device on the control panel. Their chopper was equipped with Star SAFIRE II thermal imaging. A display illuminated in the cockpit. Davis worked a joystick and maneuvered the gimbal-mounted device until it was pointed at something similar to what Gordon was describing.

"Affirmative on a heat signature in the structure. There's someone in there," Davis said.

"Get me over top of them!" Gordon shouted.

“Can I activate the lights?” Stanley asked. “We don't know what's down there and I don’t want you impaled on some piece of steel like a human shish kebab."

Gordon killed his night vision and swung it out of the way. “Go for it.”

Stanley toggled a lever. The landing lights and nose-mounted searchlight burst to life, washing the scene below them in a harsh glow. The entire crew stared down at the carnage revealed by the glare of the spotlight. Dark floodwaters surged around equipment and buildings that had likely been critical to operating this facility. Stray gear and crates of supplies bobbed in eddies.

Most concerning was the number of bodies floating or snagged on the structures. Some wore snow camo, which may have provided excellent concealment before the flood, but now revealed them in stark contrast to the dark river water. Others wore bright red parkas, which Gordon remembered from the engineers they’d recently ferried to this location.

"Poor bastards." Gordon shook his head. “Get me over that structure.”

His pilots were more cautious than he was but perhaps that was the nature of pilots. Gordon had dropped into every manner of shit-storm all over the world. He’d done combat rescues, been a door gunner, dropped onto oil platforms, and retrieved shipwreck victims from cold seas. This seemed rather straightforward compared to some of the things he’d experienced.

Davis carefully positioned the chopper over top of the metal structure built into the network of scaffolding and catwalks. They could all see that it had been a good decision to use the lighting. The place was a maze of support cables, power transmission wires, and conveyor systems. It was a chopper pilot’s worst nightmare.

Stanley abandoned his seat and clipped into a tether. In the open doorway, Gordon clipped the hoist line onto his rescue harness. He was nearly ready to swing out on the hoist cable when the copilot patted him on the back. Gordon twisted around to see Stanley holding a short, suppressed weapon out to him.

"You think I'll need that?" Gordon asked.

"Do you know for certain that you won't?" Stanley countered.

Gordon conceded the point. He'd done so many rescues that he sometimes forgot he was a warrior dropping into the unknown. He slung the rifle around his neck, then wrapped both hands around the cable, and swung gently from the open door of the chopper. He dangled in the air a moment, taking in the scene below him.

"First floor, please!" he said into his microphone.

"Roger that," Stanley replied. "Going down. First floor. Shoes, housewares, and lingerie." He pushed a button on the pendant control and Gordon began a steady descent.

Despite the turmoil beneath them, there were no weather conditions complicating the operation, other than the freezing weather. As he dropped, Gordon watched the pattern of the rotor wash in the water. He readied his weapon, making certain a round was chambered and the optic was powered up.

From the cockpit, Davis made small adjustments of the aircraft's position in order to put Gordon directly where he wanted him. He skillfully dropped him as far as the catwalk railing. They'd done similar operations enough that both men knew exactly what to do. Davis paused there, allowing Gordon to hook a foot onto the yellow pipe rail and center his body where he needed to go. When Davis got the signal that Gordon was ready, he lowered him the final feet.

When Gordon's boots hit the deck, he immediately unclipped from the hoist line and dropped to a crouch, scanning for threats. He took in his surroundings through the holographic sight on his weapon. He had no indication that he was dropping into a hostile situation. While they'd seen no bullet-riddled bodies or signs of battle, they'd been wrong before. It was a dangerous world and he needed to be ready to press the trigger if things got sketchy.

When he felt it was safe, he hurried toward the pale green structure just down the catwalk from his position. According to the thermal imaging and the satellite beacon, their target was in there. The structure appeared to be a single room, perhaps a control station or office built into the superstructure around the plant. It was around twelve feet wide and sixteen feet from end to end. There was a single steel door opening onto the catwalk in front of Gordon and he expected there was one on the other side, though he couldn't see it from where he stood.

He flattened himself against the wall and tried to listen for any sound, but all he could hear was the steady pounding of rotors above him. He cautiously tried the knob and it turned in his hand. Unlocked. Normally, he would throw open the door and step clear of the opening, waiting to see if anyone took a shot at him. The problem here was that the door was the width of the catwalk. Once the door was open, there was nowhere to hide.

With his weapon shouldered, he threw open the door and rushed into the room. There was ambient illumination from the chopper lighting and an emergency fixture in the room. He went to his right, rapidly scanning the room through his optic. He checked every quadrant of the chamber, quickly taking in the sparse contents: a desk, a couple of cheap plastic chairs, and a computer. Then Gordon saw something he'd missed. He'd been looking for something higher. Something more obvious. It was a man slumped in the corner, his back against the wall.

"Hands up! Hands up!" Gordon bellowed. He needed to identify the man before he let his guard down.

A low, guttural laugh came from the dark corner. "I hope that's a fucking joke."

"No joke!" Gordon shouted, wanting to make sure that his instructions were crystal clear over the sound of the chopper. "Hands up! Identify yourself!"

Boss extracted his arms from beneath the warmth of the rugs he'd covered himself with. He raised a single hand into the air. Then he raised the stump of forearm where his other hand had been.

"Shit," Gordon uttered. He approached Boss cautiously, rifle leveled on him, and nudged the rugs off with his toe. He needed to make certain there were no weapons concealed beneath them. What he found was a naked and bloodstained man with a satellite beacon laying beside him. "Can you identify yourself?"

Boss shook his head. "That's above your paygrade, soldier. Better you don't know."

"I need a name. Some way of identifying you."

"Captain Ballou," Boss mumbled.

Gordon knew this had to be their target. "I think I found our guy," he said into his mic. "Identifies himself as Captain Ballou. He's naked, possibly hypothermic, and has suffered a traumatic amputation of the right hand."

"He's conscious?" Davis asked.

"Affirmative."

"Do you need a rescue basket?"

"Do we even have a rescue basket?"

"We have a backboard but no basket," Stanley stated.

"Forget it. Drop me a rescue harness, a blanket, and something to put this guy's gear in."

"Stand by," Stanley said.

Gordon returned to the catwalk and shielded his eyes against the spotlight. He watched the winch cable retract and then lower again, painfully slow, with a duffel bag attached. He unclipped the bag, went inside, and dumped the contents on the floor. He turned on his headlamp and began stowing the guy's gear in the bag. All he found was the emergency beacon, his clothing, and web gear. He shut the duffel and tossed it toward the door.

"I need to lift you out of here in a rescue harness. Do you have any other injuries besides the obvious? I don't want to make them worse."

"Just the hand," Boss said, sounding exhausted.

Gordon helped Boss to his feet, replacing the grimy carpets with a wool blanket. "This will be slightly drafty until we get you out of here. We've got more blankets in the chopper."

He buckled the harness securely around the blanketed man, then grabbed the duffel bag and slung it over his shoulder. He got Boss in front of him and steered him out the door and down the catwalk, his muscles going rigid at the buffeting blasts of cold air stirred up by the rotors. Gordon's weapon clanged against the pipe railing as they walked.

He delivered Boss to the waiting hoist line and clipped him in, stepped back, and signaled Stanley that it was safe to lift him. "Ground clear. Lift the load."

Boss hooked his good hand around the line, steadying himself as the hoist took up his weight and he went airborne. Gordon watched sympathetically, knowing that the nearly naked man had to be freezing. Surely that discomfort was secondary to the severed appendage, though.

The lift seemed to take forever. Gordon volleyed between watching Boss rise toward the chopper and scanning for any other survivors. All he saw were dead men bobbing in the water. Judging by the uniforms, some were part of whatever force this injured man was part of. Others appeared to be international troops, and some he couldn't identify at all.

"Got him. Load secure in aircraft," Stanley said in his headset. *"Coming back at you."*

When the hoist line was within reach, Gordon grabbed it and guided the snap fastener to his harness. He clipped the duffel bag into the hook separately, not wanting the weight to throw him off balance as he was lifted back to the chopper. His weapon he kept at hand, ready to return fire if he drew unwanted attention.

"Lift the load," Gordon said, giving a thumbs up gesture to the chopper.

The slack disappeared and his feet were lifting off the ground. He spun slowly as he soared away from the catwalk and the rising waters. He couldn't help but look at the bodies again, wondering what had caused such destruction that only one man survived.

When the hoist was fully retracted, Stanley shot out a hand and latched onto his harness, tugging Gordon toward the chopper deck. Once his feet were firmly planted, he snapped into the chopper's safety tether and removed the hoist line from his harness. Stanley shut the door.

"All personnel secure in the aircraft. Rear is ready and secure," Stanley said into his headset.

Gordon pulled a large trauma bag off the wall and dropped to his knees beside the injured man, snapping on a pair of blue nitrile gloves. He checked his patient's pulse and carefully examined the abrupt termination of Boss's arm in the harsh glow of his headlamp. Noting that blood continued to seep from the wound, he found another tourniquet in the kit and fastened it above the one Boss had self-applied, successfully stopping the trickle of blood.

"Throw me another blanket," he instructed the copilot. The man did as requested and spread it over Boss, tucking it around him to help retain as much body heat as possible in the cold interior of the chopper. Stanley unclipped from the safety tether and returned to his seat in the cockpit.

The chopper began to rise and Gordon noticed Boss's eyes widen. "You okay, Captain Ballou?"

"Yeah. Where are we going?"

"My orders were to deliver you to JBAB if I found you alive," Gordon replied, referring to Joint Base Anacostia-Bolling in southeast Washington D.C.

"Okay."

Gordon dug back into the trauma bag and came out with a plastic packet which he opened carefully. "Captain, I need to get an IV in you. You've lost a lot of blood and we've got a two and a half hour chopper ride ahead of us."

Boss nodded. "Go for it."

Gordon pulled two bags of normal saline from the trauma kit. There may have been better fluids but it was what he had. He stuck both bags inside his shirt to warm against his skin while he started the IV. Gordon was a pro at this and got the IV started quickly and efficiently despite his cold-numbed fingers, the rocking chopper, and the bad light. When he had it going he hooked up a bag of the warmed saline and hung it from a piece of rigging. He went back into the trauma kit and came out with a hard plastic case.

"What's that?" Boss asked.

"I'm going to give you something for the pain."

"What?"

"I'm going to give you something for the pain," Gordon repeated.

"What *medication*?"

"Ketamine."

When Boss didn't protest, Gordon filled a syringe from a clear glass vial. His mind wandered to the scene he'd just left. "How is it that you're the only one who survived the flood? Didn't anybody notice the rising water?"

Boss shook his head. "It wasn't flooding that killed those men. We came under insurgent attack."

Gordon stopped what he was doing. "You're kidding, right?"

Boss stared at Gordon. "Do I look like a kidder?"

Gordon considered the man. He was powerfully-built in the way of men who lived to train and fight. His body was covered with as many scars as tattoos. He was obviously a man who'd devoted his life to...what? The military? Private security? Executive protection?

Gordon shook his head. "No, I guess you don't seem like you're in the mood for humor." He injected the Ketamine then stashed the supplies back in the trauma kit.

Boss took a deep breath, released it, and Gordon could tell the meds were taking effect. Boss's breathing slowed and the tension in his face eased. It made Gordon feel good that he could ease his pain a bit. He had to be miserable. Besides the cold and the obvious injury, Gordon had no idea what other hardships the man had experienced in the last twenty-four hours. With his patient comfortable, Gordon eased back against the wall and relaxed. He would continue monitoring his patient but the hardest part of the job was over. He was rescued and stabilized.

The flight crew was quiet for most of the return trip to JBAB. That silence happened a lot after missions when the adrenaline ebbed and exhaustion began chewing at the edges of their consciousness.

They came under fire from ground positions three different times. Once was in a rural area between Roanoke and Lexington, Virginia. The second time was over the south side of Richmond. The final incident took place somewhere over the wasteland of Northern Virginia.

This was a regular occurrence anymore. By now, the crew understood that it was not the action of an enemy force. It was probably not an attempt to harm them personally or even to bring down the chopper. It was most likely some poor soul reacting out of resentment, jealous that there was someone who had fuel when they didn't, or angry that someone was able to carry out old world activities when they were not able to do so. Gordon realized that in their same predicament, angry and desperate, he may have acted the same way, firing blindly at a blip soaring across the sky.

Their patient, Boss, was quiet too. He may have been asleep or at least withdrawn to some place where the pain of his injuries was more manageable. The Ketamine seemed to have helped. Gordon administered another dose of the medication once during the flight. As he did so, he studied the man who called himself Captain Ballou. While he hadn't said much after their initial conversation, what little he *had* said gave Gordon a lot to think about.

He couldn't imagine why insurgents would flood the power plant. Power was one of the things that everybody was asking for. True, food was obviously the top request, but he figured most people would choose the restoration of power over access to fuel. With power restored they might not be able to travel but they would have many of their creature comforts back. For this modern electronic society, addicted to devices, electrical power was the civilizing factor. It was what separated them from the animals, what separated them from undeveloped nations of the world.

The situation was not straightforward. Gordon knew there was widespread dissatisfaction with the conditions the government was attaching to power restoration. They made it simple: if you wanted power, you had to turn in your guns. That simple request struck at the heart of a very divisive issue in America, a nation built on armed resistance to tyranny. Gordon hadn't heard of any power plants being destroyed, other than in the original attack, but resistance to the government's plan was not an isolated situation. Even within the ranks of the military, diminished as it was by desertion, there were voices of dissent.

Gordon didn't take either side in the issue. He was different from a lot of folks in the military. He didn't come from a military family and was not particularly a gun guy. He was a good shot but he didn't join for the toys or cutting-edge technology. He liked the physical activity, the training, and wanted to have an adventure. He eventually found that the recruiter who'd promised him a life of daily adventure had stretched the truth significantly. Military life involved a lot of waiting.

While he enjoyed his career choice, he was not overly gung-ho about a strict adherence to the constitution. He found himself to be more of a liberal than a conservative. He was patriotic, though not to the point that he would turn on those in power. He understood the conditions attached to the restoration of electrical power and he was cool with it. There were conditions to receiving federal aid and he thought that was okay too. In his mind it was simple: if you wanted to receive aid at a camp, you turned in your weapons and quit griping.

The plan, as he understood it, was that in a few months, when the comfort camp system was stabilized, restoration of power to individual communities would begin taking place with the same general conditions. Communities who disarmed would receive power and communities who refused would receive nothing. Those in charge had presented what he felt was a logical argument for this policy. They stated this requirement was about the safety of aid workers and was about maintaining order. It would prevent the theft of supplies and the emergence of a black market built around stolen supplies.

All of that sounded legit to Gordon. A lot of the people they hauled in and out voiced concerns about this plan, feeling there was a sinister underbelly behind disarming the population, and they made it clear they were against the idea. He thought some of their talk could be considered treasonous under current orders, but that wasn't his job or his problem.

"Two minutes out to JBAB," Davis said.

"Request landing lights and remind them we need a trauma team waiting on us," Gordon said.

Before the terror attacks, base personnel could light the landing zone bright enough to see from the moon. Now, with fuel and power restrictions in place, landings were conducted in much the same way they would be at bases in war zones. That didn't bother this experienced crew. They'd landed at this same base under these same conditions hundreds of times, and it was second nature to them.

When the forward momentum of the chopper slowed and they began the gradual descent to the tarmac, Boss's eyes opened. Although he didn't speak, Gordon sensed he was being watched and found Boss staring at him.

"You okay, buddy?" Gordon asked. "Anything I can do for you before we hand you over to the professionals?"

"No," Boss said. "What's your name?"

"Gordon Brown."

Boss' voice was low but did not sound weak. "I appreciate what you did back there, Gordon. You kept a cool head and you saved my ass."

Gordon shrugged. "Just another day at the office, man. It's what we do."

"I remember the folks who help me," Boss said. "You guys stationed here?"

"We are but that doesn't mean shit. We're lucky to be on-base two days a week. We pretty much live out there in Indian country."

Boss understood that was how people were referring to the central Appalachian region now. It seemed destined to return to the frontier it had been three centuries before. "Who's your commanding officer?"

Gordon rattled off the somewhat complicated command structure that he now worked under since the shit hit the fan.

"If I need a crew in the future, I may ask for you guys. You're solid."

Gordon chuckled. "Bro, you don't need to be worrying about getting back out there. You take your time and heal up. If you do request us, though, good luck getting us. All we do is turn and burn. Some days I forget what the ground feels like."

"Don't worry about that. If I ask for you, I'll get you."

That comment made Gordon re-examine his passenger, wondering again who the VIP might be. Perhaps CIA or some military hero? Some top-tier operator with valuable information? To Gordon it didn't really matter. He didn't think it was likely he'd ever see the man again. That wound to his hand would confine him to the bench for the duration of the game.

The sun was just coming up and it would be a long time before his day was over. It was impossible to imagine what it might bring. Would he be delivering supplies to some remote outpost? Was there a team of engineers somewhere on base waiting to be shuttled to a power plant somewhere in the east?

Gordon felt the touchdown and got to his feet. The pilots began the shutdown procedure, flipping switches, and powering down the engines. Gordon opened the door saw a trauma team rushing toward them with a gurney. "The cavalry is coming, Captain Ballou. You'll be fine, brother. They'll have you back on the road in no time."

In seconds the trauma team was at the open door and men were climbing aboard to stabilize the patient for transport. When he was ready, Gordon helped them gently extricate the patient and transition him to the waiting gurney. Gordon grabbed the duffel bag with Boss's gear and followed behind as the men rapidly pushed the gurney across the tarmac to a waiting ambulance. While they loaded him, Gordon handed off the bag to one of the medics.

The ambulance door was slammed in his face and the vehicle accelerated away.

3

Two Months Later
The Valley

Jim Powell wasn't comfortable with all the chatter. While folks in the valley knew of his plan to flood the power plant, he'd had some ridiculous assumption that this piece of information would remain contained within the mountain walls of their community. He had been mistaken. The heavy snow of a particularly harsh winter had melted and the weather gradually improved. Late spring settled on them and they were having more contact with people outside the valley.

Beyond ridding themselves of cabin fever, everyone was interested in seeing who had survived. Both town and country folk alike wanted to know who was around after the tough winter. Needless to say, there were fewer people coming out of the winter than had gone into it. Starvation, disease, and hypothermia had taken a toll. While for many families there was grief and a sense of hopelessness, others found strength in the fact they'd made it this far. People were moving around and talking with one another, desperate for contact. To Jim's great displeasure one of the most popular topics of conversation was the rumor that he had destroyed the local power plant.

As he saw it, he hadn't destroyed the power plant alone, nor had he conducted the mission on his own. He remembered talking with folks about it and everyone seemed to be in agreement. It was a group effort with multiple participants. Yet the catchy headline that invariably introduced this captivating gossip was something like, "Hey, did you hear Jim Powell blew up the power plant?"

The course of life in the valley had naturally formed people into tribal groups. Jim's family was part of a larger "tribe" that consisted of Hugh, Lloyd, Randi's family, and Gary's family. That was the core of the group. On the perimeter were some families that kept more to themselves like the Birds, the Weathermans, the sheriff's family, and the Wimmers. Jim didn't think it was the folks in his tribe spreading this gossip. All of them understood he didn't like talking about it. He didn't want his name associated with the destruction of the power plant because there was an inherent risk in that information being shared too freely. All it had to do was hit the wrong set of ears and someone might decide Jim was personally responsible for a death in their family.

While Jim didn't worry so much about his core group, he didn't know about the families on the fringe, nor with whom they had contact. There were a few families remaining in the valley who had no contact with Jim and his tribe at all. It was possible they'd caught wind of what he'd done and felt no obligation to keep it secret. Folks like that, with no personal relationship with Jim's family, might spread the story not out of malice but simply because it was something interesting to talk about.

Then there were the Wimmers.

Although the Wimmers were friendly with Jim, they were not really part of his tribe, mostly because their own family was large and basically formed a tribe in itself. They had extended family outside the valley with whom they had frequent contact. Jim knew they probably discussed the action he'd taken with the power plant. He assumed it wasn't malicious, and that old Mrs. Wimmer was probably proud of what Jim had done. She was likely bragging about what a brave young man he was.

She'd often said that she didn't need "the juice.", stating that she'd come into the world without it and could go out the same way. Still, in a world devoid of news and without the normal avenues of entertainment, this juicy tidbit of information was traveling far and wide at a pace Jim was unable to halt.

On a late April day when the snow was gone and the temperature hit sixty degrees, Jim, Gary, and Randi rode to town to check the state of things. Jim promised his parents he would check on their house and make sure it had fared the bad weather. It was immediately evident that the winter had changed people. Where town folks had gone into winter wary and cautious, scared of interacting with anyone outside of their families, people were almost sociable now.

It'd been a harsh winter, with lots of cold and snow, trapping people in their houses for extended periods of time. With the proliferation of all-wheel-drive and four-wheel-drive vehicles prior to the collapse, people weren't used to being stuck at home in bad weather. Sometimes they ventured out in the worst weather just to prove they could. They'd been unable to do that this winter and were desperate for conversation and human contact. They gathered in yards and shot the shit, had group bonfires and speculated on what was going on in the world beyond them. They also came out into the streets at the appearance of people riding through town to see who they were and if they brought news.

The presence of spectators made Jim nervous. Considering how they'd lost their dear friend Buddy here in town, his small group was on guard. They trusted no one. Every rider was armed to the teeth and ready to fight if it came to that. They were not soldiers but they were haggard and hateful, dangerous because it was the safest way to be. Jim was distrustful and abrasive on the best of days, and these were far from the best of days.

They'd barely gotten past the town limits when they began to pass the first houses. From a small brick ranch, a schoolteacher Jim barely knew shot up from a rocking chair on his porch and strode boldly up to him.

“What do you have against electricity?” he demanded.

Jim was taken aback. He thought the man’s name was Rick or Rob or something though wasn’t certain. It was his first contact with anyone outside of the valley in over a month and he was surprised by the man's brazenness as well as the nature of his question.

"Excuse me?"

The man put his hands on his hips, angry and animated. "I heard about your little stunt over at the power plant.”

Everything about this interaction pissed Jim off. There was just something about being accused of pulling a “little stunt” that reminded him of the way teachers had talked when he was in school. He’d had to take it then. He didn’t have to now. His face flushed with anger for the briefest moment and then it subsided, turning to a chilling calm.

"Just what did you hear?" Jim asked.

"You know what you did," the teacher spat. "Blew up the place, didn’t you? I hope you're happy."

More teacher talk, telling Jim he knew what he did, not waiting for an explanation. God, how Jim hated this kind of interrogation. "Just where did you hear that I blew something up?"

"Where I heard it is none of your damn business."

A subtle shift of Jim’s hand raised his rifle until the barrel was leveled at the teacher’s face. "If my name is in your mouth it’s my damn business."

The teacher gave a quick look around, suddenly realizing that it had perhaps been poor judgment to confront a violent man with no witnesses. The nature of the accusation alone implied that Jim might be dangerous, at a minimum. Perhaps even unhinged. The fact that there was no safety net settled on the teacher and made him think about the consequences of his actions. There was no 9-1-1, no police, and no social media to post the interaction to. He was utterly alone.

"Well, I...well I...don't know,” the teacher spluttered. “Somebody in town. There were people talking about it and I overheard them." The man gave a stiff, inappropriate laugh. “The whole thing may have all been a simple misunderstanding.”

Jim stared at the man without moving his gun barrel. “It’s a big misunderstanding, neighbor. How about you do me a favor and don't repeat that nugget of gossip. It's not true and you can probably tell I don't like people talking about me. In fact, it downright irritates me."

The man scowled and found a second, vitriolic wind. “Well, I don’t know how you intend to shut it down. It's all anybody is talking about. They don't understand what kind of sick bastard doesn’t want the lights back on. And just what are you going to do anyway? Kill everybody who talks about it? That’s a lot of killing."

Jim flicked the safety off with his thumb. It was a world without cars, without blaring radios, and without the insular cocoon provided by earbuds. The metallic click of the safety lever was clearly audible, its meaning obvious even to the most inept. “If it’s a big job, all that killing, I should probably get started and not waste any time. Should I start with you?”

The man didn’t answer. His common sense was battling with his sense of outrage.

Jim curled his finger around the trigger. “I don’t know if you can see it or not but I’m resting my finger right on the trigger. All the training I’ve had says not to do that unless you’re ready to kill what’s in front of you.”

The man shook his head quickly. "You...don't have to do that. I'll keep my mouth shut."

Jim cleared his throat. "That’s not good enough after the *little stunt* you pulled.”

The teacher frowned and Jim smiled.

“See what I did there? I turned your own words against you. How does that feel?”

The teacher had no response.

“What you’re going to do is go one step further. You’re not just going to keep your mouth shut, neighbor. If you hear my name being discussed again, you’re going to tell folks you heard that story wasn't true. You heard it was a bunch of bullshit somebody made up."

The man looked doubtful. "I can try."

"You do that. You try real hard." Jim withdrew his finger from the trigger guard and flicked the safety back on. He nudged his horse forward and rode away, twisting in the saddle to keep the man in his view until they were a good distance away. The ignoramus had screwed up a beautiful day. Jim hated people who could ruin a good day. There was a special place in hell for them. Who was he kidding? He just hated people.

A bit further on they passed by the supercenter, the vast shopping center that had been the scene of much conflict. It was where Jim had been taken prisoner by rogue cops. It was where Jim had met back up with Hugh, a childhood friend who'd joined Jim's group as a radio operator and extra gun. It was the same place where Jim's long-time coworker Alice had died after her own perilous journey back from Richmond.

A lot of men had been killed at the supercenter, and a lot of women and children had wintered there after losing their husbands. Jim was certain it had been a miserable experience for them. This was one place where he expected hostility and resentment. He was wary long before they reached the parking lots.

He was surprised to find that the parking lot had become an open-air market of sorts. Cobbled together tables of scrap wood and blankets spread on the asphalt displayed the meager items that a handful of vendors wished to barter. There were clothes, shoes, baby items, knives and tools, cookware, and camping gear. Everyone seemed to be searching for food, medicine, and water filters, all of which were in short supply.

As the clattering of their horses' hooves became audible over the din of conversation, people turned their way. They quit their haggling and watched the approaching riders with hostile, narrowed eyes.

"People are sure throwing a lot of shitty glances our way," Randi said. "Must be because we have Prince Charming with us. He has that effect on people."

"Now I'm giving you a shitty look too," Jim said. "Can you feel it?"

Randi ignored him.

"Probably the horses," Gary said. "They resent that we have transportation."

"I hope that's what it is," Jim muttered. "I'm tired of arguing with folks. You reach a point where it's easier to just kill somebody than debate with them. I'm about there."

"Let's not get carried away," Gary said. "Debate is healthy. Murder is not."

"We'll know by the end of the day if that's true or not," Jim said. "If debate leads to a bullet in the brain bucket then I'd wager it's not so healthy."

"Remind me not to argue with you," Randi said. "I'd hate to get killed for putting in my two cents."

"You never just put in your two cents. It's always more like a buck and a quarter. Besides, you're safe," Jim said. "You have privileged status."

Randi shot him a withering look. "Oh, I feel privileged every time I'm around you. You have a way of making people feel special."

Jim ignored her and stared at the crowd as they stared at him. He spotted a woman he'd gone to high school with in the small group of traders. She lived in town, but as far as he knew she wasn't one of the folks living at the supercenter. He hoped she didn't recognize him but she did. It was too late. He looked away, and when he gazed back in her direction she was staring right at him.

"That you, Jim Powell?" she asked.

Jim gave her a weak smile and a puny wave. He'd probably have been better off not smiling. His smiles always came out resembling a pained grimace. "How you doing, Jenny?"

She put her hands on her hip and cocked her head at him. "I'd sure as hell be doing a lot better if I had power."

Jim tried to give a friendly chuckle but it sounded more like a tubercular throat-clearing. He'd never mastered those friendly mannerisms most people aren't even aware they perform. "Yeah, I'm sure we'd all be better off with a little power. I miss a cold beer."

His attempt at humor, at redirection, fell flat.

"If you wanted the juice back on, why the hell did you go and blow up the plant? I always knew you were crazy but I never figured you for selfish. Now you've gone and ruined things for the rest of us. Maybe you don't want power but some of us needed it. We all know folks who have died because they didn't have it. That's on you."

"Well shit," Jim muttered, his jaw clenching. He shot Randi and Gary a bitter look, like they should have known this was going to happen.

"That all you got to say for yourself?" Jenny pressed.

"That was a nice speech you just gave. You running for some kind of office?"

Jenny ignored Jim's jab. "So you don't deny it?" She glanced around at the crowd, trying to muster some support. "You folks heard that. He ain't denying it."

"I *am* denying it, damn it," Jim growled, losing his cool. "I don't know where the rumor came from but it needs to stop *right now*." He scanned the crowd and noticed everyone, vendor and customer alike, had stopped what they were doing and were staring at him intently. He saw anger in some of their eyes, confusion in others.

"Oh, I'd say it's true all right," Jenny went on. "The people who told me wouldn't lie about it. They said you admitted to it and now we won't have any power, any comfort camps, and no government assistance at all. They said that's what you wanted all along. People are dying and it's all your fault."

Jim was pissed but it didn't seem prudent to threaten Jenny in front of all these people like he had the teacher a short while ago. Word would travel. With the way stories inflated as they passed between people, there was no telling what the story would become by the end of the day. People would claim he'd killed her to silence her.

"Jenny, you're always accusing someone of something. You're always saying you've been wronged by the world. Everything that happens to you is someone else's fault. Best I recall, it was somebody else's fault you got knocked up the summer after high school. It was somebody else's fault you could never stay with a job or keep a husband for very long. Every damn thing in your life is somebody else's fault. Maybe you're just wanting to blame me for something that isn't my fault either."

Jenny's mouth stretched tight at having her dirty laundry flung out in the yard. "You can't lie your way out of this, Jim. The truth is out there. They ought to string your ass up for murder. You're killing people. That's what you're doing."

"Let's go," Jim said to his companions. "My ugly is about to come out." Jim nudged his horse forward and rode off, having lost his taste for going into town. He was ready to turn around and go home.

"You can't run from the truth!" Jenny called behind him.

"Sounds like word has traveled," Gary said when they were out of range of the supercenter.

"I don't get it," Jim grumbled, shaking his head. "You'd think the people that know what really happened would be aware this was sensitive information. They should know not to talk about it."

"Would they, though?" Randi asked. "You never told them that specifically. People are used to gossiping. They're used to talking. They have less to talk about these days. This was big news and I'm sure the first people to share it didn't think they were going to harm you in any way. They were probably just excited because they had something to talk about."

"Clearly word of this could harm me and my family," Jim said as if it was the most obvious thing in the world. "This type of gossip is exactly what I was afraid of. People who don't understand the big picture, who don't understand our motivations for doing what we did, are hostile. They resent me personally because they think I've condemned them to the dark ages."

"For some people, life *is* that simple," Gary said. "They're not concerned about the other issues. They don't care about giving up their guns, or even their freedom, for food and power. Not everyone sees this issue the same way we did."

"The question is what, if anything, can we do about it at this point? Is it too late?" Randi said. "Should we start a rumor of our own?"

Gary chuckled. "That might be preferable to Jim actually killing everyone who repeats the story. If he has to kill every gossip in this town, even he might eventually run out of ammo."

Jim shook his head. "I won't run out of ammo. Trust me."

"Either way, killing an entire town to shut down a rumor is not effective crisis management. It falls in the category of..." Gary struggled to find the correct word.

“Psychopathic?” Randi suggested.

Jim let out a deep breath. Some days he longed to ride off into the mountains by himself and never come back. Perhaps one day he would. "So what would be an appropriate counter rumor?"

"Maybe we go with natural event,” Gary offered. “An act of God. Rockslides are frequent in the winter. We start a rumor that there was a rockslide that dammed the river and flooded the power plant.”

Jim shrugged. "We could say there was an ice dam at a bridge and it caused the water to back up. It happens.”

"Eh, people might've heard the explosion," Randi said. "That was a serious blast. People probably felt it for miles. I think we go with something about an explosion. A gas leak at the plant."

"We could put all those stories into play," Jim said. "The more stories we have floating around, the more confusion it will cause. People won’t know what to believe."

"That's a solid strategy," Gary agreed. "We need to get more people spreading those stories. If they're coming out of your mouth it just sounds like you're trying to cover your own ass. You have a credibility problem."

Jim snarled, kicked his horse, and rode off. He was done talking.

4

Jim had soured on the bitter taste of town already. He'd never liked it, even before the collapse, but he'd promised his parents he would check on their house. For the rest of the trip he was determined to steer away from groups of people, even those along their route who boldly hailed them and waved them over. Jim had no more interest in fielding the rumors about his role in what had happened at the power plant.

He experienced a rush of relief at finding his parents' house in good condition. They would rest easier knowing that their old life, their belongings, were undisturbed and exactly as they'd left them. He rode around the house first, checking for obvious things such as broken windows, signs of forced entry, or footprints on the wet ground. He rode to the outbuildings and found them locked. From the outside everything was exactly as they'd left it last time they were here.

He dug out his key and entered through the front door. Out of habit, he felt a sense of urgency to turn off the alarm system before it sounded then reminded himself it hadn't worked since last summer. The house was cold and smelled vacant, a combination of dampness and stale, musty air. Yet beneath it all, it smelled like home.

Gary and Randi gave him space, watching from the driveway, giving him a moment to emotionally acclimate. He needed that moment. Going from room to room he was bombarded by memories in a way he was wholly unprepared for. His experience in town that morning left him angry and pissed off. It had thrown him off. Perhaps that left him vulnerable, but for whatever reason he couldn't help but surrender to the current of memories tugging at him.

There were thousands of snapshots flashing through his brain, moments from growing up in this house, memories of the life events he'd experienced there. He was completely overwhelmed. He saw himself sitting in the floor as a child while his family watched *The Waltons* on television together. He remembered stretching the cord from the wall phone into the next room so he could have a private conversation. He remembered fried chicken, mashed potatoes, and green beans. He remembered being lectured about his grades and talking about more serious topics, like college, as he got older. It was dizzying. Disorienting.

Jim shook his head, as if that simple gesture could dislodge the thoughts and stop the flow. He took off his pack and put a few pictures in there. He searched the house for other mementos his parents might appreciate. He did that every time he visited their home, taking back things that would make them feel more comfortable in their new home and their new life. It occurred to him that this might be the last life they knew. They may never get to move back into their home. The thought saddened him but his was only one small sadness in a world full of them.

Although he wasn't certain how long he spent going through the house, when he went downstairs he found Gary and Randi sitting at the kitchen table eating lunches they'd packed that morning.

"Sit down. Eat," Randi said. "You look like you need to chill out."

Jim pulled out a chair. "A beer would be nice. Got any?"

"Nope," Randi replied. "If I did, I'd share."

She was exactly right; he did need to chill out. Talking about beer made him realize he felt like a can of beer that had been shaken too hard. He felt ready to explode and spew his contents on the world. It would probably suck for both parties. Him and the world.

Jim glanced around the kitchen at the familiar objects. Many of these things he'd grown up with. When he looked at the people he was seated with, it felt strange. Although they were his friends, they were out of place. This was his parents' house and just being here without them felt wrong. The entire world was out of context.

He dug his lunch from his pack, frowned at it, and shoved it back in. He'd lost his appetite. He pushed back from the table and stood. "I'm going to poke around outside. You guys take your time."

He went outside and sat on the front steps, taking in the familiar yard with its birdhouses, benches, and decorations. Crocuses and daffodils rose through the damp soil in flowerbeds. Jim was caught in an odd limbo between the new life he shared with people like Randi and Gary and the old life he'd shared in this home with his parents.

Being in there was overwhelming. He couldn't take another minute of it. From his seat at the kitchen table he could see family photos along the wall and the sight of those injected memories into his head like a syringe of adrenaline. The last thing he wanted was the surge of emotion created by a forced journey down memory lane. He hadn't been able to stop staring at those pictures, thinking of how no one could have seen this coming. Not in any of those dozens of pictures was there any hint that the world may one day come to this.

When those family photos were taken, the entirety of Jim's world had been their family and their house. It was the very definition of a home. It had been a good life to grow up there, where he ventured out into the world each day with the knowledge there was a safe, comfortable place waiting on him at the end. He understood that not everyone in the world had that same experience of home but he could not let that awareness diminish his own experience. He would not choose to feel miserable just because others had been.

After he was married and had kids he tried to create that same experience for his own family. He, his wife, and his children had left home each morning with the knowledge that they had a safe place waiting on them at the end of the day. They did things as a family and built a life of memories and experiences.

The lines of what counted as family were blurred now. The group he shared his days with was much larger than his family or even his extended family had been. Beyond his wife and kids, beyond his parents, there was Randi and her family, Gary and his family, Alice's son Charlie, Jim's friend Hugh, and his friend Lloyd. There were other families in the valley that they dealt with each day but this was the core group. They were his new family, his new tribe.

The situation he found himself in made him shake his head. He belonged to a tribe and he was the de facto leader. What the hell?

Leadership sat odd with him, like eating an entire pizza only to have it reassemble into a large circle inside your stomach. By nature Jim was private and antisocial. He didn't like being around groups of people. He closely guarded his privacy. He didn't like people dropping in on him. He didn't like talking on the phone.

Now his family had changed. It had grown to include people he interacted with every day out of necessity. There were so many roles and responsibilities, so much work to do, that his family couldn't do it alone. There was security, basic things like providing wood for heat and taking care of their growing menagerie of animals, and there was food, always food, and the need for more of it. The world had changed and Jim's surroundings had changed with it. Like it or not, he was going to have to change too.

An idea struck him and he went to one of the outbuildings, digging around until he found an old paint can full of leftover seed packets. He returned to the house and was sitting on the sidewalk going through the can when Randi and Gary came out.

“Whatcha doing?” Randi asked.

“Thinking about spring planting,” Jim answered, holding up a pack of seeds.

"I'm excited about that," Randi said. "I've always enjoyed having a garden and I'm good at it. That's a place I can contribute."

“You've always contributed," Jim said. "That's never been an issue.

Of course sometimes all you contribute is sarcastic, smartass comments."

Randi shrugged. "Sometimes that's exactly what the situation calls for. Besides gardening, that's probably my other superpower. Being a smartass."

"Being able to shoot well is my only superpower," Gary offered.

"Not true," Randi stated. "You're the voice of reason sometimes. Don't underestimate the value of that. There's probably hundreds of people that are only alive now because of you talking Jim off the trigger."

Jim snorted. "You make me sound like a psycho."

"If the shoe fits."

Jim shot Randi a dirty look. "I'm *not* a psycho. I'm a... problem solver."

"Oh, I don't mean it in a bad way," Randi said.

"How can you call somebody a psycho in a good way?"

Randi sighed dramatically. "Okay, you're not a psycho, you big baby. But you are quick to want a *permanent* resolution to conflict."

"As I said, I'm a problem solver."

"He's a troubleshooter," Gary suggested.

Jim smiled. "Yeah, Randi, I'm a troubleshooter. When I see trouble, I shoot it."

"You have clearly demonstrated that," Randi replied.

"It's a philosophy instilled in me by my late grandfather. You never leave an enemy the opportunity to come back and settle things when he may have the upper hand. You take firm, decisive action when you can."

Gary appeared concerned. "So you intend to rid the world of all your enemies? Permanently?"

"Yeah. That a problem?"

Randi and Gary exchanged a worried look.

Jim sensed a conspiracy brewing. "Well? Is it?"

"No," Randi assured him. "It's just fine. You keep being you."

"Now you're just patronizing me," Jim snarled.

"Maybe she's scared *not* to patronize you," Gary said. "Especially since pissing you off appears to shorten a person's lifespan."

AT JIM'S INSISTENCE, they took a longer route out of town when they headed back to the valley. Knowing Jim was on edge, neither Randi nor Gary complained. They didn't want to have to deal with the collateral damage of him shooting somebody on the way home. There was another valley running behind town that eventually connected with Jim's valley. While it was a long ride through the country, whatever they ran into had to beat the hell out of dealing with the townspeople.

They walked their horses slowly, weapons at the ready. Jim's horse was loaded down with his pack and a couple of pillowcases containing things picked up at his parents' house.

"You look like something out of the old West," Gary said. "Kind of like a guy who's been stuck in the hills too long. A fur trapper taking hides to town."

Jim flashed a grin. "Sometimes I wish I was in the hills."

"I can see that, Josey Wales," Gary replied in the voice of some Western character actor.

Less than an hour into their ride Jim reined his horse to a stop in front of the burned out shell of a house. Most of the structure had collapsed inward, leaving the masonry portions behind with a few charred timbers that reached for the sky like pleading, scratching fingers.

"What's this?" Randi asked. "Some of your handiwork?"

Jim shook his head. ""You remember Buddy's story about killing those men who overdosed his daughter?"

The expressions on both Randi's and Gary's faces indicated that awareness had slammed home like the bolt of a rifle. They knew exactly what this place was. It was the house where the man lived. The one who had overdosed Buddy's daughter and dumped her body. It was the house where Buddy had come in those first days of the collapse to dispense justice.

Randi let loose with a powerful, snarling scream that sent chills down Jim's spine.

"What the fuck, Randi?" he asked. "You scared the shit out of me."

"I said I wouldn't cry anymore, dammit. If I'm not going to cry, I've got to hate that much harder."

Jim turned away from her and back to the monument to a father's revenge. A charred memorial to an attempt to right a wrong that could never be corrected. The dead couldn't be brought back. All that was accomplished was the venting of hate in hopes it would set the world right. It never worked.

Jim swallowed. "I miss Buddy too."

"I think the old guy was ready to go," Randi said. "Some days he was as much in his wife and daughter's world as he was in ours. He talked to them and I suspect they talked back. That didn't make it any easier..." She trailed off, clearly reliving the way they'd lost him.

Jim started riding and the others fell in behind him. A bit further along the road they came to a truck and Jim wondered if it was the old man's. He said he'd abandoned it here, eventually ending up being picked up by Lloyd. Curiosity tugged at Jim and he wanted to get off his horse to look for any clues that this was Buddy's truck, ultimately deciding he'd rather not know.

The truck had been vandalized. All of the windows were broken out and the doors hung open. The glove compartment lay open, the contents strewn about the floor. A harsh winter of rain and snow had matted them into a pulpy amalgamation.

They rode in silence after that, the ghost of Buddy heavy upon them. While the dark turn of their thoughts began with those memories of Buddy, they blossomed into a grim memory of all that had happened to them over the winter. All of them wanted this to be the beginning of better times. For the summer to be a period of growing and recovery, with harvest and happiness at the end. No one could see that happiness in the distance right now, no matter how hard they looked.

They anticipated the worst. They each felt within them that the bad things that had happened were not the last of the bad things. The loss they'd experienced would not be the final loss. Hardship and deprivation would continue to shape the land for as far as they could see.

5

J*oint Base Anacostia-Bolling (JBAB)*

Boss sat in a white plastic chair at a white plastic table in an empty white lunchroom. He scowled at the wall, a thick mug of cold coffee ignored in front of him. He wore short sleeves which glaringly revealed the difference between the two arms resting on the table in front of him. He stared at the angry pink stump with loathing and a seething anger. He tapped it on the table, first one way then another, provoking a pinching sensation and flares of sharp pain.

When the pain sensation proved inadequate to distract him from the turmoil inside of him he banged harder. As the intensity of his blows against the table increased, the pain grew inside him too, pushing aside everything else. When he found the perfect combination of angle and power, agony shot through his entire body. It was like being skewered by a burning arrow. Boss shoved himself back from the table and pitched forward, cradling his wounded arm while resting his head on the table.

"You're gonna reinjure that if you're not careful. It's too soon to be banging it around."

Boss snapped his head up in the direction of the voice, his face screwed into a mask of pain and rage. His eyes flared with hatred and he wanted to hurt someone. Not just hurt them but beat them to a bloody, lifeless pulp. Anyone would do. Since he couldn't injure the person actually responsible for his injury, he'd have to take it out on someone else.

The man who'd addressed him showed no fear. He'd been Boss's handler for several years and was perhaps the one man in the world who could speak honestly with him without fear of consequences. The two had a long history. Owen was not just a handler, but the closest thing Boss had to a friend. The pair had done missions together in every sandbox, shithole, and jungle between Musa Qala and Matagalpa. They'd put boots on the ground, spilled blood, and ate dust. That forged a respect between the two men that talking football at the watercooler just couldn't match.

Boss didn't respect many men in administrative positions. Usually he despised them. Owen had walked the walk. He had the gear and knew how to use it. He'd pulled the trigger and seen the consequences of doing so. That Owen had ended up running missions instead of performing them was almost a fluke, a reflection of a minute difference in each man's personality. One had a slight preference toward the chess game of strategy, the other toward hitting the ground, charging an obstacle, and making it happen.

When the rage cooled, Boss addressed his friend. "If I'm going live with this fucking thing I need to be able to use it. I need to be able to work out and handle weapons. I need to be able to fight. If I can't put it to work for me, if I have to baby it, I might as well pack my shit and go home."

"You'll be able to use it. It just takes time," Owen said. "People run triathlons and climb Everest after worse injuries. You'll adapt, but if you jam that bone through your stump there will probably be more surgeries and a longer recovery. You know that 'P word' you struggle with?"

"Patience?"

"Yeah, that's the one. You need to draw on it."

"I have to train," Boss growled.

"Then train," Owen said, throwing his hands up as if it was the most obvious thing in the world. "What you're doing now is not training. You're torturing yourself. There's a lot you could do to maintain your conditioning besides pounding your stump on a table just to feel it hurt. That's messed up."

Boss knew Owen was right, the comment reminding him that he was not talking to a pencil pusher. He was talking to a friend, a man who knew him as well as he knew himself. Owen knew exactly what Boss was doing and called him on it.

Boss stood up from the table and reached to pick up his coffee cup. He extended his right hand by reflex only to find himself nudging the coffee cup with a useless stump that could not close around it. Although he was not embarrassed by the futile gesture it rekindled his fury.

"See, this is exactly the kind of shit that will get me killed on a job. I have forty-three years of reflexes making me throw out my right hand without even thinking. Now I need to retrain those reflexes. I need my left hand to move without a thought. If I need to consciously force that hand into action I'll never be able to fight and lead operations. It's that simple."

Owen went to the stainless steel coffee urn and filled a mug of coffee for himself. He smelled it, frowned with disapproval, but took a sip anyway.

"Forget to stop at Starbucks on the ride in?" Boss quipped.

Owen chuckled. "They make this stuff superhot so you can't taste how bad it is. It scalds the buds."

Boss reached for his own cup, making sure he used his left hand this time. The motion was awkward, alien. The coffee sloshed around and threatened to spill. Owen watched without judgment.

"You're only on the sidelines if you put yourself there, Boss.

There's a lot you could be doing for the cause. There is work to be done."

Boss gave a laugh that was both sarcastic and dismissive. "Is this the coach telling the player with the trashed knee that his life isn't over? That I can always coach college ball or become a physical therapist?"

Owen shook his head. "Not at all. But I'm not going to let you sit here and feel sorry for yourself while you're on the payroll. There's work to be done and until you're released to active duty you can be running operations from the war room. You can put those years of experience to work helping me out."

"Well, I've already demonstrated I suck at carrying coffee. Plus I can only bring one cup at a time. You may need to find someone else unless I can get a serving tray attachment for my stump."

Owen shook his head in disappointment. "That attitude isn't befitting of you. You're better than that. It's not a request, it's an order. You can help out even if your heart isn't in it."

Owen turned on his heel to leave the room. He'd said all he could say.

"Owen!"

Owen paused.

Boss approached him, his eyes portraying an urgency that was outside of his normally cool demeanor. "I want the bastards who did this. They killed my team and they took my hand. All our work staffing and repairing that facility was wasted. Someone has to pay for that."

"We're writing off central Appalachia for now. In fact, folks in the war room have taken to calling it Appalachiastan. It's not worth the trouble. Hillbillies have always been difficult to manage even in the best of times. They never want to play ball, and they always overreact when they get mad. This won't be the first time in history that they've shot themselves in the foot out of stubbornness. They've delayed power restoration to their area for years and I doubt they even care. Who knows if they're even smart enough to put the pieces together?"

Boss was shocked. "You're writing the entire region off?"

"Yeah," Owen replied. "We've decided to focus our efforts on the dams operated by the Tennessee Valley Authority and those in central Virginia. Those hydroelectric facilities not damaged in the terror attack may be easier to get up and running. No coal or hillbillies required."

"What about insurgent activity?"

Owen shrugged. "It exists but it's manageable. Few other regions have experienced anything like what you saw in Southwest Virginia. Most regions are more...*civilized*."

Boss shook his head, angry but desperate to convey his need. "Owen, this is me talking. I'm your friend. You understand me and you understand vengeance. I lost a team and I owe them this. I need the people responsible."

"You don't even know who hit that facility. It could take months of intelligence gathering to even figure out who to kill. I might be able to go along with this, off the books, if you knew the target and simply needed resources to close the deal. That's not the case. You're operating in a vacuum, trying to find a needle in a haystack. You don't even have the most basic idea of where to start."

"I could get that information!" Boss insisted, his voice rising.

"I've got no doubt, but you don't have it now," Owen said. "But going beyond your personal need for vengeance, is this an appropriate use of resources? Is it even worth the effort?"

"Would you think it was worth the effort if it was your men? Your *hand*?" Boss demanded, spittle flying from his mouth.

"I would feel exactly like you do now," Owen admitted.

"Then turn me loose to do what needs done," Boss pleaded. "Don't make me beg here."

"I can't spare you now, Boss. Working on my team here, you can produce tangible results. You can do some good. You see things in an entirely different way than I do. I can't lose you on some futile mission to avenge your lost hand. That's final."

Those words stunned Boss and he gave Owen a glare. "Final?"

Owen nodded.

"You're actually giving me fucking orders?"

"You give me no choice," Owen said. "I want you in the war room at oh-seven-hundred hours." He left the room.

Boss closed his powerful hand around the coffee mug and squeezed. He stopped short of shattering it, not wanting to take a chance on damaging the function of his one good hand. Needing an immediate purge of his rage, Boss drew back and shattered the mug against the wall. Coffee splashed across it and streamed down in vertical rivulets. Boss stalked from the room.

He went straight to his quarters. He'd had several posts over the years but had been at JBAB for the last three. Aside from a storage unit outside the city, everything he owned in the world was in his small apartment on the base. Once at his quarters he found a Gerber multitool, opened it to the screwdriver blade, and went to an outlet on the living room wall. He sat in front of it and carefully unscrewed the cover plate.

The receptacle inside was a dummy. If he'd plugged something into it, it wouldn't have worked. Boss unscrewed it and set it to the side. He'd capped off the wires and pushed them out of the way to allow him to hide a few things he didn't want anyone finding. The junction box inside the wall was blue plastic. Boss had cut the bottom out of it and a piece of paracord disappeared through the hole, tied off to one of the capped wires.

He pulled the cord and a velvet Crown Royal whiskey bag appeared. It took some maneuvering to squeeze the heavy, awkward bag through the opening, especially with one hand. He dumped the contents of the bag on the carpet in front of him. Shiny gold Krugerrands spilled out. Boss raked his fingers through them. There were fifty of them and he'd never used a single one.

Several years ago he'd gone on an operation in Syria to eliminate a man known to be financing terrorist activity. Boss had tracked him to Rashidiyah, a Syrian district roughly northwest of Baghdad. He intercepted him in the process of delivering funds to two of his beneficiaries. Covered by the sound of goat bells, Boss approached through the moonlight and killed the two guards outside. When he was done inside the stone hut, three more men lay dead. The air was thick with smoke from his gunfire but Boss could make out the gleam of spilled gold on the floor.

If he left the money it would only be used in the war against America. Before anyone came upon the scene and interrupted him, and without thinking a lot about it, he stashed the gold in a goatskin pouch and pocketed it. On his way out, he tossed a grenade into the hut and double-timed it to his extraction point. Although he'd never done anything like that before, in his line of work there might be an occasion where it became important to disappear off the face of the Earth. A handful of gold coins could go a long way toward making that happen.

Intent on running a mission without the backing of the civilian and military authorities, Boss knew the only thing that motivated people beyond food and security was greed. If he wanted things done he would need to grease some wheels. It worked in every warzone and third-world dive he'd ever shown his face in. It would work here.

6

J*oint Base Anacostia-Bolling (JBAB)*

Boss didn't get much sleep that night but he did a lot of thinking. He was practical and relied on having a well thought-out plan before he acted. He was nothing if not disciplined. He understood that his own personal ambitions could not interfere with the larger course of action determined by those in power. In other words, he couldn't try to win the battle at the cost of losing the war. He was a professional after all. His desire to scorch southwest Virginia to a blackened stubble would not prevent him from doing what his country needed him to do.

He thought about his future on a personal level too. The problem of reflexively relying on his right hand persisted. He understood it was only natural in this situation, but that didn't make it any less awkward. It had taken him years to become proficient on a keyboard and now he was back to square one with that.

He couldn't count the number of times in recent days that he reached for something with his right hand only to come up short. Sometimes it was scratching or reaching for a light switch. Other times it was opening a doorknob or trying to pick up a piece of paper. Hell, he hadn't adjusted to dressing or unzipping his pants using only his left hand. He was having to relearn things he'd done his entire life.

Although it was an inconvenience, he wouldn't let it stop him. He thought about adaptability. How could he best adapt to his current situation? What could he change or modify to retain his combat effectiveness? That was the question.

At some point in the night, lying awake in his austere bedroom, Boss had a moment of insight. He'd always understood that he was a tool to be utilized by men with grand goals. That was his role within the special operations community, as well as his role within the government and the military. When someone needed a specialized tool for a difficult job, Boss and other men like him became that tool. Some days he was a scalpel, surgically removing someone impeding the goals of the United States. Other days he was a hammer, flattening everything that got in his way.

He accomplished his various assignments using his mind, his stamina, and his weapons. Sometimes he needed a different set of tools, though, and through hundreds of missions he'd learned how to get the specialized equipment he needed. At times it was a specialized weapon, designed to fight under a unique set of circumstances. Other times it was different clothing, a unique optic, or some offbeat electronic device. There had been missions that required rifle rounds different than what he normally had available and he'd had them made for a single mission. It was the same with explosives.

He'd learned that if he needed something and couldn't find it, it was time to locate someone who could. He'd find the guy with the skills to make what he needed. A specialist. That approach made Boss more successful than some of his colleagues. He didn't simply make do with what was available. He went to every length to make sure he had exactly what the job required. In the sleepy spiral of his thoughts, he understood this was the approach that would be required. He needed to make some modifications.

To *himself.*

At some point he gave up on sleep and rose to prepare for the day. As he'd been ordered, he appeared outside of the nondescript operations building before 7 AM. Although he was harboring some hostility over the way things had gone with Owen yesterday, he'd chilled out some. It had been an emotional reaction, something he wasn't proud of. It had been the same when he woke up in the hospital with his hand missing. He was tempted to strike out on his own and find the people responsible. Fortunately, he'd talked himself off that ledge. It wouldn't have been smart. He had to do the same now, keep the emotions in check.

His role was a lifetime assignment. It wasn't something you stepped away from, something you quit because your feelings got hurt. He couldn't leave and go find an equivalent position with a competing firm, at least not without leaving the country and completely switching his allegiances. He had to die in the saddle or get so old they'd put him out to pasture.

At the operations building, he entered the exterior door and found two guards positioned outside a second windowless door with a biometric scanner. As soon as he saw it, Boss swore loudly. The system only had data on right hands. If you had a right, they scanned it in. Boss's right hand was in the system but his left was not.

Unaware of the reason for his outburst, the guard said, "Right hand on the scanner, sir. Hold for the green light."

Boss scowled and held up his right arm. "What right hand?"

The guards glanced at each other with uncertainty.

"I'm Captain Ballou. I have my ID," Boss said, reaching into his pocket for his Common Access Card. It didn't bear his real name but matched the rank on his uniform and was issued specifically to get him around this base.

"Sir, we don't have a protocol for granting SCIF access to visitors unable to utilize the hand scanner. Who are you here to see?"

SCIF stood for Sensitive Compartmented Information Facility.

Getting past this door required a security clearance. Boss had it but had no immediate way of proving it. He rattled off Owen's name, credentials, and the name of his division. One of the guards picked up a phone and dialed a number. After a brief discussion Boss was turned over to one of Owen's flunkies and permitted entrance to the operations center.

"We'll get that left hand scanned in today," the flunky promised. "I apologize for the inconvenience."

Boss was proud of himself. He'd maintained his cool. No cursing and no middle fingers. As far as the inconvenience went, it was only one of many.

DESPITE THE AWKWARD START, his first day in the war room passed quickly. There was a lot going on around the country and a lot of decisions to be made. It was like being in Mission Control during a rocket launch. There were thousands of simultaneous operations underway and a buzz filled the room. Besides Owen, there were dozens of officers and civilians. Some of them Boss recognized, though there were others he'd never seen before. Perhaps they were folks like Boss, men who were rarely seen but had a long reach.

It was impressive and Boss saw why Owen needed the help. There were nonstop logistical challenges and questions that Boss did indeed find he was perfectly suited to address. He rose to the challenge and did what he could to further the mission. The time flew by.

"Sir, I need you to come with me for a moment."

Boss removed his headset to find the flunky who'd escorted him back earlier.

"We need to get that left hand scanned into the access control system," she reminded him.

Boss scooted back from the workstation. "I need to tell Owen."

"Already taken care of."

They left the room, bypassing another guard, and went down a stark hall. At other doors he could hear the buzz of activity similar to what he'd just left. His escort stopped at an unmarked door and presented her hand to a biometric reader. When the light changed, she opened the door and led Boss inside.

The whir of tiny cooling fans grew to a collective roar. The air was cooler to combat the heat generated by the massive server farm that filled half the room. Around the exterior walls of the vast room, people sat at workstations clacking away at keyboards. The girl led him to an overweight bearded man at a wraparound workstation. He had multiple lanyards and ID cards hanging around his neck. Nerd bling.

"Heath, I need a palm scan for Captain Ballou," the lady said. Captain George Ballou was the name Boss worked under on-base. It corresponded with his identification and uniform. He hadn't used his real name in a long time. In the databases, the soldier Boss had entered the service as had died early in the war in Iraq and he'd had a long succession of aliases since then.

Heath stopped typing and regarded Boss. He sighed as if doing his job presented him with a great inconvenience. That type of attitude from glorified civil servants irritated Boss and he briefly wondered what it might feel like to jab his stump into his eye. Would it fit? Could he make it fit with enough force?

Heath performed a few mouse clicks and rolled his chair down the length of his desk, stopping in front of Boss. "Right hand on the scanner." He gestured at a book-sized device glowing with a cool white light.

"That's the problem," his escort said. "His right hand is already in the system."

"It's not working?" Heath asked.

"You could say that," Boss said, raising the damaged limb between them.

"Oh, I see. Sorry about that," Heath said. He didn't miss a beat, scooting back to the computer, making a few adjustments, and rolling back to the scanner. "Left hand please."

Boss did as he was told, placing his hand firmly against the glass.

Heath examined it, pressing Boss's hand a couple of times to make sure it was properly positioned.

"Okay, that should do it," Heath announced. "Don't move." He clicked a button and observed the screen of his computer, watching the scanner's progress.

Boss checked out the room while the machine did its thing. There were perhaps ten folks including Heath. All were pecking away at keyboards or watching banks of monitors. While his eyes wandered, he checked out Heath's row of monitors. There were nine of them in an array. Some displayed scrolling data in a brightly-colored stream. One displayed electronic transactions that Boss assumed were people entering and exiting by way of the various biometric and keycard scanners. Another screen rotated through pages of thumbnail images that obviously came from security monitors.

"All done," Heath said, clicking his mouse to save the data. "All I need to know is where to grant him access to."

The girl handed Heath the identification Boss had given her on the walk down the hall. "Attach it to this profile. All permissions should be the same. Grant access wherever his role allows him to go."

Boss was distracted by the monitors flicking through security camera feeds. "You monitor security cameras? I would have thought those feeds would go to the police and security office."

Heath shot a glance to the side to see what Boss was looking at. "Oh, those aren't on this base. Those are feeds from various project sites around the country."

"Project sites?"

"Comfort camps, power plants, and power restoration projects," Heath said, rolling his chair back from his desk and crossing his arms. "We're all done here. It should work now. Give me a call if there are any problems."

Boss didn't move, focused on the security camera feeds, his brain going down a path he couldn't pull it back from.

"If we're done here, we need to let Heath get back to work," the girl said, noticing that Boss hadn't taken the hint.

"I have some questions for Heath," Boss said. "If my access is working now I should be able to find my own way back to the war room."

"You should be squared away," Heath confirmed. "You can go anywhere you're allowed to go."

"Questions about what?" the girl asked.

Boss shot her a look. He didn't know who she was to be questioning him. "Questions above your pay grade and outside of your directorate. Please excuse us."

The girl's lips tightened and she frowned.

"If Owen asks, I'll be there in a few minutes," Boss said, his voice low. "This is important. And confidential."

The girl appeared uncertain, but was aware she'd been dismissed. "Okay, fine. Just don't be long."

Boss waited for her to go before turning back to Heath. "Do you archive those camera feeds?"

Heath gestured toward the banks of servers. "We do. Right there."

Boss leaned forward and lowered his voice. "I was at the coal-fired plant in southwest Virginia that flooded. Did you capture footage of that?"

Heath looked as if he were recalling a bad memory. "That was a real shit show, wasn't it? I didn't know if anyone survived or not."

"There was one survivor and you're looking at him," Boss replied. "Everyone else was killed."

Heath pondered that for a moment before snapping back to life. "We did get some footage. I caught the highlights when I got to work that morning and I know folks higher up the chain viewed it. As far as I know the footage should be archived."

Boss had never considered that while his men were fighting for their lives there were spectators watching it like a World Cup match. He didn't know what he thought about that. Did the observers understand the gravity of what they were watching or was it like a video game to them? He knew some of those men. They were his team. The others, the engineers and NATO troopers, he didn't care about.

"I need you to find that footage," Boss said. "I need to see it."

Heath's mouth tightened and he shrugged. "I'm not sure if I can do that, Captain Ballou."

"I have the required clearance. I'm sure you saw that in the record you just accessed."

Heath sighed. "It's just that there are policies about reviewing archived footage. People can be sticklers about those kind of things. You have to request access and your request has to specifically detail what you're wanting and why you need it. There's just this *process*. The server records every access so we have a data trail." The hand gestures and expressions that accompanied the word "process" made it clear it was such a pain in the ass Heath was certain Boss would be deterred.

He was wrong.

Boss glanced around to make sure no one was looking, then casually dug a finger into a shirt pocket. He came out with a gold Krugerrand and displayed it to Heath like a magician preparing to perform a trick. "I'm sure you know that the cash you're receiving in your paycheck is relatively worthless right now. It won't buy you anything."

Heath nodded, his eyes focused on the gold coin.

"Some things never lose their value. Some methods of payment thrive regardless of the state of things. You put me in a room with that footage and I'll give you this coin. No one will ever know about it. As far as that data trail goes, I'm sure you can find some way to take care of that."

Heath looked nervous but leaned forward. "Come back tonight."

Boss smiled. "Thanks, Heath. You've been very helpful."

7

J*oint Base Anacostia-Bolling (JBAB)*

It was a mentally exhausting day and Boss was glad when it was over. He wasn't cut out for office life. He was used to more action, more physical exertion. Being caged up in an office all day put him on edge. He wanted to go for a run to clear his head but he needed to make a stop before it got too late. Without returning to his quarters, he made a beeline to the base machine shop.

He'd never been there before and it took him a while to find it. Inside, there were dozens of men running machines, grinding, welding, and making a racket. It was a hive of activity and pallets holding completed work and pending jobs were sitting everywhere. After he stood politely in the open roll-up door for several minutes, a stocky man dropped the stinger of a large arc welder and walked in Boss's direction, tipping his welding helmet up on his head. His demeanor was that of a man irritated at being interrupted.

"Can I help you, Captain?" He was in his fifties and wore a leather welding jacket with a lot of miles on it.

"I'm looking for the chief."

"You're looking at him," the chief replied.

Boss studied his grimy coveralls. "You're working the shop floor? I thought you guys just worked the computer and the phone these days?"

The chief shrugged. "No choice. This base is busting at the seams. We got troops showing up from every branch and more jobs than I can cover. Speaking of which, what do you need, cause I got shit to do."

Boss held up the stump of his severed hand. The chief raised his eyebrows and regarded it with confusion.

"I need to do something about this," Boss said.

The chief reached inside his leather jacket and dug in his pocket for a pack of cigarettes. He pulled one out, lit it, and took a deep inhale. He shook his head, exhaling smoke from his nostrils, and spoke in the comforting tone of someone addressing a confused person with dementia.

"Buddy, I'm sorry about your injury but I think you want Walter Reed. I hear they're operational with limited services. I don't know if you can get a prosthetic right now with all the shit going on but that would be the place to start. Nothing I can do for you. Now I need to get back to it." The chief turned and started off, shaking his head at the poor, confused sap he'd been talking to.

"We're not done!" Boss growled.

The chief stopped in his tracks and glared at Boss, assessing him now as a potential opponent. He wasn't used to being addressed in that tone. Sure, he got yelled at on a regular basis by people wanting their jobs done, but they weren't threatening. They knew being threatening could get their job delayed inevitably. This sure as hell felt like he was being menaced, though, and it didn't sit right with him. He couldn't let it pass.

He took a final drag off his cigarette, flicked it away, and squared off with Boss. He was ready to throw a punch. "What are you? Force Recon? Special Operations? Some other kind of shit like that?"

"Let's go with some other kind of shit for now," Boss replied.

The chief raised a hand and pointed a greasy finger at Boss. "I don't give a damn if you're Chesty Puller himself. I don't take orders from you."

This guy was playing the Chesty Puller card? He had to be old school. Even with his angry posture, Boss didn't feel threatened. The man hadn't made any of the precursors to an actual attack. He wasn't telegraphing a punch. Besides, even with the impediment of his missing hand, Boss could have taken him to the ground and broken his arm. He could also do much worse. That wasn't why he was there, though. He needed this man.

Boss held his hands up in a placating gesture. "I'm sorry, Chief. I'm not here to start shit. I need your help."

The chief dialed it down a notch but didn't back up. "Listen, I appreciate your predicament but this is not the way we do things around here. If you want something from me, you submit paperwork, and you get on the schedule. We're running three shifts right now and can't keep up with demand. My ass isn't even supposed to be out here making sparks. I'm supposed to be sitting in that air-conditioned office over there scheduling work and ordering materials. However, due to downsizing, we outsource a lot of our work to civilian contractors anymore. Most of them aren't in operation at the moment so every bit of repair, machining, and fabrication falls on this shop. I've got work stacked higher than King Kong's asshole and I'm too old for this shit. I should be retiring. I should be picking out a boat and finding a house in Florida."

The chief's face was bright red and he spat as he vented. Bringing him a special request was obviously bad timing. He was not in the mood. Unfortunately for him, his problems were not Boss's problems.

Boss spoke slowly, like a man facing a vicious dog. "Chief, I appreciate *your* predicament, but this is a very special circumstance. Feel free to ask around about me. You'll find that I'm a good friend to have and about the worst fucking enemy you could ever imagine. If you ever wondered who the devil sees in his nightmares, you're looking at him."

The chief was used to people trying to push him around. Everyone always thought their emergency was the most important. This man did seem different though. He seemed like he was really dangerous and not just a big talker. You had to take men like that seriously.

"Captain Ballou? I ask about that name and men will crap their britches? That what you telling me?"

Boss grinned. "You need a day to ask around and find out?"

The chief whipped off his welding helmet and pulled a handkerchief from his pocket, mopping at his face. Rivulets of sweat ran through the gray stubble on his head. "So just what the hell are you wanting anyway?"

"Chief, I have a deep appreciation for what machinists are capable of and that's why I'm here. I'm looking for a mechanical solution, not a medical solution. I'm not after some rubber hand so kids won't stare at me. I'm not here because I want to feel better. I'm here because I want to get maximum effectiveness from what's left of this arm. I need this to be a tool and not an impediment."

The chief took a deep breath and let it out slowly. He met Boss's eyes again and was certain that gave him all the background he needed on this man. He didn't need a day to ask around. He just needed to give the guy what he wanted, if that was even possible, and let him go on his way. He'd dealt with this type before. "We'll try to work you in. Exactly what is it you would like to be able to do with that appendage?"

"A simple request, really. I want something that will help me fight and kill. Bonus points if it's operational in an office setting too."

The chief scratched his head. "You mind if I bring over a couple of other folks? I have a good team."

Boss gave what passed for his version of a smile. "Glad to see you come around. You won't regret your decision. There may be a time when you need me and there are very few men I grant favors to. You'll find yourself in a very select club."

"Whatever," the chief said. "If I had a buck for everyone who owed me, we'd be having this conversation on the French Riviera."

He led Boss to his office and poured them each a cup of bad coffee. Boss noticed the sprawling stacks of ignored paperwork on the chief's desk. Were people really still using forms to get things done? It appeared they were. The door behind him opened and three men of varying ages came in. All appeared tired and dirty.

"This is my A-team," the chief said, nodding toward the group of men. "Ratliff there is a Machinist Mate First Class and knows his shit. The two youngsters there know how to do all the fancy computerized stuff. They do 3D printing, CNC, and cutting with water jets and lasers. I'm not knocking it. They can make a part in seconds that would take me hours."

Boss sipped the nasty coffee and watched the group as the chief explained to them the basics of what Boss had requested. Rather than responding with the same attitude the chief had, these men were enthusiastic. That made sense to him. Making replacement parts and repairing equipment all day was probably not as mentally stimulating as the challenge presented by turning an amputation into a weapon. This may have been the kind of project that got them excited about being machinists in the first place.

"You'd be like Jay J. Armes," Ratliff said when the chief was finished.

Everyone else looked at him blankly, missing the reference.

"He was a detective," Ratliff explained. "They made a toy based on him back in the 70s. I had one. He was missing both his hands and there were crazy attachments that replaced them. He was a real person. He was famous for rescuing Marlon Brando's son from kidnappers."

The rest of the men appeared skeptical. Perhaps Ratliff was one of those guys who was always throwing out obscure tidbits of information that people didn't know whether to believe or not.

One of the younger machinists, identified by his name tape as Altizer, spoke up. "If you don't mind me asking, how important is comfort versus durability? Is it more important to have something you can wear all day that might not fit as securely or do you want something that's absolutely not coming off if you bang the shit out of it?"

"I want as much as you can give me. Obviously comfort would be nice, but my intention is to fight with it. I want it designed with that level of durability in mind."

"Modularity is the key here," Meadows, another of the younger machinists, said. "We can make a comfortable socket with friction retention. For combat we can have a removable harness that anchors itself across his back and onto the other arm. Then it's not going anywhere."

The men chattered excitedly for several minutes before the chief put a stop to it.

"We've got to get back to work. We've got work that has to be finished today," he announced. "I need one of you to take some measurements."

"A mold too," Ratliff suggested. "A mold of the stump would be helpful."

Meadows shook his head at Ratliff. "Make your mold if it makes you feel better but a 3D laser scan is the way to go. It's a virtual, digital mold. We're making a precision device not some Bronze Age casting."

The chief nodded. "Meadows, you get scanning, and the rest of you go back to work. Scan, mold, measure." He gestured at Boss. "I'm going to turn you over to Meadows to get what he needs. Then I'll need to know where to find you when we're ready for you to come back."

"I'll check back in with you," Boss said. "Don't worry about that."

The chief couldn't hide his dread. Nobody liked to work with someone staring over their shoulder.

"It will be okay," Boss said. "I'll give you all space to work. I appreciate your assistance with this. It won't be forgotten."

"You know anything about machining?" the chief asked. "We could use some help around the shop."

"No, but do you need anyone killed?"

The chief broke into laughter. As funny as it was, he was certain Boss wasn't joking.

8

The Valley

JIM HATED MEETINGS WITH A PASSION. He hated attending them, hating planning them, even hated seeing them on his schedule, back when he had a job, for the pure sense of dread that came along with knowing they were approaching. Before the collapse, when he was working every day at the state mental health agency, the knowledge that he had a meeting on a particular day was enough to dampen his mood from the moment he woke up in the morning. He came up with all sorts of ways to miss them. He would ask friends to call him during the meeting so he had an excuse to leave. He would set an alarm on his phone that sounded like a ringtone so he could claim he had to take the call. Anything to escape.

With the world gone to shit, here he was in a meeting again. The irony of it was that he was the very person who'd called it. It made him feel like a hypocrite, that the person in the valley who probably hated meetings the most had found it necessary to have one.

The fire pit area behind Jim's house had been the informal meeting space since the early days of the disaster. It was where they made important decisions, gathered to support each other, or shared meals together. While everyone could fit into Jim's house if they had to, it was not comfortable. The house had been cramped before the collapse, but now it was worse. Moving Nana and Pops in led to things being stored in the hallways. Also, gear that used to be stored away—packs, Go Bags, tactical gear, weapons—was now stored in easily accessible places. This usually meant piled on the floor beside the front and back doors. The clutter and congestion in the house was something the family could tolerate if it was just them. With twenty more guests thrown into the mix, it was too tight.

The day was sunny with a blue sky and temperatures in the mid-fifties. After a particularly brutal winter the day felt nice and some folks wore short sleeves, basking in the warm spring sun like cats in sunbeams. The tribe was gathered. There was Randi's family, Gary's family, Charlie, Hugh, and Lloyd. The sheriff and his family had been invited but chose not to attend. Jim had the feeling that the sheriff's family was struggling. They had supplies but were in a dark place emotionally. He was going to have to do some outreach and see if he could get them to engage. They were going to have to work this summer to survive another winter. They needed to plant food just like everyone else. They would have to accept, just like Jim had, that they could not go it alone.

Jim scanned the assembled faces. The adults looked back at him expectantly, waiting for him to get this show on the road. The children wouldn't be particularly interested in what he had to say but they needed to hear it. It wasn't only the heads of households who would be part of the spring planting, but every able member of the assembled families. Like it or not, there would be work for everyone.

"I'm sorry to make you come to a meeting on such a pretty day. God knows I hate them as much as the next guy, but we need to talk about getting some crops in the ground. It's going to be labor-intensive and will require every set of hands we have."

"It's kind of nice to see everyone," Ellen said. "A meeting isn't such a bad thing."

Jim curled his lip into an involuntary sneer. "We see each other all the time. Having a meeting just takes a relaxed, casual interaction and turns it into drudgery."

Ellen held a hand up toward Jim, warding off his negativity. "Don't project your grumpiness on me. It's a beautiful day and I'm glad to see everyone here."

"Yeah, Mr. Grumpy Man," Ariel piped in. Jim could always count on his daughter to keep him humble.

Jim tried to give her a glare but couldn't hold it. It turned into a smile, then a laugh.

"I agree," Pops said. "It's good to see everyone. You're all looking well."

Jim sighed and launched into the reason he'd called the meeting in the first place. He wanted to get it over with and go on about his day. "The sooner we get this started, the sooner it's over with. We need to talk about planting. Several of us have been scouring the valley for seeds and had pretty good luck with it. From this point forward we'll need to make an effort to save seeds every year, or until such point as we can go to the store and buy them again. We have enough for a good start. We'll need to utilize existing garden spots right now. The soil there has been prepared before and will be the easiest to deal with. If it comes to it, we can try preparing some new ground in the future, but it will take a lot more work, especially without machines. Just getting the sod out can take a serious effort."

"Will we have any machines to assist with gardening?" Gary asked. "Tillers? Tractors?"

"We will. There's a little gas left and I'd recommend we go ahead and use it. It probably won't last much longer. Machines running it might be hard to start so we may have to use starting fluid. There're a couple of gas tractors in the valley we can outfit with plows, disks, or tillers."

"What about diesel?" Gary asked. "I would assume we have more diesel tractors out there."

"We do have some diesel left stored in heating oil tanks. It's been treated and should last a while longer but we don't have much. I'm really hoping to save it for emergencies. If we have to make an emergency run in a vehicle that diesel will be nice to have around. Even it won't last forever, though. The days of no fuel will be here soon if the world doesn't get back on track."

That statement fell on everyone like a wet blanket. Any moods elevated by the beautiful day were soured by the thought that things could get worse than they already were.

"So where do we start?" Randi asked. "Do we all grab what we like to eat and start planting our gardens?"

"Definitely not," Jim said. He gestured at his dad. "Pops has more gardening experience than any of us. I'd like him to take a look at each garden and figure out what might best grow there. He can help plan the planting. What needs to go where and all that. Once the seeds are in the ground, it's a matter of watering, keeping the weeds beat down, and fencing out the animals."

"We'll be using some of those solar-powered electric fence units," Pops said. "Scarecrows would help too and that might be a good project for the children"

"Oh, I can help with that," Nana offered. "I've got all kinds of ideas."

"We need more gardening implements too," Jim said. "People used to throw a tool away rather than attempting to repair it. I'm guessing that there are damaged gardening tools all up and down this valley that could be repaired and put back in service – hoes, rakes, shovels. Even if you just find a head, we can make a handle for it."

"So, be on the lookout for old hoes?" Randi asked with a smirk.

Jim cracked up but there were some disapproving expressions that didn't bother Randi in the least. "Glad you said that and not me," he said.

"When do you want to get started?" Hugh asked. "Takes me longer to get down into the valley so I need to plan in advance. It's a long walk up and down that mountain. And there's no good garden spot up that high. The soil sucks."

"We can start today. We need to burn the old gardens off if they're dry enough to plant," Jim said. "I want to do them one at a time with everyone present so there's no chance of the fire getting out of control. We can't call the fire department if we catch this valley on fire." Jim shot Gary a look.

"What?" Gary asked. "What's that look about?"

"Nothing," Jim said with a smirk.

"Something!" Gary shot back.

"You *know* what it was for," Jim replied.

Gary sneered. "A guy starts one wildfire and he's labeled for life."

"Just one?"

"Two!" Gary admitted. "Fine, okay? Two wildfires. For anyone who doesn't know, I've started two wildfires from burning brush in my backyard. It's all out in the open now. Happy, Jim?"

Jim grinned. "Yep."

Randi cackled.

Pops cleared his throat. Gardening was serious business to him. "We can start planning immediately. I'll try to get around to everyone's garden spots today and check out the soil conditions. Then we'll see what seeds we have and go from there. It would be good if someone could collect all the seeds and make a list."

"Is that it?" Jim asked, rubbing his hands together and already preparing to get up from his seat.

"No, it's not," Pops said. "Everyone should be on the hunt for solar fence chargers, extra rolls of electric fencing, and the yellow clips that hold the wire to t-posts. If we don't find enough we'll have to take down some existing fence and reuse it."

"Got it," Jim said, pointing at Pops and repeating his list. "Fence posts, wire, solar chargers. Anything else?"

"Do you have to go to the bathroom or something?" Ellen asked. "Why are you in such a hurry?"

Although Jim didn't want to get into it and this certainly wasn't the place to address it, he wasn't comfortable with the role he found himself in. He felt like he was in charge of this group, which was honestly the last thing in the world he wanted. Every time something came up they turned to him. He couldn't escape it. Some days he wanted to take his family and move further back in the hills. He wanted to disappear and leave this feeling of responsibility behind him.

He couldn't do it. He hadn't been able to do it on that long walk home. It had been a constant struggle to accept he was part of a group and they needed him. He didn't want either of those things. He didn't want to be part of a group and he didn't want the responsibility of being needed. The whole experience of surviving up until this point had been a lesson in accepting what the world threw at him. He didn't get to control every single facet of his life. If he wanted the people gathered around him to survive this challenge then he had to push aside his personal feelings. He had to lead even if he hated leading. He had to accept responsibility even when he hated to do so.

He had to be a better person even when he was content being a selfish bastard.

"What are your thoughts on going into town?"

Jim was surprised. It was Gary's wife, Debra, asking, and she was fairly quiet. "Uh, I think town sucks and I hope to never go back. I'd prefer to go hours out of my way than to pass through there ever again."

"What about for the more normal of us?" she asked.

Randi and Ellen cracked up. Jim was taken aback.

"I'm joking," Debra said. "It's just that Gary mentioned there was some sort of flea market thing going on in the supercenter parking lot and there are things we need. I have things to trade and I was hoping to do some bartering. I've been growing some herbs, spices, and greens by the fire this spring."

"They asked me about that this morning, Jim, and I wasn't sure what to tell them," Gary said. "I have a few things I'd like to barter off too. Some of the men we killed since coming here had decent knives on them and I've got more knives than my family needs. I thought they might trade well."

Jim processed the information. Part of him wanted to stand up and shout, "Are you people nuts? Stay out of town!" yet he couldn't do that. Already uncomfortable with being seen in a position of authority, he didn't want to move on to being dictator.

"That's a decision every family will have to make for itself," Jim said. "I wouldn't recommend taking children because it can be ugly and hostile. The risk of violence is pretty high, especially if you have anything that someone else may want to take. You have to go prepared for a fight and stay on your guard."

"Can we borrow horses?" Gary asked.

He directed the question to Jim. Some of the horses belonged to Jim and others to Randi. They were all living at Jim's place because it was better set up for caring for them. When Jim hesitated a bit too long, Randi spoke up.

"You can take my horses. You should double up, though. You don't want to give the impression that you have a wealth of anything. People would probably try to trade them from you. If you refuse, things could get out of control."

"She's right," Jim said. "Those of you who haven't been out in a while have no idea how bad it's gotten. We've probably lost more than half of the folks in the powerless areas of the country."

"I don't get it," Lloyd said. "Why aren't trucks rolling in with aid already?"

"The scale of the disaster is too big," Jim said. "There are too few areas that have power and fuel for them to take care of everyone."

"Plus, we haven't exactly welcomed them with open arms," Hugh said.

"You guys know why we did that," Jim said. "They basically wanted to trade food for freedom and I'm not making that trade."

"Hence the anger of the people in the community who feel you made the decision for them without giving them a vote in it," Randi pointed out.

Jim was getting pissed now. They were only stating the obvious but he felt the comments were attacks on him, or at least put him in a position of having to defend his decision.

"To hell with those people!" Jim snapped. "I'm not sitting by and watching something like that happen. Even if we agreed to give up our rights *temporarily*, just until order was restored, they'd never agree that the time was right to give our guns back. If we accept surrender, you can't back up and change your mind. Once your rights are gone, you don't get them back."

"Sit down," Ellen said, trying to soothe him. "No one is attacking you. We're just making sure everyone understands the situation."

"Along those lines," Gary said, trying to change the subject, "we need to make sure that anytime anyone says they heard a rumor that the folks in this valley were involved in the attack on the power plant, we need to shut it down. We need to tell them we heard there was an ice dam on the river that flooded the valley. Or you tell them that you heard there was an explosion that caused a landslide. Whatever you say, do *not* further the rumor that we played a role in that. We saw some hostility about that on our last trip to town, though most of it was directed toward Jim."

Jim grimaced and bit his tongue. He wanted to unleash a torrent of profanity but not in front of the children. "I need to go split wood," he growled. "You all can keep talking if you want to. I'm done."

He stalked off toward the wood lot, mumbling as he went, the occasional stray word indicating that his profanity had found its voice.

9

Joint Base Anacostia-Bolling (JBAB)

Boss gave the machinists a couple of weeks to work on their project unmolested. He resisted the temptation to lurk in their shop and watch them. They'd probably have found his presence menacing even if it was not his intention. He had that effect on people. He didn't want to rush them and he didn't want to alienate them. He had a respect for the precision of machinists–they were technicians like himself—and he wanted them doing their best work. That would not come from him hanging over their shoulders and making them nervous.

He assumed they'd contact him for more measurements, to test the fit, or at least ask questions, yet it never happened. The complex measurements they took in the beginning with the 3D laser scanner had measured his arm with a precision that no hand tool could match. It took thousands of measurements from thousands of individual data points in the time it would have taken Meadows to close an old-fashioned manual caliper around his arm. Apparently, they had all they needed. He truly hoped that was the case. He would be extremely disappointed if they'd not contacted him because they hadn't been able to commit any time to his project.

During his wait Boss distracted himself with his new assignment in the war room. He wasn't just going through the motions; he put his extensive field experience to work running teams for Owen. Despite the state of things, Boss was surprised by how much was going on out there. Besides the general effort to get power restored to as many regions as possible there were projects aimed at building, supplying, and staffing "comfort camps" in the affected areas.

Getting fuel to places it was needed required a tremendous effort. There were heavily-armed tanker convoys transporting fuel on the interstates. Many secondary roads were blocked by abandoned vehicles. Clearing the roads was part of the effort. There were airlifts of fuel, filling massive bladders on the ground in remote locations. A lot of manpower was required to work on repairing the damaged refineries. Finding parts and getting them where they were needed was a logistical nightmare. The functioning refineries required significant defensive capabilities to deter theft. Raids were constant and the assignment had a high mortality rate.

On the black ops side of the coin there were covert missions being run every day, in every corner of the world. Communication challenges, as well as a lack of news coverage, made it the ideal time to strike against anyone you didn't like. The powerful were eliminating their enemies in business and in government. Politicians were silencing those who had dirt on them. The intelligence community was assassinating their enemies at an alarming rate. Anyone who didn't play ball with them disappeared. Around the world, terrorist leaders were being killed in their sleep, poisoned in cafes, or shot by snipers when they crawled from their holes. With scant oversight and no press, it was a great time to settle scores.

Everyone in Washington was familiar with the expression about not letting a good crisis go to waste. People with the ability to do so were taking full advantage. They were hustling to gain ground and increase their personal power. One man's rise meant another's decline. One man's gain meant another's termination. Boss knew the American public wouldn't be able to sleep at night if they fully understood just how many men in the world had private armies and skilled killers at their disposal. Boss knew. He was one of those skilled killers. At least he had been before his accident.

When he finally got word via secure email that the machinists were ready to meet with him, he rushed to the machine shop in excitement when he got off duty. The fact was not lost on him that these men should have been off duty. He fully understood they'd likely put in long hours to accomplish his request on top of their already extensive workload. If they'd taken their assignment seriously, he would make it worth their while.

Greetings were rushed and tentative. Boss was not a warm, chatty guy. Besides, everyone knew why they were there and were anxious to get to the main event. The chief led Boss to a private workroom in the back of the shop. Plastic distribution totes and cardboard boxes were stacked around the walls. In the center of the room the men gathered around a plastic folding table covered with a white sheet. When everyone was present, Ratliff reached forward and dramatically whipped the sheet off the table, exposing the fruit of their efforts.

Boss was taken aback by the display in front of him. It was beyond any of his expectations. While he'd hoped for some type of more durable prosthetic than he could obtain through normal channels, these men had delivered an entire system. He had no idea what all the pieces were or how they worked but it was definitely impressive.

The men didn't know how to take his silence. Was he happy? Sad? Angry and preparing to kill all of them for disappointing him?

The chief cleared his throat and pointed to one of the devices on the table. "We've tested everything but fit. The computer says it should fit but that doesn't guarantee comfort. We'd like to test the sockets first and make sure they fit properly. I'll let Ratliff explain the details. He spearheaded the project."

"The sockets? As in plural?" Boss asked.

Ratliff pointed to two of the larger devices on the table. "We call those 'gauntlets.' We couldn't come up with a single gauntlet that would serve all the specialized functions we had in mind and decided it was better to create a light-duty gauntlet and a heavy-duty tactical gauntlet. Light-duty would be optimal for casual and office use. The design is more focused on comfort and usability."

One of the junior machinists gestured to another piece of kit on the table. "That's the tactical gauntlet. It's optimized for combat. It's heavier due to the materials used but it incorporates a number of functions we think you'll find very impressive."

Ratliff carefully picked up the smaller gauntlet and held it before him. There was both pride and protectiveness in the way he delicately cradled the object. "This one is of carbon fiber construction. It's ridiculously strong and lightweight. The interior is molded to exactly fit your socket. It's lined with a thin silicone layer which will aid in retention. Friction alone should hold it in place."

He turned the device socket side down and showed Boss the end. "Both gauntlets accept interchangeable attachments. We've used titanium alloys where we could to keep things lightweight. In some places we were forced to use steel because it's all we had available. We can make any number of attachments based on your needs but in this first set of deliverables we've included some that we came up with. I think I speak for everyone when I say we enjoyed this project. It was a nice break from the routine."

Ratliff pointed to the various attachments lined up on the table. "That's a lightweight stylus made of electroconductive material allowing you to use touch keypads and tablets, dial a cell phone, and perform delicate tasks such as typing on a computer keyboard."

Boss picked up the slender and surprisingly light stylus from the table. He examined it from one end to the other. It was useful but not the kind of cool he got excited about.

"There's a light-duty hook and a light-duty clamping mechanism that can be used to pick things up while wearing this gauntlet," Ratliff continued. "We don't have robotics capability at this shop so all of this is simple mechanical function. When you choose to change attachments we put in a locking mechanism that allows the previous attachment to eject under spring tension. It's easy to do with one hand. The locking mechanism is designed so that you're unlikely to accidentally discharge an attachment while it's in use."

Boss was impressed but reserved. Although not prone to enthusiastic outbursts, he was indeed excited. This was exactly why he'd wanted to use machinists. They didn't just do things, they *overdid* things. They overthought things. They thought like he did, simply applying their minds to a less violent task.

"What about that other gauntlet? How is it different?" he asked, gesturing to a similar item on the table.

Ratliff put down the sleek carbon fiber gauntlet and picked up a more substantial chunk of gray metal from the table. He couldn't hold back a smile and the rest of the machinists joined him like they were controlled by a common mind. They were proud of themselves.

"We call this the tactical gauntlet. It's a combat-duty equivalent of the device we just showed you. It functions much in the same way as the carbon fiber version but we didn't feel that friction alone would be sufficient to keep this one in place."

"What's it made of?" Boss asked.

"Titanium," the chief said. "It's expensive shit left over from another job. Some of the mechanical components in the latch mechanism are steel but the titanium shell has its benefits."

"Like what?"

Ratliff's face took on a serious expression and without warning he began violently bashing the device against the table in front of him. The neatly organized attachments rattled and bounced. He did not stop until he'd bashed a hole in the thick plastic top. The rest of the machinists grinned like children.

"See? No damage," Ratliff said. "It would do the same to a man's head. It's incredibly tough, and the steel internals add ballast to the end. It gives you incredible striking ability even without the tactical accessories fitted into the gauntlet."

Boss raised an eyebrow in curiosity. "Tactical accessories?"

One of the junior machinists reached beneath the table and came up with something like a laptop case. He placed it on the battered table, unzipped, and opened it. The machinist hesitated a moment, staring at the contents, then made his selection. He drew an eight inch spike from the case and slid it into the opening in the business end of the gauntlet. It locked in place with a firm click.

"We call this 'the ventilator,'" he announced proudly, handing it over to Boss to examine.

Boss studied it carefully. He grabbed the spike and tugged at it, pleased to find that the mechanism held it securely. There was no give, no wobble, no play. He was anxious to see how it would hold up in testing.

Ratliff reached into the same case and withdrew a thick double-edged fighting blade and held it up for Boss. "We kept the blade short to reduce the chance of you snapping it off if you get...*overzealous.* The weak point is probably where the blade transitions to the stem. You're going to have to test it and see how it holds up. We made several extra blades just in case."

"Oh, I will test it thoroughly," Boss replied. "Trust me on that."

"The attachments for the light-duty carbon fiber gauntlet will also work in this one," the chief added. "There's universal compatibility in the latching system."

"You mentioned that it might require more than a friction fit to hold it in place?" Boss asked.

Ratliff nodded. "A harness system. Yeah, we apologize that it's not more aesthetically pleasing. We didn't have time to reinvent the wheel so we constructed a harness with what we had at our disposal. It fits much like a shoulder holster would. It will take some fine tuning but basically the idea is that it will be strapped across both shoulders to put some tension on it. That should keep it from slipping off during the most vigorous...use."

"Can I try it on? Is it ready to use?" Boss asked.

"It's ready," Ratliff said. "Let's start with the lightweight one and test the fit. It may be a bit snug."

Ratliff continued talking but Boss was not hearing any of that. He had the carbon fiber gauntlet in his hand and was inserting his arm into it. When he had it most of the way in Ratliff showed him that he should place the base against a wall or table so he could press his arm fully into the socket. When it slid fully into place there was the faint flicker of a smile on Boss's face. It felt ridiculously natural.

"See? You can tell when it's on right," the chief said. "You can feel it."

Boss stepped back from the table and swung his arm gently through the air, practicing a slow motion martial art strike. "That feels incredible. If I was to close my eyes I would think I had a hand just based on the balance and weight of the thing."

Ratliff cleared his throat. "We estimated your body weight at 104 kilograms. Typically a human hand represents 0.58 percent of total body weight. With that in mind, we estimated the wrist-forward portion of this gauntlet should weigh 610 grams to best approximate the weight and balance of your old hand. Most, but not all, of the attachments are designed so that they extend no further than the point where the natural tip of your fingers would be. Your mind is already trained that this is the extent of your reach and we wanted to take advantage of that. The stylus, the hook, and the claw all stop where your fingers would've stopped."

"Fucking amazing."

Ratliff picked up the stylus attachment and showed Boss how it inserted and locked into the gauntlet. Boss made a few tentative taps on the table with it, studied it for a moment, and then removed the attachment.

"I'd like to try the tactical gauntlet."

"Sure." Ratliff removed a hook attachment from the case and passed it to Boss. "Insert this into the gauntlet. We couldn't wear the gauntlets to try them but we made the assumption they would come off easier if you could hook onto something and pull. You have to overcome the friction."

Boss did exactly that, looping the hook attachment over the edge of the table and lifting. The table lifted easily and the cuff didn't loosen.

"Try something heavier," the chief instructed.

Boss hooked the device around the door frame and pulled. Just as the machinists had described, the carbon fiber gauntlet gradually came loose from his steady effort. Once it was removed, he handed it off to Ratliff and the machinist tucked it away neatly in a plastic storage case with a padded foam interior.

One of the junior machinists passed Boss the titanium gauntlet. "You put this one on the same way. The fit should feel exactly the same but the attachment will be heavier. We weren't able to balance this one out like your natural hand. Once you have it on we'll show you how the harness works."

Boss inserted his forearm into the socket and pressed down to make sure it was fully seated. Though it was a little heavier it fit similar to the previous gauntlet. It ran a good deal higher up his forearm than the carbon fiber version, stopping within a couple of inches of his elbow. When he was done waving it around Ratliff approached him with an elaborate nylon harness.

"That shit looks complicated," Boss said warily.

Ratliff shook his head. "It won't be. Once we have it adjusted to your body you won't have to go through this process each time. You can just leave it adjusted like you would with your plate carrier or any other piece of web gear."

Ratliff helped strap Boss into the nylon harness, adjusting several Velcro closures to get the best fit. When it was securely fastened, the machinist hooked the harness onto metal tabs on the gauntlet. "You don't want this to be too tight. Think of it more like a retention lanyard than a belt. The molded silicone lining will do most of the work. This simply keeps you from losing it if you get a little *aggressive*."

Boss smiled at that. "I can assure you I will be very aggressive in my testing."

Ratliff exchanged a grin with the other machinists before returning to Boss. "We predicted as much. It was built with you in mind."

When this gauntlet was secured, Ratliff stepped back and Boss gave it a tentative swing, getting the feel for it. He performed the same range of strikes he'd done earlier with the carbon fiber cuff.

"Not bad at all. As you noted, it's slightly heavier, but the straps are not binding. I can move freely. I could fight in this with no problem."

"We tried the harness under a range of clothing and gear. We located the Velcro closures in places where they wouldn't cause too much pressure or chafing. Of course, if you find something uncomfortable or not to your liking we can modify it. Satisfaction guaranteed and all that."

Boss acknowledged Ratliff's comment with a nod and checked out the attachments again. "Give me something fucking brutal."

The chief laughed and reached for the case of attachments. "Let's try one of the fighting knives. Simple but effective." He withdrew a knife blade that extended about six inches below a metal collar. The collar was flush against the gauntlet when attached. There was a satisfying click as the chief locked it into place.

Boss held it in front of his face, grinning from ear to ear. "That is one wicked piece of steel."

Ratliff touched the collar welded around the device where it inserted into the gauntlet. "We decided it might be a good idea to have some type of shielding that prevented fluids from getting into the mechanism. We refer to it as the 'gore shield.' You'll have to let us know how it works out."

Boss was happy as a kid on Christmas. "I'm dying to try this thing out."

The machinists exchanged the same sneaky, conspiratorial look they had earlier.

"We thought you might feel that way," one of the junior machinists said. He went to a cardboard box near the wall and removed a heavy object wrapped in a garbage bag. He took the bag to a battered, greasy worktable mounted against the wall and dumped out the contents. He stepped back to reveal the severed head of a black cow.

"The officer's mess is butchering their own beef," he said. "They were glad to let me take a head."

Boss looked from the cow head to the chief. He pointed his spike at the head and raised a questioning eyebrow. The chief, Ratliff, and the other machinists all nodded in unison.

"All yours," Ratliff said. "Wear it out."

Boss stalked toward the cow head while the machinists all put on their safety glasses. They flinched when Boss struck a lightning fast, powerful blow that plunged the blade between the eyes, sinking fully to the hilt. The cow was mostly bloodless at this point so there was minimal splatter, but there was the revolting sound of bone and tissue crunching, then scraping against steel as the blade was withdrawn. The skull presented no more resistance than an eggshell against Boss's muscle power concentrated into that razor sharp piece of steel.

He pulled it out slowly, then leaned over to study the wound. He probed it with his fingers, measuring the extent of the destruction. The machinists watched with a mixture of distaste, fascination, and pride.

Boss struck again, varying his angle of attack, seeing how the blade and the gauntlet responded to the forces placed on it. When he was done, he stepped back, studying the gauntlet and blade. He tried to wiggle the blade, seeing if the attack had loosened it, but it was as solid as it had been when he'd started.

"Well done, my friends," he said. "This exceeds my expectations."

The machinists beamed with pride.

"I was concerned about the time it took," the chief said. "With our schedule it's hard to fit in anything extra. We enjoyed this one, though. Probably the first fun project we've done in a long, long time."

Boss removed the gauntlet and placed it on the table. "Can you pack that away for me?"

Ratliff and one of the junior machinists started wiping down the gauntlet and packing the attachments in the travel case they'd put together for it. While they were occupied with that, Boss fished around in his pocket. He came out with an object that he placed on the table before him. All activity stopped as the item clicked solidly against the table surface under the pressure of Boss's finger.

It was a one ounce gold Krugerrand.

Boss removed three more from his pocket under the watchful eyes of the men. When he was done, he slid one in the direction of the chief, Ratliff, and the two junior machinists. They watched in silence. No one reached for the coins. They almost seemed scared, as if he'd pulled out a weapon.

"That's for your trouble," Boss said.

No one moved.

"That's a lot of money," the chief finally said.

"You went above and beyond," Boss said. "And that's for keeping this project between us. The job, the money, all of it. Do I have your word?"

He went around the table and each man nodded. Ratliff finished packing away Boss's gear and extended the case toward him.

Boss took it. "Gentlemen, you all have a good day," he said, leaving the room.

When he was gone, the chief leaned forward and placed a finger on a Krugerrand. He slid it to the edge of the table closest to him and dropped it into his waiting palm. From there it disappeared into a pocket. "I suggest you men do the same. Pocket that shit," he said, heading toward the door. "And somebody get rid of that head."

10

The sheriff lived in one of the empty houses near Buddy's house. The sheriff, his wife, and their children had experienced a difficult winter after the sheriff's mother died. For him, it probably seemed that the collapse of the country, the rise of chaos, and his mother's death were all bound together in a single, tragic event. His grief for his mother and for his damaged community alike held him in a gloomy embrace that he had not yet risen above. People visited and came away shaking their heads, fearing the worst.

The sheriff's state of mind had kept Jim from talking to him about his plan to destroy the power plant. Jim wasn't certain if the sheriff would have participated anyway, the action potentially being too lawless for a career law enforcement officer to participate in. Deputy Ford had no such reservations, having given his life in service of the mission. Jim didn't know how much the sheriff knew about the operation. They'd never discussed it. Despite Jim's appreciation at the sheriff joining them in the valley, there were certain things he withheld from the lawman. In this time of moral ambiguity he could not be certain where the sheriff's allegiance stood. Was it to the obsolete laws he'd promised to uphold or was it to the wellbeing of the community that faithfully voted him into office?

The sheriff's house stood a good distance back from the road. When he approached, Jim spotted Ford's empty mobile home in the distance. He'd tried to convince Hugh to move in there but he refused. He liked maintaining his separateness. He liked living on the fringe of the wilderness, high on the Clinch Mountain range.

Jim shouted a greeting from the gate, waving an arm to show he was friend and not foe. He called until the sheriff walked around the house and waved back, then slipped through the gate and closed it behind himself. Although there was no livestock on this property, it was good country etiquette to close the gate back if that was the way you found it. He slipped the rusty link of chain back over the bent nail that secured it.

It took Jim two or three steady minutes of plodding up the gravel lane to reach the sheriff, who stood in the driveway leaning on a spading fork. Mud caked his shoes and pants legs. Overalls would have been more appropriate for his task but he still wore his sheriff's uniform, clinging to that one thread of normality. For him, it was the workday and that was what he wore to work.

"Gardening?" Jim asked.

"Trying."

"Was there at least an old garden to start with?"

"There was. We burned it off and I'm trying to turn over the soil some. It's hard going."

Jim pointed to the spading fork. "It is with that. You should've come to the meeting we just had about gardening. I left a message in your box about it. There are some areas where being a team player is helpful and gardening is one of them. We're trying to coordinate our effort to get the best yield. This is an area where we can't afford to fail. This isn't gardening to show off your pretty tomatoes at work. This is gardening to keep your ass from starving to death next winter."

The sheriff leaned forward on the handle of his gardening tool. "Yeah, I started to come. I've been in a rut since my mother died. I knew her death was coming but dealing with every single aspect of it ourselves was challenging. I mean, you plan for the funeral but you don't plan for cleaning and wrapping the body these days. Most people gave that up a generation or two ago."

"I guess we're used to other people taking care of the more unpleasant aspects of it," Jim said. "The process has been sanitized and we just show up to grieve."

The sheriff stood up straight, turned to the side, and spat. "For your sake, I hope things are back in order by the time you have to deal with this. Shitty time to bury people you love."

"Somehow I doubt things will be back in order anytime soon."

The sheriff appeared uncomfortable at that statement. He got that way anytime people suggested this might be a prolonged event. "Did you need something in particular or did you just come by to make sure I hadn't gone off the deep end and killed my family?"

"The latter," Jim admitted.

The sheriff adopted a smug demeanor, his suspicions confirmed. "I appreciate your concern but we're fine here."

"Listen, it's not my place to tell you how to take care of your family but I can tell you that engaging with the rest of the folks in this valley will improve your odds of survival. If you're going to live here, you might as well take advantage of the help that's available to you. Pops is helping people plan their gardens. We even got a gas tractor running and we're using it to prepare the soil. Those are resources you can take advantage of. Have you even found any seeds?"

"I found a few things in a junk drawer in this house. I figured I'd grow what I found and count on trading it for other things to round out the pantry."

Jim dialed it back a notch. He was pushing too hard, trying to make the sheriff see things that were obvious to him. "Look, I already learned the hard way that going it alone is not possible. If I learned anything from this experience that was it."

The sheriff held up a hand, warding off further debate. "I get it. If Pops is willing to come around, I'd appreciate his insight."

Jim was never much for small talk and he was already tired of talking. He wanted to visit Lloyd and have a sip of moonshine. "I've got to go see Lloyd. I'll send Pops by tomorrow. You might as well hold off on working that dirt until you talk to him."

The whole time he was talking, Jim was already walking away, speaking back over his shoulder. He only made it a few steps before the sheriff spoke.

"Jim."

Jim stopped in his tracks. Something about the sheriff's tone concerned him. He turned to face him.

"I was planning on coming and seeing you before the day was out, anyway. I had a visit this morning from a couple of men in town."

That irritated Jim. They'd become slack over the winter about manning their guard posts. They'd gone weeks at a time with no visitors and people decided it wasn't worth it to sit there. They'd convinced Jim to let them lapse. This was the result. Men walked into the valley and visited the sheriff and he had no idea it had happened. "About what? They want to buy beef?"

"That came up but that wasn't the reason for their visit."

"That right?"

The sheriff sighed, dreading this conversation. "They said there were a lot of folks in town who had planned on utilizing those comfort camps the government was setting up. Widows, the elderly, families with children, all kinds of folks. A lot of them hiked down there together, prepared to camp outside in the cold until the camps officially opened and they were allowed entrance. Turns out when they reached the comfort camps there was a big sign announcing that all recovery efforts in the region had been canceled due to insurgent activity."

Jim's gut knotted up. He didn't have to ask what that meant and why this conversation was being directed at him. He was pretty sure he had a good idea. "Why were these men here to discuss that?"

"It was kind of an informal thing. They said they represented a group of concerned citizens of the county. They wanted to know what I, as the chief law enforcement officer of the county, was doing to arrest the aforesaid insurgents."

"Well, technically, I'm not even sure the power plant is in your jurisdiction. Isn't it over the county line?"

"I mentioned that," the sheriff said. "You know what their response was?"

"Surprise me."

"They said that it was my jurisdiction if the insurgents were based out of this valley."

Jim shook his head bitterly. It took him a moment to reply. "Where did they get the idea that this valley was the source of *insurgent activity*?"

"They didn't say exactly, but I got the impression it was Wimmers talking to more Wimmers. The valley Wimmers talking to the town Wimmers. I'm not certain that's the *only* way that the story got legs but it's made its rounds. They told me the people in town accept it as fact."

"Accept what as fact, exactly?"

The sheriff hesitated before replying. "That *you* were behind that attack on the power plant."

"I've heard that same rumor."

"What was your response?" the sheriff asked.

"I may have threatened to kill the person who asked me about it. I may also have mentioned that they had faulty information."

The sheriff became pensive. "I don't think you can kill men fast enough to stop this rumor. It's spreading like wildfire."

"I guess the thing I need to know is whether you intend to do anything about it," Jim stated. "We're telling folks it was an ice dam under the bridge that flooded. If they hear enough contradictory information no one will know what is true."

"That might be a believable story if it wasn't for the gunshots and the fact that the residents of low-lying areas around the plant were warned of the flood risk in advance. They said a woman and two young men were waking people, shouting warnings that the river was backing up. Now I know I'm a sheriff and not a detective, but their descriptions sounded an awful lot like Randi, Pete, and Charlie."

Despite the sheriff's questioning look, Jim gave no visible reaction to that piece of information. "What's your official position on this?"

"That I will look into it."

"Unofficially? Between us? Do I need to watch myself around you now?"

The sheriff shook his head. "No. Law enforcement is pretty low on my priority list right now. I just want to keep the rest of my family alive."

Jim nodded. "I'm not sure we've seen the end of this."

"I'm afraid you're right."

"My advice would be you warn them not to push me."

"If I see them, I'll pass it on."

"You do that," Jim said, starting back down the long gravel driveway. He definitely needed that drink.

11

Joint Base Anacostia-Bolling (JBAB)

THROUGHOUT HIS RECOVERY Boss trained obsessively. It connected him with his old life. Regardless of who he was embedded with, regardless of the assignment, that was what special operations folks did. They worked every day to make themselves the best at what they did. It wasn't about vanity. It wasn't about gym muscles or appearances. It was about survival, endurance, and being the baddest man on the battlefield. It was about being able to annihilate anyone who got in the way of your mission.

Recovering from the initial surgery to clean up the amputation, he focused on cardio because he couldn't put direct pressure on the wound. The doctors didn't want him doing anything at all. He was supposed to take it easy for several weeks, but not doing anything would impact his conditioning in a way he just couldn't accept. Besides, for Boss, running a half marathon before breakfast every day *was* taking it easy. There were no weights, no sandbags, and no combatives. He wasn't getting bruised, tossed, punched, or face-planted in the dirt so he considered it an easy day.

When the wound appeared to be healing properly, closing up with no infection, Boss broadened his workout routine. He added sit-ups and worked his core. He worked the medicine ball with his left hand, trying to develop the reflexes on his left side that he'd had a lifetime to develop on his right. In his practical way of thinking, he didn't see the loss of his right hand as his biggest problem. It was that his left hand didn't have the reflexes of his right.

Like every career gunslinger, he'd trained for offhand shooting. Everyone understood that there could be a time when their strong hand, their dominant hand, became injured and they'd have to defend themselves with their offhand. He was already proficient with aiming and shooting with the left hand. He knew all the tricks for offhand mag changes and transitioning the weapon.

However, he'd only treated those techniques as backup measures. He'd never approached left hand shooting as if it might become his primary means of doing his job. That had to change. Left-handed holsters and ambidextrous weapons would be the easy parts. It was the retraining that would be difficult.

With that goal in mind, he spent hours at the range running drills. He ran through every function of his handgun. He did hundreds of mag changes every day, cleared jams, loaded magazines. It felt weird. Even moving with a gun felt weird when he was relying on his left hand to do all the work. He wished the machinists could make him a handgun attachment for his gauntlet system. Even if they could, they had no way of enabling him to fire it without using a second hand. He would just have to suck it up and become as proficient as he could.

Boss was running through an especially challenging drill when he felt like he was being watched. He whipped around to find a short, white-haired man with a bushy handlebar mustache watching him. He made no effort to hide that this was what he was doing. Already uncomfortable with his performance and more than a little frustrated, Boss was not in the mood to be providing entertainment to some old codger. He felt like he was being evaluated and that pissed him off. Who did this guy think he was to be watching him that way?

"Can I help you?" Boss growled, attempting to express all of his aggravation in his question. His tone would have sent most people scurrying if the death stare didn't get them first.

The old man was nonplussed. "No, just watching."

"I don't like being watched," Boss said. "Fuck off, you old buzzard."

"I might be able to help you."

Boss snarled. "I'm not in the mood for coaching, Grandpa. Beat it before you piss me off."

The old man came closer. Boss was surprised by his audacity. Could he not take a hint? Did he not sense the danger in ignoring Boss's warning?

The old man gestured at the gun in Boss's hand. "I see you're a fan of the 1911 platform. Me too. Totally wrong choice for you, though, considering your impediment."

Boss glared at him. "I don't remember asking your opinion, but my duty assignment allows me to choose my own sidearm. I prefer a .45, thank you."

"You need to minimize mag changes. With a few changes you could reduce how much work you have to do to run a handgun."

"What do you know about it?" Boss growled. "Range Safety Officer? Appleseed instructor?"

"I'm a Marine, asshole. When I was on active duty I was an armorer. Depending on the mission I was probably embedded with every kind of special operations unit you've ever heard of and probably a few you haven't. For some damn reason they brought me back when the attacks hit. I'm not sure if it was because they needed me or because someone felt like they owed me a favor. Either way, here I am."

"What a sweet story," Boss muttered. "All heartwarming and shit."

The armorer didn't react to Boss's sarcasm. Maybe he was senile. Perhaps he'd dealt with special ops egos before. "I could set you up with a better handgun. Something more suited to your particular needs. I think you'd be impressed at the difference."

Boss had a fleeting moment of indecision. As much as he was irritated by the intrusion into his training, perhaps he should listen to him. It was like using the machinists to build special gear for him. He should chill his attitude a second and listen. He might actually know what he was talking about. "Okay, I'll play your game. What would you recommend?"

"A Glock 17."

"Why a Glock?" Boss asked. He was not a fan of "the block."

The old man shrugged. "Availability of aftermarket accessories. You should have an extended slide release. We could put a magwell on the Glock that would make rapid mag changes easier by funneling the mag into the grip. We can outfit your mags with extended base plates so they're easier to grip. There's even an extended charging handle available for the Glock that would make it easier to rack with one hand. No more fighting to snag the sights. Hell, you could even run thirty-three round mags if you wanted."

Boss considered the information. The old bastard had persisted in trying to help him even when he was being a jerk. Boss saw value in everything the older man suggested. He definitely knew his stuff.

Boss walked toward him and extended his hand. "Sorry I was an asshole."

The old man took it and shook. "Son, you're not going to hurt my feelings. I've worked with all kinds. I've been cursed in more languages than you've even heard. What do I call you?"

"They call me Boss."

"They call me Gabby."

"I'd like to try a Glock set up like you're talking about," Boss said. "This is a struggle under ideal conditions. It'll suck worse in combat. Throw in some sweat, blood, and adrenaline and it could turn into a shit show."

"Not to be nosy, but are you going to be around base for a while?" Gabby asked.

"I'm temporarily reassigned here until I get a medical clearance for field work."

"Then give me a couple of days to pull together the supplies I need. Have you considered a rifle setup?"

"I wasn't sure if there was an option for that," Boss said. "I hadn't really considered it."

"When I get the Glock set up, I'll meet you here to test function. I'll bring a couple of bullpups. You aren't one of those guys who hates a bullpup are you?"

Boss nodded.

Gabby smiled at that. "I love changing attitudes. A bullpup is going to be your best friend."

"I'll believe it when I see it."

From the range, Boss headed for the racquetball court at the base fitness center. He was almost embarrassed to be seen going into a racquetball court. He'd always associated the sport with assholes, but for him, it was about one thing—reflexes.

He didn't like playing with other people. In general, he didn't like the kind of people who played racquetball. Sometimes folks banged on the clear wall to inquire if he wanted a partner. His murderous glare sent them on to the next court. He wasn't interested in making friends. He was interested in teaching his left arm to lash out without him having to think about it. The high speed environment created by batting the ball around the small room was the perfect way to build that skill. In his mind, it wasn't a racquet he was wielding but a combat knife.

After he sweated out his demons, he took a quick shower and headed for his next destination. It was late evening and hot. Even though his apartment had functioning air conditioning, he'd much rather be out in the field. It was where he felt at home. He desperately wanted back in action but had no idea how long it might be before that happened.

He hadn't given up on revenge. Since his injury he'd knocked around thoughts of how he might exact his revenge without compromising his obligation to Owen. In fact, when he was not actively engaged in some task or working out to the point of puking, it was where his mind settled. It was the low spot in the landscape of his thoughts. He'd eventually come to the conclusion that even though he couldn't personally launch a scorched earth campaign on the residents of southwestern Virginia, it didn't mean a mission couldn't be run. He could treat it like any of the other dozens of missions he was personally overseeing now, at least until it was time for the grand finale. Then he would step in and get his hands dirty.

When he had a rough plan fleshed out he started monitoring chopper traffic in and out of the base. Occasionally, he saw Gordon's team, the people who'd rescued him from the power plant, coming and going. He was aware they'd come in the previous night. When he made an inquiry he found out they'd be on base for forty-eight hours while their chopper underwent routine maintenance. A further inquiry led him to the quarters they'd be staying at while their chopper was serviced. That was his next stop for the evening.

While Boss didn't know where Gordon and his crew were based out of, they were overnighting in some of the temporary quarters that had sprouted up in every empty corner of the base. People, both military and civilian, were showing up every day. Boss had no idea where they were all coming from but he understood the influx included government VIPs in need of shelter, engineers on their way to power generation assignments, and military folks from all branches. There was no shortage of supplies, but there was a shortage of space inside the wire. Some base personnel were currently being fed in tents instead of the normal dining facilities. Boss assumed they'd been displaced to make room for the VIPs who didn't want to eat without air conditioning.

The placement of the temporary housing units created tight alleys not even wide enough for a vehicle to pass through. With the gun emplacements, armed troops, and the general atmosphere of urgency, the facility more closely resembled an operating base in Iraq than an urban base on American soil. After months where the city surrounding them had no power, the area was even developing the smell of a war zone. Large diesel generators hummed like trucks, powering lighting and climate control for the congested tent city. Boss couldn't imagine the civilians sleeping in the noise but the military folks wouldn't even notice it.

The base was operating with limited services. They had fuel, generator power, and the toilets flushed. Millions in the city around them had a lot less. If Boss was in charge, he would have shut the damn place down and pulled all personnel back to a facility that wasn't surrounded by so many folks wanting what they had. There were a ton of bases within range of a truck convoy.

Remaining there was supposed to be symbolic. Those in charge didn't want to vacate the seat of power. They didn't want to surrender Washington, D.C. for fear they'd never get it back. They didn't want to vacate the White House or the Capitol Building for the message that sent to the public. They had the whole area surrounded by a security perimeter, complete with concertina wire and sniper nests. Although the center of power was safe for now, it was a tenuous foothold. If the angry residents decided to overrun them, it would be a difficult wave to put down.

Weaving his way through the maze of brown air beam tents and hastily erected plywood buildings, Boss was certain there was some type of organizational system in place but he couldn't figure it out. There were markings on the structures, though nothing to tell him which way he needed to go. After finally asking the right person, he found the right tent.

He entered an airlock system that used two separate doors to keep the cooler conditioned air trapped inside. The interior of the tent was a vast open space the size of a gymnasium. While some of the tents had plywood interior walls with individual rooms this one didn't. Cots were neatly aligned in rows throughout most of the floor space. This wasn't a home, it was a crash pad. Only a few were occupied, which should make Boss's job easier.

He went from cot to cot, searching for a familiar face. It took him a half-dozen to finally spot the guy he thought he was looking for. The last time he'd seen Gordon it had been under different conditions. Boss had been drugged and delirious. Gordon had been wearing a helmet and flight gear. Boss had done his homework, though. He'd accessed Gordon's service record while he was developing his plan. He'd gotten a good gander at his picture and refreshed his memory.

He leaned over the bunk and nudged him. "Gordon."

There was grumbling from some of the bunks.

"What the fuck, dude!" one man grumbled, raising up and glaring at Boss. The expression he got in return made him lay down and shut his mouth.

"Gordon!" Boss repeated, shaking him harder.

Gordon groaned, turned his head, and opened his eyes. "What the hell? What do you want, man?"

"It's Captain Ballou. You pulled me out of that power plant. Remember?"

Gordon blinked a few times, trying to focus. Boss was cleaner, less rough around the edges, than the last time he saw him. "Give me a minute."

"I'll be out front," Boss said.

He left the dim sleeping quarters and took a seat on a crude bench in front of the tent, watching the activity taking place around him. He couldn't imagine this base had ever seen the level of activity it was seeing now. There was a steady stream of choppers flying in and out, and convoys of vehicles were running missions, armed up like they were on patrol in Iraq or Afghanistan.

Gordon came staggering out in a pair of running shorts and dropped onto the bench beside Boss.

"Late night?" Boss asked.

"We hit the base around sunup," Gordon said. "I hadn't slept in twenty-four hours. Everything has been turn and burn the last few days. I'm surprised they haven't grounded the pilot for exceeding his flight hours."

“Nobody is grounding pilots right now. We fly them until they drop.”

“Obviously,” Gordon said.

"Sorry to drag your ass out of bed."

Gordon yawned. "It’s cool. I guess I have shit to do anyway." He pulled a cigarette from behind his ear and stuck it in his mouth. He had a lighter in his palm and lit the smoke, taking a deep inhale. First of the day. It was the moment smokers lived for, up until it killed them.

"I need a favor," Boss said.

Gordon exhaled then turned to look at Boss, seeing no clue in his face as to how serious a favor it might be. "What is it?"

“You fly on a regular basis over that region of southwestern Virginia where you picked me up?”

Gordon had both hands on his thighs, almost like he was holding himself up. His cigarette dangled from his lip, defying gravity as he spoke. "I don't know our exact schedule, man. Shit has been chaotic, but we’ve been that way at least twice a week or so. It’s a regular flight path."

"I need you to do something for me on your next trip west. It has to be in that same area."

Gordon’s expression changed. People were always asking him to do things. They wanted him to stop and ask about their parents, search for their family, or even feed their dog. Gordon didn't mind helping out when he could but his crew ran on a tight schedule. They could fit in a few unsanctioned stops but couldn't exactly be stopping to launch missions in hostile areas without command approval.

“What is it?” Gordon asked hesitantly.

"No landing, no boots on the ground. I just need you to throw a loop in your flightpath and circle over that general region once or twice."

Gordon took another drag on his cigarette. It was starting to get dark and solar powered floodlights kicked on near them, bathing the ground in a harsh yellow light. "You looking for someone? You think you got a team member out there still alive? We didn’t see anyone else when we picked you up but the conditions were pretty bad."

Boss shook his head. "Nothing like that. Just a little information dissemination. I’ve got some flyers that I need you to throw out over the population centers."

"What kind of flyers?"

"Does it matter?"

Gordon shrugged. "I guess not. Just being nosy, but I guess I should know better, right? It doesn't sound like a big deal. I’m sure we can help you out."

Boss smiled. “I appreciate that. I told you before, I'm a good man to have in your debt. This favor won’t be forgotten."

Gordon flipped his cigarette into a bucket by the door. "No problem, man. I’m just glad to see you're doing okay."

Boss held up the arm with the missing hand. "I guess, as long as you consider this okay."

Gordon stretched and stood up. "You’re on the right side of the dirt, brother. Not every man can say that."

Boss knew that to be true as well. He’d buried his fair share of friends. Yet, he was struggling to adapt in a field of expertise where physical prowess was such a significant part of his identity.

Boss stood and patted Gordon on the back. "Thanks, Gordon. You'll be hearing from me. Go on back to bed."

“Shit, Captain, it’s Miller time. I’m off-duty tomorrow.”

12

J*oint Base Anacostia-Bolling (JBAB)*

THE NEXT DAY, Boss slipped out at lunchtime to pay a visit to a supply clerk he'd befriended several years ago. He'd run missions before where he needed custom maps printed, and the supply clerk was his connection for getting things printed on weatherproof paper. The stuff was like those crinkly white suits that painters wore but it was difficult to tear and wouldn't smear under the worst of conditions.

The printing office was a good distance from the operations building Boss was working out of. He took the opportunity to run, not wanting to waste good training time after being cooped up inside all day. He had a good sweat going when he stepped into the long, low building where copying and printing took place. The first thing he noticed was the air-conditioning. Most places on the base didn't have functional air-conditioning since it required so much additional electric power.

"Can I help you?" a scrawny girl with tattoos and a nose ring asked. She appeared to be about twenty-two. Or twelve.

Boss regarded her before replying. "You have air conditioning?"

She smiled. "I know, right? We tried going without it and all the paper products started curling. People griped because it wouldn't go through the copiers and printers anymore. Something about the humidity. Next thing you know, we have air conditioning." She threw her hands up like it was a gift bestowed by the gods and she had no inkling from where it came.

"I'm looking for Fuller," Boss said.

"Uh, he doesn't work here anymore," the girl said. "My name is Marsha. Can I help you?"

She had to be new. She was too damn helpful for someone working on a military base. "Where's Fuller?"

She threw her hands up again, as if he'd poofed out of existence right before her eyes. "Something about being short-handed somewhere. They made him somebody's aide. They said civilians could handle this job just fine and that's what I'm doing."

Boss considered this. He wasn't certain if her being a civilian would increase or decrease his chances of getting what he wanted. Either way, his approach would be the same as he would have used with Fuller–an appeal to greed. "I need something printed on that weatherproof paper."

"Weatherproof paper..." Marsha repeated, scratching her ear.

"They use it for maps."

She pointed a finger at him. "Oh, I've seen that. Map paper!"

"Yes, map paper used for maps. Can I take a look at it?"

"You want me to bring you a piece of it?" she asked.

"No," Boss said. "I need to see the supply. I need to know how much you have."

Marsha regarded the long counter separating her from Boss. At the end, a plastic chain stretched between eye hooks kept him out of the "employee only" section. "I don't know about that. Are you allowed back here?"

Boss raised an eyebrow at her. He thought of all the places he'd been in this world, both officially and unofficially. That this girl would question his ability to step behind the counter at the base print shop was nearly laughable. Boss glanced around. “I don’t think anyone will say anything. We’re good.”

"What are you using it for? ‘Cause, like, we have this process where you requisition stuff. Like, you request it *officially* and then we’re like ‘that’s cool, man, come get it.’"

"I can’t tell you what it’s being used for. I’m familiar with the requisition process but this is an emergency. Something just came up."

She screwed her mouth up in uncertainty. "I don't know. I'm new to this base. How do I know I won’t get in trouble?"

Boss assessed the young girl. “How did you get this job?”

She smiled. “My dad. He’s assigned here. I was in college at Virginia Commonwealth University and he brought me up until things got safe again. My whole family is here.”

That explained a lot. "You want to earn some money?”

Marsha became cautious. She’d obviously had a bad experience with that particular question at some point in her past. “I don’t have to do something creepy, do I? Not that I wouldn’t, but I’d have to think about it.”

"Nothing creepy,” he said. “It would have to be confidential though. This is related to a top secret operation. National security and all, you know.”

“No problem. I’m all about patriotism and shit. Seriously.”

“Then let’s see what you have in weatherproof paper.”

She led him back to the paper section of the storeroom but couldn’t point out specifically which paper was weatherproof. Boss found it himself after about ten minutes of digging around. In the same section, he found two pallets of high-visibility weatherproof paper. He’d used the same stuff in psy-ops before, dropping pamphlets over occupied territory in the Middle East. That would be even better than map paper and there was a hell of a lot of it.

“This is what I need,” Boss said.

She grabbed a ream of five hundred sheets from the top. "How much do you need?"

"All of it."

Marsha's eyes widened. "All of it?" She studied the pallet, trying to figure out just how many reams were in the two pallets before her.

It was time to cut to the chase. Boss slipped his hand in his shirt pocket and came out with a shiny gold coin which he raised between two fingers. It was another of the Krugerrands. "Do you know what this is?"

"It looks like gold, man."

"It is a gold coin. It amounts to damn good compensation for work you can do while you're already working here at this job. No extra time but a good bit of extra pay. You can't say anything about it to anyone. Not even your dad."

She nodded seriously. "Got it. What do I need to do?"

"I'm going to give you a document. I need that document printed on that paper."

"Easy enough."

"Then you stack the printed flyers back in the boxes and I'll have someone pick them up."

She eyed the coin pinched between two of Boss's fingers. "How much is that thing worth?"

Boss shrugged. "Around thirteen hundred dollars when I got this one. Since the shit hit the fan, who knows?"

"More than that now?"

Boss nodded. "Much more."

She smiled. "Where's the file? I'll get started tonight."

He handed her a USB thumb drive. "Take it to a machine and open it now. I want to make sure you don't have any trouble with the file."

She did as he asked. When the document opened, she read it. When she was done, she turned to Boss with an alarmed expression on her face. "What the fuck, dude?"

Boss held a finger to his lips. "Remember, not a word to anyone. This is a matter of national security."

EARLY THE NEXT morning before his shift in the war room, Boss ran by the print shop. The place wouldn't open for another couple of hours but Boss knocked on the back window and found Marsha in the final stages of her marathon copying session. Fueled by energy drinks and God knew what else she'd pulled an all-nighter and earned the money Boss had promised her.

She opened the back door and he slipped inside, locking it behind him.

"Dude, that was a long night. I've got, like, paper cuts everywhere and I'm pretty sure I've got a toner buzz going on."

Boss was impressed. "You took on a job and you kicked its ass. That's something to be proud of."

"Hell yeah, I kicked its ass!" she confirmed, as if there'd been any doubt this would be the outcome. The girl had bravado if nothing else.

Boss liked her attitude. That was part of the reason he never felt that an overtone of menace was required with her, as it often was with other people. This girl was down to play along. A challenge with money at the end was fine with her.

"How long until you finish?" he asked

She threw a quick glance at the running copiers, the boxes of open paper, and the nearly full pallet. "Like an hour," she replied hesitantly. "I'm running five copiers at a time and it's kept me hopping all night. I've run my ass off."

Boss checked his watch. "Will that give you enough time before other employees show up?"

"It'll be enough. Then what?"

Boss glanced at the two pallets with concern. This was going to take some coordination. He may have been a hair ambitious in getting this many flyers made. He hoped Gordon was heading out empty or there would be no room for a cargo of this weight. They could transport it in the cargo net, but then how would Gordon be able to scatter the flyers? They needed to be inside the aircraft so he could scatter them by the handful.

Then there were the fuel considerations. The additional weight of all this paper could impact their fuel consumption enough to throw off the refueling schedule. Boss checked one of the boxes of paper and recorded the weight, then did a quick calculation based on how many boxes were on the two pallets. He raised his eyebrows. It was considerably more than he had anticipated at around one ton per pallet. He was going to have to compare notes with Gordon and figure out how they would pull this off.

"I'll have a truck come by here to pick this up in one hour. Wherever you are in your work when the truck gets here, that's where you stop. You got it?"

"Got it."

"Do you have a forklift?"

"Of course, and I can run it too."

"Why am I not surprised?"

She stuck her hands in her pockets. "Not to seem like a greedy bitch or anything, but when do I get paid?"

Boss laughed at her directness. With the right training, a girl like this could be good on a team. She had the right attitude. He reached inside his pocket and pulled out a single Krugerrand.

Her eyes lit up at the sight of the coin and she held out her hand. He placed it in the center of her palm and locked eyes with her.

"You don't lose this. Don't show it to anybody. And don't spend it anytime soon. Got it?"

She nodded enthusiastically. "I know how to keep secrets, dude. I got a stash and no one will see it."

"You do that, Marsha. I can't afford people asking questions. As I said, this is a confidential operation. I expect you to maintain operational security. If you follow the rules, there could be more work for you in the future."

She clearly liked the sound of that, although Boss wasn't sure if it was the money that held her attention or the intrigue that she was contributing to a secret operation.

"Nice doing business with you. You know where to find me if you have something else."

"Appreciate it. Now remember – one hour. You'll need to button all this up and make sure everything is cleaned up. Flush that thumb drive down the toilet and clear the memory on all the printers, and make sure there's nothing in the trash. Shred everything."

Marsha gave him a weary thumbs-up and Boss headed out the door.

He double timed it over to the motor pool and spoke with a friend. Boss wouldn't waste a Krugerrand on this service but he did offer him a top-notch bottle of rye whiskey to transport the pallets of flyers to a special hangar. He had already arranged for a friend there to receive the pallets and keep them under wraps until they were ready to load on Gordon's chopper.

Boss wanted this whole operation to commence quickly. The longer those flyers sat around base, the greater the likelihood that someone could find them. It wasn't like he would face serious repercussions for distributing the flyers but if they were discovered it might scuttle any further plans. Owen might put a guard on him or start having him followed.

He checked his watch again, then looked at the sky. The sun wasn't up yet, though the black was turning to gray and it would be light soon. He had time for another couple of miles before he had to be at work in the war room. He kicked up his pace to a steady run and burned through the cool morning air.

13

Despite Jim's reservations, Gary, Debra, Will, and Gary's daughter, Sara, made plans to travel to town one morning. Sara was doing a lot better after Randi gave her some tough love, basically telling her to snap out of it or crawl off to die somewhere. Her instability had been a drag on the family but she was back with a vengeance. Everyone processed grief in their own way and hers had been a hard way. She had to stare her own death in the face and choose to come back among the living.

In the days leading up to the trip, Debra used colorful yarn to tie small bundles of greens and herbs for trade. They were all about the same size, making them a consistent unit of barter. Gary and Will dredged through the odd bits of gear they'd accumulated from the skirmishes they'd had since coming to the valley. When they killed men in battle, they stripped the bodies of useful gear. It was not something anyone was proud of but there was no sense in leaving it there to ruin or be stolen by someone else. In this manner they had accumulated plastic bags of ammunition that didn't fit their weapons. They had a few extra flashlights and some cheap knives they would take to the market with them. They intentionally chose not to take too much, wanting to feel out the market first.

They went to the effort to make a list of the specific items each person in their family wanted. It included those hygiene items they were running low on, diapers, and baby formula. They were also after seeds, vitamins, and hot sauce, an item Will was craving. They didn't have high expectations of what they might find at the market but they wouldn't know unless they went. Before stores came along, this was how it was done and here they were again.

They'd be riding in on horses instead of walking. The tribe as a whole had accumulated more horses over the winter, both through trading, spoils of skirmishes, and rescuing starving animals. They had a growing herd but Jim convinced them not to take too many to town. The valley tribe shouldn't appear to have a surplus of animals. That might make them a target for thieves. After all, he reminded them, Buddy had been killed by folks wanting his horse for food. Not everyone saw the same thing in a horse anymore. While one man saw a ride, another saw a steak dinner.

They chose to ride double, the four of them taking just two horses. Debra filled an old bushel basket with her trade goods, making a strap of paracord that allowed her to carry it over her shoulder. She hoped it would allow her to carry her greens without mangling them.

Debra plied Gary with questions, trying to get an idea of what they might find there in town, but he was of little help. He hadn't paid enough attention to the vendor tables on his last trip into town, mostly because he was so concerned Jim was going to kill someone. He had no idea if it was the same vendors every time or a rotating assembly of desperate peddlers. They would have to see what awaited them when they got there.

Their ride in was the most relaxing activity the group had undertaken as a family since being driven from their neighborhood. The spring sky was robin's egg blue and it lifted everyone's mood. The grass was greening up in sporadic tufts. The trees were sprouting buds and diminutive leaves. Birds were everywhere, their lives relatively unchanged by the strife of humankind. Chipmunks scurried erratically. The riders caught occasional glimpses of timid fawns, camouflaged by their spotted hides. Baby rabbits, smaller than softballs, scurried from behind clumps of grass, torn between curiosity and fear.

At the river crossing, the water ran high from spring showers and melted snow but was low enough to cross with no worries. This crossing was used long before cars came along. In a previous century, folks had rolled away the submerged rocks to create a relatively smooth lane beneath the water. It had probably been a pleasant task on a hot summer day.

Just beyond the crossing, where the paved road ran along the riverbank, was the wreckage of a previous battle. Bullet-riddled cars sat askew, tires in the ditch, or tangled together by crumpled bodywork. The very sight of it changed the mood of the group. For a few brief moments between the valley and town they had been able to forget that they were in a survival situation. That moment of euphoria was over.

Death was never far away. The reminders of its presence were constant. If they let their guard lapse it could be them dying on the road next time. If they didn't work hard enough it could be them starving over the winter. If they didn't plan sufficiently their family might be smaller come this time next year. Gary had heard the expression many times that dying was easy and living was hard. There was proof of that at every turn. There were more ways to live than there were to die.

"What happened here?" Debra asked, seeing the way Gary looked at the cars.

She'd heard stories about the various fights they'd gotten into but they were out of context for her. She'd never made this trip to town, never seen the sites where the battles took place.

Since he'd brought his family to Jim's valley, Gary had done what he could to spare them from the ever-present carnage. To some extent it had worked, though the stories of death and sounds of gunfire were inescapable.

"There was a gunfight here. Men were killed. Some of them were good and some were the bad. There was a deputy killed here and it isn't far from where Alice died, in that cornfield over there. That's how this whole experience has been. You can't enjoy a beautiful day without hitting a reminder that things are far from perfect in the world."

"You have to find some way to enjoy life," Debra said. "If not, why stick around and live it?"

"That's the struggle I go through." Gary sighed. "If you become so hardened that things like this don't bother you anymore, have you become *so* hardened that you can't enjoy the good things?"

"Then tell yourself these cars are here because of an accident. Back when we were growing up there used to be cars laying down over steep hills all over the place. People wrecked them and never went back for them. When those wrecks first happened, I'm sure there were stories attached to them. Eventually everybody forgot the stories. Treat this the same way. There was a wreck and the car just hasn't been towed. Change the old story. Forget the old story."

Gary couldn't imagine he could actually convince himself of that. He couldn't pull the rose-colored glasses over his eyes and pretend bad things didn't happen. Wasn't that a disservice to the people who had been lost? Didn't they deserve to be remembered? If he tried to lie to himself, tried to rewrite the narrative, his brain would speak up and remind him of the truth.

"I've noticed your friend Jim is getting that way," Debra said.

"What way?" Immersed in his own thoughts, Gary had lost track of where the conversation had left off.

"He's allowing himself to become so hardened that he struggles to let the good emotions in. The light isn't reaching him anymore."

It was an interesting way to think of it, that the light wasn't reaching Jim anymore. It was an apt description of the darkness that ruled his personality lately. Gone was the sarcastic smartass, gone was the joking. Jim was angry. He was a smoldering firework that had not yet exploded but everyone was afraid to get close to.

"He probably struggles with that every day," Gary finally said.

Debra frowned. "He's losing the fight."

"He might be surrendering the fight," Gary countered. "I think he sees it as the only way he can save his family. He had to become that way so they don't have to."

"I never considered that," Debra said.

"It's a sacrifice people sometimes have to make in hard times. If you let yourself become the kind of person it takes to survive, you can become unreachable. You win but at a very high cost."

"That makes me very sad for him."

"Me too, and I don't want to go down the same road. I worry about that a lot."

Debra shook her head. "It won't happen to you. You're different."

"How am I different?" Gary asked. "I'd really like to know. It might make me slightly less worried about what I'm becoming."

"I can't tell you. It wouldn't make sense to you. I know it, though. I know it like I know my children. I know it like I know the back of my hand. You're not Jim and you'll never be Jim. You're made different."

Gary thought about that. He didn't know where to put that information. Was that good? Was it bad? Was it a judgment against him or praise for him? Going beyond his own selfish concerns, what did it say about his friend? What did it foretell for his family?

"You ready?" Debra asked, seeing no more reason to stand around at the scene of bad memories and past history.

"There will be more of it," Gary said.

"I expect there will be."

Five minutes of slow riding brought them to the side access to the superstore parking lot. Gary and Will had both been here before but Debra and Sara had not. They'd gotten used to seeing those stores a particular way. They were always open, always illuminated, things were always orderly. None of that was the case now.

Plate glass windows, broken during periods of violence, were patched with plywood and signs ripped from other storefronts. Cars were overturned and pointing in all directions, bullet holes riddling their sheet metal, glass shattered. Trash that would not burn was scattered everywhere.

"It reminds me of the pictures you see of what the Woodstock festival looked like after all the people left," Sara said.

Debra nodded. “It does.”

Gary reined his horse to a stop and told his family the story, how a few corrupt cops had walked off the job and built a small army. “This was their base. They fortified it with cars and terrorized people who went by. This is where Hugh came from and where Alice died.”

"Why are there so many cars here?" Sara asked.

"Most of them probably came off the highway," Gary said. “They were driving along and got low on gas. They pulled in here thinking they could fill up. When there was no gas available some of them chose to park their cars here."

"What happened to the people?" Sara asked.

"Who knows? The entire country is littered with vehicles like this now. The road back from Richmond was like this. That's why the magnitude of this disaster is hard to comprehend, and why the recovery will be so difficult. Whenever I hear people say we’ll be back to normal soon, scenes like this are what I remember. Even if the power comes back on, how many folks don't have a car or a home anymore? Will insurance companies pay for this or will they all be bankrupted by the scale of it? If they don’t pay to rebuild people’s damaged homes, what will people do? The nuts and bolts details of what’s required to get this country back on its feet are overwhelming."

Debra nudged their horse into motion. "Let's do what we came here for."

Gary held the reins but his mind was elsewhere. Perhaps she was right. Maybe he thought about it too much. Had he let the scale of it overwhelm him when he just needed to focus on the immediate future? People like he and Jim—the prepared folks all around the nation—had been validated. Although they had been singing about infrastructure vulnerabilities and the public’s general lack of preparedness for years, what good had it done? Were they expecting someone to pat them on the back and congratulate them?

That wasn't going to happen. There was no prize for being right. The reward for being right was misery, suffering, and loss, which was exactly the same prize you got for being wrong. It may have been lessened a bit because of the preparation they'd made but that didn't spare them from the suffering. There was no mercy.

At the farthest end of the parking lot near the gas pumps was the vendor area. The metal canopy covering the pumps provided the vendors some protection from the sun or rain. The size of the event had grown since the last time Gary, Randi, and Jim came through. The better weather might have put people in a trading mood, or at least made them want to get out of the house.

Gary halted his horse and told Will to hold up. "Slide off, Debra."

"Here?"

"Yeah," Gary said. "We're going to leave the horses here at this restaurant."

Seeing her mother dismount, Sara did the same and asked, "Will the horses be safe here?"

"Will is going to stay and watch them," Gary said.

"Will *he* be safe?" Sara asked.

"As safe as any of the rest of us."

"I'll be fine," Will assured her.

"Will, I want you in front of the restaurant there on that grassy patch. Tie the horses off to one of those trees so you can give your full attention to your surroundings. Stay where we can see you. You're covering us and we're covering you. Got it?"

"Got it."

"Check your weapon," Gary said. "Round in the chamber, ready to go. Same for the rest of you."

Everyone did as he asked. They'd all been excited about going to the market until they were confronted with Gary's serious demeanor. He acted like they were going to an open-air bazaar in a war zone. The idea that this might be a relaxing outing had fallen by the wayside.

With their weapons dealt with, everyone made certain they had the trade goods they were willing to part with. Sara was carrying the list of things they were searching for. Will collected the reins and led the horses to a patch of overgrown grass directly in front of a chain restaurant.

"Let's go," Gary said, starting off toward the gas pumps.

Sara and Debra fell in behind him. They walked on the road but the surface crunched beneath their feet in a way it hadn't before the collapse. The highway department and vehicle traffic used to keep the roadways relatively clean but they were strewn with clutter now. Broken glass and spent shell casings ground beneath their feet. Rotting paper, discarded packaging, and empty cans aggregated against the curbs. Tattered shopping bags were caught in the trees and fluttered like bullet-riddled battle flags.

Nearing the gas pumps, Gary could see that the space beneath the metal canopy was fairly packed with vendors. There were tarps and blankets thrown out on the ground displaying a scant assortment of items the vendors hoped might hold some value. Others dispensed with the formality of any sort of ground cloth and simply lined up their goods on the dirty pavement, hoping they might catch the eye of someone wanting to trade.

Other vendors had elaborate booths like those set up by professional flea marketers. They built crude tables of cinderblocks, pallets, and scrap lumber. They sat on overturned buckets, faded camping chairs, or directly on the ground. Some booths had crude signs listing items they were needing or items they had for sale but hadn't brought with them to market. One sign advertised that the vendor was wanting to trade eggs for shotgun shells. Another promised live chickens or salt bacon for vials of insulin.

All eyes were on Gary and his family as they approached. Conversation between the vendors and the scattered customers faded.

"Why are they staring?" Sara asked.

"Maybe it's our guns," Debra suggested.

They were displaying their rifles and handguns openly. Gary had his rifle held across the front of his body, ready to raise it and fire at a moment's notice. He found being here with his family more stressful than being here with Jim and Randi. These people were his responsibility. Jim and Randi were not.

Gary's family didn't know it but it was not their weapons, their clothing, or anything of that manner. What gave the vendors pause was the direction from which these newcomers arrived. From the direction of the valley. Rarely did anyone come from that direction. Most of the vendors at this market were townspeople, as were those who came to trade with them.

There were no greetings when Gary, Debra, and Sara reached the first of the vendor tables. Conversation remained stalled, as if someone had lifted the needle on the phonograph and had yet to set it back down. Gary's family didn't let the awkwardness of the moment deter them. This was what they'd come to do. Besides, after a long winter of being shut in with no socialization, perhaps all interactions with strangers were a little awkward. People had to figure you out. They had to grasp your intentions.

The shoppers from the valley found nothing good about the goods before them. Most of what people displayed were cast-off items and housewares they had no need for. There were cooking pots, manual can openers, and broken camping stoves. There were some tools and a few old guns of the hunting variety. There were small piles of loose bullets and shotgun shells alongside knives and the singed stubs of used dinner candles. There were tattered matchbooks advertising used car lots and colorful butane lighters priced according to how much fuel remained. There were old faded spices and canning jars with no lids. The only food available was the dregs of every pantry – dented cans of olives, pimentos, peas, and beets.

Debra shot Gary a disappointed look. She'd seen none of the things on their list. They'd seen nothing worth even trading a single bundle of greens for. She wondered if they needed to engage the vendors and talk with them to find out if they had additional wares that weren't on display. It was reasonable that in this lawless world, the best items might remain out of sight.

14

Jim prayed that whatever compelled him to follow Gary's family into town was simply misplaced paranoia. Watching through binoculars from a treeless hill across the river, everything happening before his eyes told him his suspicions had been correct. There was furtive whispering taking place in the vendor area. Gary and his family either couldn't see it or mistook it for conversation. Witnessing it only increased Jim's sense of dread.

With an urgent pat on the back, a child was sent tearing across the parking lot and into the main entrance of the superstore. He emerged moments later with a handful of armed men. The boy pointed to the restaurant where Will stood guard over the horses. When the men slipped off in a crouch, ducking between shot-up cars, Jim knew it was time to act.

"Shit."

His curse wasn't merely an expression of alarm at the danger headed Will's way. It was for the whole sordid mess he was certain would eventually land in his lap. Stories would spread of Jim Powell killing more people. His reputation would continue to grow in a way that was not beneficial, nor did it promise long life and a peaceful existence. Yet he couldn't worry about that now.

Jim dug his heels into his horse, headed toward the restaurant where Will waited. Hopefully he could get there before the men closed in on the young man. Will's eyes were dutifully glued to his wife and her parents. He was not watching his six and Jim couldn't imagine Gary leaving the kid there without a lecture about monitoring his perimeter. Will was young, though, and his eyes were on his wife, concerned more with her safety than his own. The boy didn't yet understand that sometimes you had to keep yourself safe to keep others safe.

Jim dropped into the trees and lost sight of the supercenter complex, hoping he got there in time. Stealth would slow those armed men but he still had a river crossing and a stretch of road beyond that. The icing on the cake was that Jim was not a very competent horseman. He could stay atop the beast most days but held no illusion that he'd mastered the skill. If he was going fast, it was only dumb luck and random chance that kept him in the saddle.

He slowed at the bank of the river and eased the horse into the water. He let it go at its own pace, picking its steps and moving when it felt comfortable to do so. Once it was nearly across, Jim kicked it and the horse lurched, taking several great lunges to pull itself up the riverbank. Now on smoother terrain, Jim pushed the horse to a run but chose to stay just on the shoulder of the paved road. He didn't want the clatter of hooves to give his approach away.

Halfway to the supercenter he dismounted and tied his horse off to a guardrail. He sprinted up the last stretch of road, then diverged from it when he was closing in on the restaurant parking lot. He bounded up a steep bank of clumped, overgrown grass and crouched at the top, peering beneath the guardrail and into the restaurant's parking lot.

While he couldn't see Will from his position he could see three men clustered behind the restaurant, whom he assumed to be the same three he had seen crossing from the superstore. To approach without having caught Will's attention, the men must have come around the long way, travelling through fields and ditches to reach the back of the restaurant. That detour may have bought Jim the time he needed to intercept them.

Two of the men held long guns, and another was creeping toward the front of the restaurant, an aluminum baseball bat at the ready. Jim could see how this was going to play out. At least, if the men had their say. They would club Will and take the horses. Jim had no idea what lay in store for Gary and the rest of his family at that point but it could be bad. They were caught between the vendors and the armed men hidden behind the restaurant. If they were even able to flee on foot, they would do so while taking fire from two different directions. It would suck badly.

Jim played out scenarios in his head. Could he salvage this without having to kill anybody? If he yelled at the guy with the bat, alerting Will, it was likely the gunmen would open fire on him. Predicting the moves of armed and desperate men wasn't like chess. The possibilities weren't defined by a strict set of rules. It was chaos.

He was down to seconds now. He had to do something. Bat Man was a mere six feet from the corner of the restaurant now. After that, Jim would lose sight of him and there would be no easy way for him to intervene. In six feet, Will would be another valley resident lost to violence and there had been too many of those recently.

The bat wielding man flattened himself against the corner of the restaurant and listened. He was trying to guess Will's position, planning his attack. He raised the bat in front of him with both hands, hefting the weight. His chest flared in and out as he steeled his nerves.

"Fuck it," Jim hissed.

His red dot optic on Bat Man, Jim pulled the trigger twice in quick succession. At less than a hundred yards' distance there was no chance of missing a center mass shot. The first caught the bad guy square in the sternum and flattened him against the building. The bat clattered to the concrete sidewalk. Jim's second shot was a hair to the right, a heart shot. He slid down the side of the building, leaving a blood smear on the bricks behind him.

Jim swung toward the two armed men at the delivery entrance to the restaurant. He expected to find them panicking, perhaps already on the run, but they were cool under fire. In fact, they'd already spotted him. One pointed a finger in his direction while the other was doing the same with a scoped bolt-action rifle.

A screech of panic burst from Jim's throat as he flattened himself into the grass. There was a *BOOM* from the high-powered rifle and the round punched a hole in the guardrail above his head. It was immediately followed by a shotgun blast. Tiny pellets peppered the grass around Jim and pinged ineffectively off the guardrail. Jim rolled back up, his eye already on the optic, and found the guy with the rifle cycling the bolt.

As soon as the red dot crossed his body, Jim pulled off two quick shots. One round caught meat and the other ricocheted off the brick wall. The rifleman dropped his weapon and clutched at his shoulder. Jim swung back onto him and squeezed off another round. He screamed and dropped like his strings had been cut.

The man with the shotgun was backpedaling when Jim swung toward him. He pulled off one round, then another. The man was half-running, half-falling, and Jim couldn't track him fast enough. Rounds pinged off brick and concrete on all sides of him, then he was around the corner and gone.

15

Everyone in the vendor area froze at the sound of gunshots. They were too close to mean anything but trouble. Gary spun and saw Will crouched down near the grazing horses, trying to locate the shooter. From his vantage point, able to see sides of the restaurant that Will couldn't see, Gary spotted a man. It was the one with the shotgun, the one who'd escaped Jim, easing alongside the restaurant. He was heading for Will.

"Will!" Gary yelled.

Will looked in Gary's direction. Gary gestured in the direction of shotgun man. Will could see the gestures but couldn't interpret them. Did Gary want him to gather the horses and head that way?

Gary didn't have time to yell another warning; the armed man was getting too close. Sara screamed at her husband but he didn't know what the screams meant. Gary made a decision. He saw no other course of action. He raised his rifle and flipped the safety off.

Many of the vendors were startled by the gunshots, though not all of them. Some knew what was happening, knew men had been dispatched in Will's direction. Gary taking out one of their men was not part of the plan. They couldn't let that happen. One of the vendors went for a gun.

Debra caught that flicker of movement in the periphery of her vision. Following the movement, she spotted a grizzled old man pulling a revolver from the pocket of his denim jacket. Debra didn't hesitate. Her left hand shot out, pushing Gary away from the line of fire as she drew with her right. Just as Gary had trained her, she never took her eyes off the attacker. She drew and pushed out with the pistol. When the front sight centered on his chest she pulled the trigger. He jerked and sprang to his feet but did not drop the gun. She put another round in him and he sat down hard, the gun flying from his hand.

Then all hell broke loose.

Gary flinched and spun at the gunshot mere feet away from him. He saw his wife with a gun and, following the direction in which it was pointed, spotted a man writhing on the ground. Torn between helping his son-in-law and getting his wife and daughter to safety, Gary was pulled by blood. He swung his rifle toward the vendors, watching for additional threats.

It was sheer chaos. People were running, hiding under tables or beneath cars. There was screaming, crying, and shouting. Then there was another gunshot and Gary saw Sara fire a round into a woman levelling a shotgun on Debra.

"Behind that car!" Gary barked, pointing toward a gold Taurus.

He prodded Debra in that direction, then Sara, his head whipping between them and the vendors. There were people everywhere and it was impossible to tell who was a bystander and who was a threat until they pointed a gun. In the distance he saw people flooding from the superstore and running into the parking lot. Some had guns, some had baseball bats. Were they investigating the shots or there to take part in the attack?

Gary backed away from the table, sweeping his muzzle across a ninety-degree range of activity. He never took his eyes from the red dot. When that dot landed on an angry, bearded man slapping a hunting rifle across the roof of a car and pointing it in Gary's direction, he pressed the trigger. Blood sprayed and he dropped from sight.

Gary ran sideways and dropped behind the Taurus with his family. He made sure Sara and Debra were protected by the engine block, then turned his attention to Will. The guy intent on ambushing Will had thought better of it. Perhaps the gunfire had scared him and he assumed the young man would be on guard now. For whatever reason, he was backing away from the front of the store and returning in the direction he'd come from.

"Get down," Gary told his family. "Watch under the car to make sure no one is coming this way. If you see feet, blow them off."

Gary rolled onto his stomach and drew a bead on the man retreating from Will. Before he pulled the trigger, Jim flew from around the corner, dumping rounds into the approaching man. He did a staggering dance step and then dropped, blood pooling around him.

"Will!" Jim called.

"I'm here," came the young man's terrified voice.

"You're safe. Get back here with those horses."

"Got it."

Jim sprinted from the back corner of the building to an abandoned car about forty feet across the parking lot.

"I've got you covered. Go now!" Jim yelled.

His rifle dangling from its sling, Will fast-walked around the corner of the building, a set of reins in each hand. He made a beeline for the back of the restaurant. Jim crouched at the front wheel of the abandoned car, his rifle pointed across the hood, ready to provide cover. He looked for Gary and his family but didn't immediately spot them.

"Gary!"

"Here!" Gary replied.

The first wave of armed attackers from the superstore reached the perimeter wall of damaged vehicles. They took positions and began firing at the gold Taurus sheltering Gary's family, riddling it with bullets. Others from the group opened up on Jim, shattering the windows in the burgundy LTD he stood behind.

Jim ducked, shards of safety glass raining down on him. "Is anyone hurt, Gary?"

"No, just scared to death.

"You've got to come this way. We'll cover you. Can everyone run?"

Gary got wide-eyed nods. They were terrified.

"We can make it!" he yelled back.

"Will, you with me?" Jim yelled.

"I'm here," he replied.

"We've got to lay down cover fire. When they start running, let it fly. Got it?"

"Got it!"

"You guys ready?" Jim asked.

"Ready," Gary replied.

"*MOVE*!"

Gary sent his daughter first. At her appearance, Jim and Will sent rounds into the fortified wall of vehicles hiding their attackers. So as not to cluster everyone up and present a bigger target, Gary waited a full second before sending Debra on her way. She ran a bit slower, past the discarded basket of herbs and greens she'd hoped to barter. One second later, Gary followed behind her, sidestepping and joining in with the suppressive fire.

The cover fire worked against the shooters huddled behind the beat-up cars but it was at this point that gunmen on the roof of the superstore opened up. Sara had already reached the safety of the restaurant but screamed when rifles began firing from the parapet wall around the top of the supercenter. Rounds skittered off the pavement around Gary and his wife. A round hit a concrete curb and ricocheted with a distinctive whine. Panicking at the eruption of gunfire, Debra's pace broke. She faltered and her feet tangled. She went down hard, her handgun skittering across the pavement.

Gary dropped to a knee beside her and continued firing with one hand while offering an elbow to his wife.

Jim was unable to locate the source of the new gunfire until he caught a flash on the roof. "The roof! They're shooting from the roof! Light those fuckers up!"

Jim did a quick mag change and dumped rounds at the parapet wall above the main door of the supercenter. At this point he didn't care if he hit anyone or not, it was just about making them quit firing. No, forget that. He wanted to kill them. This was becoming personal.

Behind the restaurant, Will and Sara broke a quick, terrified embrace to peer around the wall and see what Jim was yelling about. Noting the angle of his fire, Will took aim at the parapet wall and started chewing through his own mag. Terrified that her parents were exposed to this withering fire, Sara got on her knees, leaned around the corner, and fired her 9mm rounds at the superstore with wild abandon.

The shooters at the superstore paused under the barrage. Gary got Debra on her feet. She loped toward the restaurant with Gary behind her, moving and shooting. He paused long enough to retrieve her handgun, never taking his eyes off the superstore. By the time he ran dry, his wife was safely behind the masonry walls of the restaurant. He broke pace and made a mad dash to join her, falling into the waiting arms of his family.

Forty yards away and crouched behind a vehicle Jim shook his head. His position was taking all the fire now. "Quit reuniting and cover my ass!" he barked. "I'm coming in!"

Gary did a quick mag change, then a pair of rifles and a pair of pistols poked around the corner, spitting hot lead. Jim bolted to join his friends, sending wild rounds in the direction of his attackers as he ran.

“What? No hugs for me?” he gasped as he blew by his friends and reached cover.

Gary quit firing long enough to throw him a look, trying to figure out if he was serious or not.

"It was a joke. Let's get out of here," Jim said. "If we don't get ahead of them, they'll box us in. There are too many to keep track of."

“What the heck even happened?" Debra asked. "One minute we were just standing around and the next, bullets are flying everywhere."

"I was watching from across the river," Jim said. "Three men came out of the superstore and headed for Will's position. I figured they were going for the horses. It was all I could do to get over here and intercept them."

"You followed us?" Gary asked between bursts of firing, his face a grimace of fear and determination.

"I had a bad feeling." Jim gestured at the dead men lying a few feet away. "We need to get out of here but I want to search these bodies first. There's this guy and two more like him around the corner. I'll be damned if I'm going to leave weapons and ammo that can be used against me the next time I come into town."

"I got this one," Will said, reaching out and snagging the dead man's pants leg.

He dragged the man around back and went through his pockets. Sara took his shotgun, checked the chamber, and kept watch around corner.

"You get this one, Gary," Jim said, pointing at the second man he shot. "I'll get the one around the far corner."

Gary crouched over the dead man, picking up his hunting rifle and slinging it over his back. He frisked the body, finding a Ruger 9mm in his belt and a pocket full of loose rounds for both weapons. Gary hesitated at shoving his hand into the blood-drenched pocket so he slit it open with his folding knife and scooped out more rifle rounds, shoving them into his own pocket.

Jim flattened himself against the wall and moved toward the first man he'd shot, the one with the bat. He found a hefty .357 magnum and one speed loader containing more rounds. The guy had a black-handled Buck knife on his belt. Jim wouldn't leave a knife behind but had no interest in unbuckling the dead man's belt. He cut the belt loose, taking knife and sheath both, shoving them in the cargo pocket of his pants.

The direction of their attacker's voices changed, as did the rate of fire. They were moving. That meant they were coming for them. They needed to wrap this up and get the hell out of there. Jim made a cursory pat-down of the shirt pockets and found a folded rectangle of Day-Glo green paper. He unfolded it, seeing the word "wanted" in bold, block letters, but was interrupted by the clatter of hooves on the pavement behind him.

"We have to go, Jim," Gary said, fear and urgency in his voice. "I think they're getting ready to rush us." His family had already mounted their horses and were ready to ride.

Jim jumped to his feet and shoved the folded paper into his pocket.

At a sudden barrage of gunfire the horses skittered. Sara made a panicked sound and grabbed Will tightly. He yanked the reins, trying to regain control of the horse.

"That way!" Jim said. "Keep this building between you and the shooters. My horse is over that bank. I'll meet you at the road."

They dug their heels into their horses and scurried toward the back of the parking lot, passed the dumpster, and disappeared over a shallow embankment. Jim followed, not wanting to expose himself to gunfire by taking the most direct route to where he'd left his horse tied. He ran behind Gary's family, then angled away to his horse tied in the woods. In less than a minute he was mounted and galloping to catch up. They couldn't ride nearly as fast as he could with two of them on each horse.

He cut them off at the intersection, just before they were to turn in the direction of the river crossing. "I'm afraid to go that way. We gave them too much time. They've probably got a trap set. They know we'll go that way and they'll cut us down."

"Then what do we do?" Debra asked.

"We cross somewhere else," Jim said. "There's another shallow crossing but it's harder to get to."

"Where?" Gary asked.

Jim pointed in the opposite direction. "The river widens out about a half mile in that direction. It's rocky so we'll have to be careful. Let your horse set the pace."

"Then let's go," Gary said. "I'll feel better when I get that river between us and them."

"It's only water," Jim said. "It won't stop them if they're determined."

Jim nudged his horse into a trot, the fastest pace they could maintain with the rest of them riding double. It would have to be fast enough. Remembering the piece of paper in his pocket, Jim dug it out. His curiosity was nagging at him. After seeing the word "wanted" printed so boldly, he assumed it might be a list of things that people needed.

He couldn't have been more wrong.

He unfolded the paper and his gut knotted. He was confronted with a grainy but terrifying image. A familiar face stared back at him.

His own face.

It took him a moment to put the image into the context. Where had he been that he would have been dressed in such a manner? Then he recalled. It was at the power plant on the night they attacked it. He'd been trapped in the frigid, rising water and was at risk of hypothermia. He'd entered one of the heated buildings and shed his clothes to warm up.

The picture, mercifully, only showed him from the chest up, but he was certain he'd been walking nude through the corridors of the control room when the image was captured. It had to have been from a security camera. That same camera would likely have caught him killing the NATO guards just seconds later.

He reined his horse to a stop. Below the image bold letters proclaimed:

WANTED FOR DOMESTIC TERRORISM
THE BOMBING OF A FEDERAL ENERGY INSTALLATION
AND THE MURDER OF TROOPS ACTING UNDER THE AUTHORITY
OF THE UNITED STATES GOVERNMENT.

REWARD OFFERED FOR LIVE CAPTURE ONLY

Reward of one year supply of food for a family of four;
One thousand rounds of 9mm ammunition;
And one thousand rounds 5.56 ammunition.

Reward may be collected at your local high school football field
On the afternoon of the 4th of July.

Build a signal fire to attract our attention.
Tie the prisoner to the goal post.
Once we have landed and confirmed his identity,
The captors will receive their reward immediately.

Happy Hunting!

"WHAT IS IT?" Gary asked, catching up with Jim.

Wide-eyed and pale, Jim handed the flyer over to Gary. He held it so that Debra could lean around him and read it.

"Was today about you, Jim?" Debra asked. "Did they attack us because of you?"

Gary shook his head. "I don't think so. They didn't know Jim would be there. It was probably about the horses. That's why they went for Will." He finished reading the flyer and handed it off to Will and Sara.

"They might have remembered you were with Jim before," Debra said. "From when you guys came through with Randi."

Jim shrugged. "It's possible but I'm thinking it was about the horses."

"Where did they even get that flyer?" Gary asked. "It's on some weird kind of paper. Like waterproof map paper or Tyvek."

No one answered her because no one even had the vaguest idea.

"We need to get moving," Jim said. He took the flyer from Will's outstretched hand, folded it, and tucked it back into his pocket.

A few hundred yards later Jim dismounted and used a multitool to cut a high-tensile fence. He continued on, leading his horse down over a bank and into a thicket of saplings and blackberry bushes. The rest fell in behind him. He led the horse with one hand, the other firmly wrapped around the grip of his rifle. They ended up on a narrow cow path that followed along the river.

"Hold up," Sara whispered.

The group came to a stop, expecting she had a rock in her shoe or had snagged herself on a vine but she was crouching by the river.

"What is it?" Gary asked.

She stood, a soggy sheet of waterproof map paper in her hand. She shook it off and held it up for the others to see. It was another copy of Jim's wanted poster. Before they reached their crossing, they found nearly a dozen more.

"How the hell did they get down here?" Will asked.

Gary, an amateur pilot, had an idea. "I would guess they did an airdrop. They scattered them from a plane or chopper."

"Dammit," Jim muttered. "That means they're everywhere. We have no chance of containing this."

"If they chose to saturate the area surrounding the power plant there could be hundreds of thousands of these floating around, based on how many we're finding here," Gary said, the gravity of that weighing on him.

"We're going to have to tighten shit up," Jim said. "We got slack this winter about manning gates and guard posts. When people quit coming around, we quit watching for them. They'll start coming again. I don't know how long these damn things have been floating around but someone will eventually recognize me. There are people in town who know where I live."

"None of us will be safe," Debra said. It wasn't an accusation, just a statement of cold, hard fact.

"This just proves it. We need to get out of this valley. We need to go back home," Sara said, tearing up. "Our own homes."

"We can't go home," Debra said, her voice stern, her jaw clenched. "It's not safe."

"It's not safe here!" Sara replied, shrill, nearly hysterical.

"Stop it! Calm down. We don't do anything yet," Gary said. "We were only able to move all our possessions to this valley because we basically stole a truck and the fuel to get it here. We can't do that again. If we have to leave the valley it will only be with what we can carry on our backs. Are you prepared to live that way?"

"Surviving out of a pack is not feasible for most families," Jim said. "It's a prepper fantasy."

"Then what the hell do we do?" Sara demanded.

"We go home because that's all we can do for now. Then we figure this shit out," Jim said. He stalked off, tugging at the reins of his horse.

After a tense, silent walk, they were able to mount up and cross the river. On the far shore, Jim guided them up into the woods and they traversed the ridge, protected by the concealment of the hardwood forest. Though most of the trees were not fully green, they broke up the profile of the riders.

Perhaps a half hour later they breached the last gap and the valley opened up before the riders. Clinch Mountain rose boldly to their right, the shoulders steep and the spine straight as a board. Knowing this was the point where radio reception in the valley began, Jim pulled his from a pouch on his vest and powered it up. "Ellen, can you hear me?"

Jim was forced to repeat the message three times, unsure if her failure to respond was due to poor reception or the fact that she often wandered around without her radio. He'd lectured her about it and she didn't take it well. It usually ended with her giving him a lecture right back about all the things he did that bothered her. It was a long list.

"Jim! This is Ellen. You okay?"

"Are Pete and Charlie nearby?" he asked, ignoring her question.

"They're in the barn skinning something they caught in their snares this morning."

"Can you get them in there with you? I need them to do something immediately."

"What's wrong?"

"I don't have time to explain it twice. Get them *now*."

He lowered the radio to his chest, waiting on her to return. He saw worry on the faces of the people in his group. This short trip had frazzled them. Taking rounds had a way of doing that to a person. In less than minute she was back.

"I got them. We're all here."

"Put Pete on."

"What is it, Dad?"

"Pete, I need you to listen to me very carefully. We ran into a little trouble in town. We're all safe and we're headed into the valley now, but we need to close our defenses up tight. Load up with all your sentry gear and get to the observation post near Buddy's old house. Stay there until you hear from me. Your job is to let us know if anyone approaches that gate. You got it?"

"I got it, Dad. Is Charlie supposed to go with me?"

"No. I need Charlie on the gate near Gary's house. Same deal. He'll need all his sentry gear, but put him on a horse so he can get down there faster. I don't know for certain we'll get any trouble but I don't want any gates unattended. Any questions?"

When neither boy had any, Ellen got back on the radio. *"What's this about Jim?"*

"This is not the time, Ellen. I don't know who might be listening. I'll tell you when I get there. Can you help get those boys on the road?"

"I'll do it," Ellen said. *"Are you close?"*

"About twenty minutes out. Make sure you're wearing your gun. Keep everyone but the boys close to home."

"Okay, Jim. I guess I'll see you when you get here." Her tone revealed that she was not happy with the lack of information. They weren't

talking on any high-tech secure radios, though. These were thirty dollar radios from the superstore. Anyone could be listening. Jim shoved the radio back in the pouch on his vest.

"I guess things have to go back to the way they used to be when we first moved to the valley. When we wore guns all the time and lived in fear." It was Debra speaking and it was not a question. It was merely a comment on the state of things, her thinking out loud and confirming all their own gnawing feelings.

"Will, when we reach the woods, do you mind manning the observation post there?" Jim asked. Of all the roads, this would be the worst to leave unattended. It was the most direct route between their homes and the angry folks they'd just done battle with.

"Why Will?" Sara asked, not wanting to part with her husband.

"We need to have an emergency meeting when we get back to the valley," Jim said, trying to be patient. "I need representatives from every family. Anybody we can spare needs to be manning an outpost."

"Can I stay with him?" she asked.

She was asking Jim but it wasn't his decision to make. "I don't care," he replied. "That's between you, your husband, and your parents."

When she expressed her desire a second time, Sara did not phrase it as a question. She'd made up her mind and was merely informing them of her decision. "I'm staying with Will," she told her parents.

Jim watched Gary, watched the concerned father cue up a response, a list of all the reasons she couldn't remain behind. Before he could put voice to them, Debra responded to her daughter.

"That's fine, honey. You do what you need to do."

It clearly wasn't fine with Gary. He looked at his wife like she'd grown a second head. The experiences they'd had since the collapse hadn't exactly turned her into someone different, as it had with many others, but it had given rise to a new pragmatism within her. It was tough for him to accept that his daughter was a grown woman and had every right to make her own decisions. She would be his little girl until the day he died. That fact was an uncontested truth of nature.

"Do you two have a radio?" Jim asked.

Will tore back the Velcro flap on a belt pouch and extracted his radio, holding it up for Jim to see.

"Power it up and let's test it."

Will did as he was asked and they tested the radio. The group rode a short distance further and stopped at a heavily forested section. Will and Sara pulled off from the group and dismounted. A few feet away, a log observation post was camouflaged into the edge of the forest.

"This isn't the Alamo," Jim said. "I don't need you trying to make some last stand if you see people coming from town. No dramatics, no hero shit. Get us on the radio. If they get close and you can't scare them off, pull back. Your main function is detection and early warning."

The pair nodded somberly.

"You guys good on ammo?" Gary asked.

It hit Jim that the question was phrased as if he were simply a dad asking his daughter if she and her date needed some extra money for the movies. How times had changed. The world had changed.

The pair pulled out their magazines to see how many rounds they'd fired. It was easy to lose count during battle, not even realizing how many times you changed magazines. Wanting to make doubly sure they had plenty of firepower, Gary handed over four full AR mags and two thirty-three round Glock mags.

Will held up the long 9mm stick mag curiously. "Will this even fire from my pistol?"

"Yes. It will stick out the bottom a little."

"A little?" Will asked, eyebrow raised.

"Okay, a lot, but those are my last resort mags. When things are hot and you're just laying down fire, they're perfect for that."

Will and Sara exchanged a look. It was the same expression millions of kids have given parents when they did something that children thought was ridiculous.

Sara tied their horse off near some grass to a short lead hanging from a nearby branch just for that purpose. Will hustled around adding fallen branches to the front of the shelter, improving the camouflage where it needed touching up.

Jim, Debra, and Gary said their goodbyes and pulled away, though Jim could tell Gary's heart was not in it. He wanted to stay. They trotted their horses toward Jim's house while he worked his radio. By the time he neared his home he'd managed to contact someone from every family associated with their tribe, explaining that they needed to have an emergency meeting and everyone should have a representative there.

Despite the crushing workload facing each family, all agreed to send someone. This excluded about a half-dozen families in the valley who had little or no interaction with Jim's group. He felt like they should be part of this but they'd shunned his efforts to be part of the group. None of them had ever participated in the valley's radio chatter, even though Jim had left messages in their mailboxes explaining the procedure. He wasn't going to be pushy. He understood people wanting their privacy and he was trying to respect their wishes.

"I've got a bad feeling about this," Gary repeated several times. "A *damn* bad feeling."

Gary rarely swore. Him emphasizing a statement with a "damn" nearly carried the same tone of finality as a judge slamming his gavel on the bench or a pastor saying amen at the end of a prayer. It carried weight. It lent a seriousness to his words as if the very future of this entire valley had been pronounced by an oracle.

16

When they reached Jim's yard, his entire family was waiting on him. The only exception was Pete, who'd already headed off toward the observation post near the house Lloyd was currently living in.

"What's going on?" Ellen demanded before he was even off his horse. She didn't like being put off on the radio, being left to wonder. There were too many truly awful possibilities in their world anymore. Then, noticing the absences among the group, her eyes widened. "Where's Will and Sara? Are they okay?"

"They're fine, Ellen," Debra assured her. "We dropped them off at the observation post on the way in. They're watching the road to town."

Ellen took a deep breath and let it out slowly. "What's going on that you needed to leave them there?" There was a tinge of panic in her voice. Things had been going so well since the battle at the power plant. She'd had a fantasy of a nice quiet summer where the worst would be behind them. Why did everything have to be so difficult? Why was the world conspiring against them?

She had no idea just how bad things were about to get.

Jim dismounted and tied his horse off to a fence post. It would have enough room to graze but he wanted to keep it saddled in case he needed to leave in a hurry. Gary and Debra did the same, tying their horse off a couple of posts away from Jim's.

Jim faced his parents, his wife, and his daughter. "I followed them into town because I had a bad feeling, but it's way worse than I thought."

Ellen had her arms folded over her chest, literally holding herself together. "Were they attacked at the market? Over that rumor about the power plant?"

"They were attacked in the market but I don't think it was over the rumor. I think it was over the fact they had horses and no one else did. But then there's this." Jim dug into his shirt pocket and removed the flyer he'd taken off the dead man, handing it to his wife. "It's worse than any rumor."

Ellen's panic meter pegged out as she read the flyer. She waved it in front of her face. "What the hell is this?"

Pops reached for the flyer. "Can I see that?"

Ellen shoved it toward Pops without taking her eyes off Jim. They were pleading and imploring. Demanding. "What is that?" she repeated slowly.

"I've got no idea. I'm nearly certain that picture is from a security camera at the power plant. There was a point where I was nearly hypothermic and had to ditch my clothes. I took shelter in some kind of control room to warm up."

Pops was shaking his head in disbelief as he read the flyer. His reaction wasn't panic but disgust. He'd had enough of violence and the worry that came along with it. He was tired of seeing his community like this.

"So is this from the government? Did they hand those out? Is the government after you now?" Ellen asked. "Because if it's the government we're fighting now we don't have a chance."

Jim shook his head quickly, trying to cap the well of surging fear. "Those guys we intercepted back in the winter, Scott and his crew, the ones walking the power lines. They talked like the government was pretty fragmented right now. Like there wasn't any single unified government making unanimous decisions and acting as a whole. This could be any one of a number of fringe elements. Hell, it may not even be anyone in the government at all. It could just be somebody local trying to stir all those rumors up into something more serious."

"I doubt the locals have access to working copy machines and that quantity of high-tech waterproof paper. They sure wouldn't have access to power plant security footage," Gary surmised.

Jim shot him a look that said *you're not helping.*

"It could be a power company," Pops suggested. "They've got power and probably copiers too. They could have obtained that camera footage. Maybe this is their way of sending a message that interference with power plants won't be tolerated."

"The whole part about the reward and showing up in a chopper to collect their *prisoner* makes me think it is some wing of the government," Jim said. "Besides, it's the government running the power plants now so I doubt there's a private corporate entity known as the power company anymore. I bet every power company employee is a government employee right now."

"That *prisoner* you refer to so calmly is *you*, Jim Powell," Ellen snapped. "It's *you* they want hauled onto the football field to be taken away in a chopper. We can't let that happen."

"You mentioned Scott and his people," Gary said. "If we can get them on the radio, they might be able to ask around and see if they can find out where this came from. It wouldn't hurt to ask."

"That's a good idea," Jim said. "It'll take Hugh a good hour to get down here. He'll probably be late for the meeting, but when he arrives, we can turn him loose on that. They left him with some radio frequencies he could use to reach them."

"What do we do in the meantime?" Ellen asked. "We can't just sit here waiting for people to come after you."

"We watch our backs," Jim said. "Keep our guard up. We watch our borders and stay armed."

"Perhaps we should try to reason with the community," Pops said. "We hold some kind of town hall meeting and you explain your reasoning to them again. We make sure everyone understands that you did this in their best interest. They just can't see that now."

"I'd never come back from that meeting," Jim said. "They'd mob me and fight over who got the reward. I'd probably get killed in the process."

Gary sighed. "And half the town would die along with you."

Ellen nodded in agreement. "There's no way we'd stand by and let them take you."

"I knew this was going to happen," Nana said. "I told you it was ridiculous to choose keeping your guns over getting the power back. I'm afraid most of the town is going to feel the same way as me."

Jim gritted his teeth. *Respect your mother and father*, he reminded himself. "If that's the way you feel, you should probably stay inside with Ariel during this meeting I'm about to have. You're definitely not going to want to hear what I have to say."

Gary glanced toward the gate coming in from the main road through the valley. "Somebody's coming now. Judging by that horse I would say it's Mack Bird."

"I need to grab a drink of water before everybody starts rolling in," Jim said. "I'll see you guys in a minute." He headed off toward the house, glad to be done with that conversation.

Ellen rushed off after Jim. Ariel hugged her grandmother tightly.

17

A sizeable group was soon gathered around the fire pit in Jim's backyard. Bird had been the first and Weatherman wasn't far behind him. One of the Wimmer boys was there, though "boy" seemed an ill-fitting term for Mrs. Wimmer's middle-aged son. Fred Wimmer was in his late forties and had always lived on the family farm. He called himself a farmer but held a full-time job with the highway department. He was a stocky man who had maintained his stockiness despite the current conditions. While most folks in the valley were losing weight, the only thing different about Fred Wimmer was that his beard had gotten longer and his clothes a bit grubbier.

Jim assumed Hugh was on the way down the mountain. If he was walking off the mountain, they'd likely be done by the time he got down there, so Jim couldn't wait for him. Randi and Lloyd showed up at the same time, which was no surprise to anyone. She was often at Lloyd's place anymore but she refused to acknowledge it. If anyone asked, she said she was taking banjo lessons. Jim had dared raise a skeptical eyebrow at her once and she threatened to slap that very eyebrow off his head.

As representatives from the various families showed up, Jim

gravely handed the flyer over and watched their reaction as they read it. Nearly everyone within their tribal group had participated to some extent in the action at the power plant. They understood the risks and everyone appeared to agree that it was the right thing to do.

As far as Jim knew, there wasn't a person among them who felt that giving up freedom for electricity was a good idea. It was a classic socialist trap. If you let the government take care of you, they'll make sure you have everything the person beside you has. The only problem was that the system never worked out.

The end result was always oppression and tyranny. If they surrendered the tools by which they could fight back, then they had no chance. If they handed over their guns and their freedom, the government would take their spirit next. Then there would be nothing left. They would have become soulless vessels at the end of a government feeding tube, completely at the mercy of whoever was changing the bag.

Jim believed death was preferable to that, as bitter a pill as it was to swallow.

As the flyers were going around the circle, the sheriff arrived. Jim was uncertain if he would attend so he was glad to see him. He was one of the few in attendance who'd had no part in the raid on the power plant. Jim wasn't sure how he would feel about the discussion they were about to have but he was a resident of this valley now. He'd expressed his intention to remain there for the immediate future so he needed to be included. Not long after the sheriff arrived, Hugh came riding in bareback on a thin Palomino with a handmade rope bridle.

All eyes turned to him. He was thin and shirtless. His weapons and gear were draped across his bare upper torso like some outlaw reluctantly dragging himself to town. With his long hair and beard he'd have looked at home in an early Clint Eastwood movie.

"Where'd you get that horse?" Jim asked, not recognizing the animal.

"I heard him walking in the woods yesterday. I thought it was a deer or bear at first, but when I tracked it this is what I found. I had some black licorice in my pocket and that's all it took to win him over. He followed me home."

"We should have set you up with a horse earlier," Jim said. "That'll really shorten your travel time."

"It's okay. There wasn't much point back in the winter. There's no grazing up there in the woods."

Hugh rode away to tie his new horse off. Jim left the circle and followed him, handing over the flyer.

When Hugh finished reading it he looked back up at his old friend. "You've sure pissed somebody off."

Jim grimaced. "We stirred a hornet's nest."

Hugh handed the flyer back over to Jim and they returned to the circle around the fire pit. Before he took a seat, he held the flyer up. "Has everyone had a chance to read this?"

There was a chorus of mumbles, a few scattered curses. Everyone had read it.

"This is bad," Jim said. "Most of you know this story has grown all winter as a rumor. Several of us have run into hostility from townspeople already, basically accusing us of depriving them of power. They think we denied them the opportunity to find relief at the government comfort camps."

"Well, didn't you?" Fred Wimmer piped in.

"Yes, we did," Jim admitted. "But that was the plan. Those camps are no way for the government to treat its own citizens. Our tax money and our blood built this country. I will not accept being forced to turn in my guns to take advantage of resources we already paid for. This is not the government giving us anything. This is the government distributing supplies that already belong to us."

There were nods of agreement around the circle, though not from everyone. It was evident the glowering Fred Wimmer had more to say about the subject. When Fred first spoke up, Jim felt like he was just voicing the obvious. Yes, the attack on the power plant may well have resulted in the comfort camps not opening, but Jim saw that as a success. Fred Wimmer might not think so.

"Dude, you know they're coming for us, right?" Weatherman said.

"If they're pissed enough to go to all this trouble, to hand out all those flyers, they're going to want to make an example out of someone. They don't want this shit happening all over the country."

"It may already be happening all over," Mack Bird countered. "We wouldn't have any way of knowing."

"There are pockets of resistance," Hugh said. "I've heard radio chatter about it. We may be the first to actually knock a power plant offline though."

"Good for us," Weatherman said, a broad grin splitting his face.

"Gary and some of his family were attacked at the market today. That's where we found the flyer. We're not sure if they were attacked because they were from this valley or whether it was an attempt to steal the horses. Everyone needs to be on high alert."

The sheriff appeared alarmed at the news of the attack. "Was anybody hurt?"

"Not our people," Jim said.

"Not for a lack of trying," Gary spat. "We were out in the open and were lucky not to be killed. In fact, if Jim hadn't been concerned and followed us into town, they'd probably have killed us all. We would have been boxed in."

"How many of them did you kill?" the sheriff asked, a man waiting for bad news. He was tired of losing residents of his community. He took each death personally.

Jim, Gary, and Debra exchanged glances as if telepathically trying to arrive at a number.

"I don't know," Jim finally said, taking the lead. "I killed at least three but there could have been more. I took a lot of shots at a distance and didn't wait to see if they dropped."

"I shot two," Debra added. "We were all firing. I saw people fall but I'm not sure how many we actually killed."

The sheriff lowered his face to his hands. He removed his Sheriff's Department cap and ran his fingers through the hair. "I'm not saying you all did anything wrong, but when things like this happen it makes me look bad. It seems as if I'm taking sides just by virtue of living back here with you."

"Sorry if keeping our family alive makes you look bad," Debra said. "We'll remember that next time."

The sheriff shook his head regretfully at her, as if she weren't understanding his point.

"If you don't want to be here, you can go. No one is holding you back," Jim said, the statement perhaps coming out harsher than he intended. "Remember, I brought you to live with us because I was trying to *avoid* bloodshed. I thought if you were living back here with us the bad cops at the supercenter would leave us alone. That problem is solved now so you're free to move on if you're not onboard with the way we do things."

"I don't know what to do," the sheriff said.

Jim was growing impatient with the sheriff's inability to make a decision, his lack of drive. "I don't know what to tell you," Jim replied. "But there's going to be a point where you have to choose sides."

"I don't know if I can choose sides," the sheriff retorted. "You guys may not be in the wrong but you're not necessarily in the right either. I don't feel like I can side with you and *against* everyone else out there in the county. That's what you seem to want and it's not the kind of decision I'm prepared to make."

Mack Bird, usually a man of few words, spoke up. "If you stay long enough, the decision will be made for you by virtue of your presence here. If you want to be on the other side of the fence, you'd best be getting there."

The sheriff stared at the ground, no closer to making a decision than he had been an hour ago or even a month ago. Fred Wimmer, on the other hand, had been stewing this whole time. He stood up, shouting at the people in the circle.

"I don't think any of you assholes are in the position of telling people who has to go and who can stay. My family was in this valley two hundred years ago. Hell, we were the *only* people here. We cut this place from the wilderness and made it what it is now. Up until about forty years ago every farm back in here belonged to an uncle or a cousin of ours. If anybody should be making the rules here, it should be us. If it was up to me, I'd tell every one of you to get the hell out of here."

Jim didn't like being yelled at. Everything had been civil up until this moment. He got to his feet and faced Fred. "You sure as hell aren't making rules for me or my family. I respect your parents and I respect what your ancestors did here, but if we're going to be honest and lay everything out on the table, your family is part of the problem. While there's no denying that the picture on that flyer is me, nearly all the gossip about folks in this valley attacking the power plant can be traced to your family. It's you all running your mouths that's got the town stirred up."

Fred's face turned red. He stomped over to Jim and got in his face, yelling so loud, so venomously, that spit flew from his lips. "Hell, I admit it. Don't even blame the rest of my family for it. It was me. I've been telling everybody I see about it because it pissed me off that you took it upon yourself to make this decision for the rest of us. How many people in this county are going to suffer because of you?"

"Your parents were informed of this," Jim reminded him. "Your mother was fine with it."

"My mother don't speak for me!" Fred bellowed. "Hell, she don't even know what year it is."

Jim stared him in the face. He was disgusted by his greasy skin and the pig eyes that were too close together, his foul breath and reeking body.

Fred leaned closer. "I hope whoever sent that flyer kills every fucking one of you."

Jim threw a short jab and hit Fred Wimmer right on the button. The punch was a quick snap. He didn't take the time to load it and he didn't telegraph his plan. He just threw it with all his strength and caught Fred right on the side of his chin.

Fred stiffened and fell like a tree in the forest. No one had seen this turn of events coming, least of all Fred Wimmer. Everyone sat there in shock, Fred's body seizing in front of them, until Randi jumped up to attend to him.

No one said a word. Then Weatherman started clapping. "He deserved that. He *so* deserved that."

Around the circle, Jim saw nothing but shocked faces. Then, as much as he didn't want to, he turned to see the reaction of the one person in the group whose opinion he actually cared about. Ellen was staring at him with an expression of confusion. It was the look you gave someone when you no longer had any idea who they were or who they were becoming. Jim wasn't certain he knew either but he was certain that from this point forward, his enemies would not all be outside the valley. Some of them would be within its hills. He had no idea how the rest of the clannish Wimmers would respond to his attack on one of their own.

Jim was no longer paying attention or listening to what happened in front of him. His adrenaline was up and he was in that place where violence was at the tip of his fingers. Had Jim not been surrounded by people, he had to wonder if he would have killed Fred Wimmer.

Randi, Hugh, and the cackling Weatherman slid the barely conscious man across the back of a horse to deliver him home. Hugh and Weatherman volunteered, heading off in that direction. Then Randi was in front of Jim and she was reaching carefully toward him, explaining what she was going to do. He wasn't listening. She took his hand and examined it. She tried asking him how certain movements felt but he didn't respond.

"It could be broken," she told Ellen. "He probably deserves it. If you're going to punch everyone simply for being an asshole then you'll eventually be the only one left standing."

Ellen agreed.

Jim yanked his hand back and walked away from the group. The meeting was over. He was done. There was no way he was going to be able to bring himself down to a place where he could talk logically about the situation before them. When he reached the corner of the house he threw a quick glance back and saw the group was talking among themselves. Maybe they could figure something out but they would have to do it without him.

At the front of the house, he angled off toward his shop building.

There was a bottle of Jim Beam in there and he needed a drink. His back was to the house when he heard the screen door open and then clatter shut. He waited on Ellen to tear into him, lecturing him on his behavior.

"Go ahead," he growled. "Say what you need to say."

When no one spoke, he spun around, ready to explain himself, and found Ariel on the front porch. He wondered if she'd seen what he did. What had she thought about it? Would she be scared of him now?

"Daddy?"

He didn't answer her. Not because he didn't want to, but because he didn't know what to say. Ariel skittered down the porch steps and ran across the yard toward him. She took his hand and examined it, touching the place his knuckles had split. Seeing her soft, tiny fingers holding his dirty, bleeding hand reminded him of how her hands had looked as a baby.

How much those hands had changed over time.

Again, he thought of how much the world had changed.

She swung her pink purse from her side to the front of her body and dug into it, taking out a first-aid kit he'd put together for her when she was going to 4-H camp. She withdrew two colorful Band-Aids shaped like crayons and applied them across his rapidly swelling knuckles, smoothed them with the pad of her little finger, and put her trash back inside her purse. She didn't like to litter. He'd taught her that.

"I don't have any medicine," she said.

"That's okay, baby. The best medicine would be a hug."

Ariel grabbed him tightly and held on. He wrapped his arms around her and they were a pocket of right in a world gone wrong. A tear worked its way from his eye.

What had he done to them? What had he done to them all?

18

In late evening they switched sentries at the observation posts. Pete, Charlie, Will, and Sara were all brought in and replaced with folks who would hold their station until around midnight. Another of Gary's daughters and one of the Weatherman girls teamed up to man, or "woman" as they called it, the observation post near their homes. Hugh relieved Will and Sara at the post on the river trail into town. Jim relieved Pete at the post near Buddy's old house, wanting time to himself, and taking a solitary duty was a lot easier than telling everyone to leave him the hell alone.

He didn't get the privacy he was after. From the front porch of the house he'd shared with Buddy, Lloyd spotted Jim walking toward his post. By the time Jim changed out with Pete and sent him on his way, Lloyd joined him with a banjo and a jar of blackberry moonshine.

"Do you even have a gun with you?" Jim asked when he saw his old friend ambling toward him.

Lloyd paused. "I left it on the porch. My hands were full."

"You remembered your banjo and liquor but forgot your gun?"

"Priorities, my friend."

Jim was disgusted. "This shit is serious. You shouldn't be drinking when the weather calls for an elevated chance of lead showers."

Lloyd started picking *Ruben's Train* on the open back banjo. He paid no attention to Jim.

Jim studied Lloyd's banjo. "That damn thing is an antique. You're going to destroy it dragging it all over the place."

Lloyd shook his head. "They didn't baby them in the old days. They went to war. They went to the fields. People threw them over their backs and walked to barn dances through the rain and snow. I suspect a good banjo prefers to be treated that way. They like an active life."

Jim went back to watching the road through the ports of the crude structure. "You're a nut case."

Lloyd rolled his shoulders as if conceding the point. "You really think they'll come for you?" he asked, muting the strings with the flat of his hand.

Jim was slow to respond, as if hating to admit the truth. "Eh, the idea of a reward is pretty tempting. Somebody will try."

Lloyd plucked absently at the banjo. "While I can take it or leave it, a lot of folks are really attached to their electric power. They got all those gizmos they need to charge. Even though I prefer life without it, you can almost understand people's position. Assume that your mom and dad didn't have you taking care of them. What if they were facing a slow, undignified death by starvation and the comfort camps could have stopped that? How would you feel about someone ripping that away from you?"

Jim threw him a glare, though it probably wasn't visible in the rapidly darkening structure. "If you're trying to make me feel better, you're not doing much of a job."

"I'm not trying to do anything. I'm just processing."

"Well, your processing is pissing me off. You think I'm not wrestling with this already? Although I knew there were consequences and I weighed them out before I announced the raid on the power plant, this is about a bigger question. It's about the future of the country and how it survives. It's about what kind of country we're going to have when we get back on our feet again. After two hundred years of freedom, we could lose it all in a three to five year disaster. I don't want to see that."

"I'm not sure that one attack by a small group of people can affect what direction the country takes. That's a bit ambitious."

"There could be other people ready to fight back if they know they're not alone."

"Then it's going to get real ugly," Lloyd said. "I don't know if you're talking a coup or a civil war, but a lot of people could die."

"I'm tired of people telling me that things are going to get ugly," Jim snapped. "I'm well aware."

"Fine," Lloyd muttered. "No need to get pissy. I was just making conversation. If you're going to be an asshole, I'll just take my jar and go home."

"Don't drink all that blackberry," Jim warned. "That's my favorite."

"You're dead to me," Lloyd said. "No more blackberry for you."

"Go home and go to bed."

Lloyd wandered off in the near darkness, stumbling because he hadn't brought a flashlight either. Jim could have lent him one but thought a good spill in the failing light might teach him a lesson.

After Lloyd's departure things were quiet for a while and Jim was left alone with his thoughts. It was what he wanted, why he'd chosen to man an outpost that evening, yet his thoughts were merciless and brutal. It was hard to avoid the awareness that what he saw as a stand for freedom had possibly screwed him and his neighbors good.

For as much as he'd never wanted any responsibility for his friends and neighbors, he found himself in that position. He led them, fought for them. They turned to him for answers. Like it or not, that was the state of things. He was their leader and he'd let them down.

Had any of this been avoidable or would all roads have led to the same destination? Would *any* choice he'd made have led to this same place? There was no way of knowing. Yet he couldn't back up and change anything.

A bright moon rose full and bold, restoring a pale light to the valley. Jim climbed from the observation post to admire the beauty of the night. In the distance, he heard a faint whistling. He froze, the hair on the back of his neck standing up at the spooky, mournful sound coming from somewhere in the darkness. He raised his rifle but couldn't imagine anyone with ill intentions announcing themselves by whistling. This was someone who wanted to be heard.

"Who is it?" Jim demanded.

A light clicked on nearly fifty yards behind his position. It was pointed at the ground. Jim pointed his rifle in the direction but squinted his eyes, not wanting to lose all of his night vision.

"Easy, it's just me."

"Shit," Jim mumbled.

Of all the people he didn't want to see, the sheriff was in the top two. Jim couldn't imagine what made him want to come up for a visit. Unless he had something new to say, there was no point in talking anymore. Jim took a seat on a chunk of firewood and glumly watched the sheriff's light approach.

"Evening," the sheriff said.

Jim frowned. "I notice you didn't say *good* evening."

"I'm not certain there's anything particularly good about it."

"At least we agree on something. What brings you out here? Got something on your mind?"

There was no use going through the motions of a congenial evening visit among neighbors. It was best to cut right to the chase.

"I do have something on my mind."

With only silence between the men, the sound of katydids rose in their ears. Spring peepers chanted from a nearby pond. When the sheriff wasn't immediately forthcoming with the reason for his visit, Jim started grumbling.

"Why the hell is it that people tell me they got something on their minds and I practically have to pull it out of their face hole? Wouldn't it be so much easier if the people simply came out and said it? Everyone makes some big announcement, they got something to say, but they never say it. Are you wanting me to beg or is this just a dramatic pause?"

Jim could sense the sheriff tense up at his outburst. The air changed around them. "Well, pardon me. Forgive me for being polite when delivering information. That's just how I was raised."

Jim remained silent. He'd be damned if he was asking again. This was about to become his permanent position on people who came to him with news. Silence.

"When I got back home from that meeting at your house there were people waiting on me," the sheriff said. "A couple of men from town."

News of people walking into his valley raised his hackles. "How did they get to your house? Did they walk right by this outpost?"

"I asked them about that. I wanted to make sure they hadn't harmed your boy since I knew he was keeping watch here. They said they figured the road was being watched so they approached from the woods. There are logging roads and game trails all through those mountains."

"Yeah, I understand there are vulnerabilities," Jim said. "I guess we've never faced folks determined enough to come in through the woods."

"They knew which house to come to. They knew exactly where to find me. That was interesting."

Jim didn't like that at all. The fact these men had visited the sheriff's house only reaffirmed that there was no way they could watch everything at once. Having outposts on the road only deterred the people dumb enough to approach by the roads in the first place. Anyone intent on doing bad things would skulk in like a pack of coyotes coming for lambs.

And how did they know where the sheriff lived? Did that mean they knew exactly where Jim lived? Did they know who lived in all of the houses? If that was the case, then men coming for him might know right where to go. Instead of searching the valley for him they could perform a targeted strike on his house. The thought of that made him sick.

"What did they want?"

More hesitation, more reluctance to put it into words. "They want me to bring you in," the sheriff finally said.

"For the reward?"

"Nah, they say it's for justice, though I reckon they could serve both masters. They could lock you up to serve justice and still turn you over on the 4th of July to whoever sent that flyer."

"I reckon that brings us around to the inevitable question of what you intend to do about it, Sheriff."

"I don't supposed you're interested in surrendering yourself, are you?"

Jim barked a laugh, but it was not about humor, it was the release of tension. "Not hardly."

"When you take this job, people see you as a figurehead. I ain't a lawman anymore. I ain't doing the job but I reckon I'm a figurehead of sorts. People are going to come to me with their problems and I don't reckon I can do anything about that."

Jim shifted his body, discreetly positioning the side of his body with the holstered pistol away from the light. He eased his hand down to the grip and rested it there. He tugged it gently and it broke free of the friction that held it in the Kydex holster. A calm chill settled over his body, like slipping into cool water on a hot day. "So is Sheriff Figurehead here to make an arrest or merely pass on this information?"

The sheriff's response would decide his fate. The lawman was so near to dying that Jim was already planning how he was going to drag Lloyd out of bed to help him dispose of the body. He was already coming up with a story to cover for the shot he was about to fire.

"I'm not here to arrest you," the sheriff said.

Jim tried to relax his shoulders and his neck. Perhaps he'd make it through this long day without inflicting anymore violence. "I reckon that's the safest play for you, Sheriff. The day you come to arrest me is the day you don't go home to your family. I respect you as a man but I won't allow you to take me in. I got a job to do here, looking after my family, and it's not nearly done yet."

He bobbed his head in the ambient glow of his flashlight. "I don't expect that you're my problem, Jim Powell, but I appreciate that warning."

Jim was walking on a razor's edge at that moment. It was like when he lashed out against Fred Wimmer. He felt like he'd stepped too close to killing the sheriff and part of him didn't want to back up from it. Part of him felt like it was the right thing to do, like if he didn't do it now he'd only have to do it later. That was a lesson of his grandfather's that had proven correct time after time.

The constraints that kept Jim a civilized man were failing as often as they worked these days. Sometimes it felt like something was taking over his body, something that knew how to handle these times better than he was rationally able to. Jim wondered if the sheriff knew how close he was to dying. Perhaps sensing that very thing, the sheriff began to retreat. Jim noticed he did not turn his back, as if he did not trust Jim at this point. Likely he sensed within Jim that same thing that Jim sensed within himself, that emerging berserker who was growing weary of struggling with the line between right and wrong.

"Sheriff?"

The sheriff stopped in his tracks. It was not a comfortable pause but a concerned one. Perhaps he thought this was when it would happen, when this would turn into a fight for his life.

"Who were they?" Jim asked.

"Who?"

"The men."

"The ones who came to see me?"

"Yes."

The sheriff hesitated, perhaps uncertain this was a wise thing to do. Would disclosing their names put those men at risk? The answer was obvious. Most definitely.

"I'm just questioning their motives," Jim explained.

"They feel that laws have been broken and you're the likely suspect. They want order restored to their community. They think you should answer for the crimes if you committed them."

"If they come back, tell them I'm going to come looking for them next time. They can make their accusations against me in person."

The sheriff's profile was outlined against the night sky. He was pensive, perhaps stirred to thought by the questions Jim raised. He seemed more relaxed, less concerned that this conversation was going to end badly.

"I'm assuming that's a threat?"

"Most definitely."

19

Hugh's outpost was the first to be tested. It was almost predictable. He was manning the outpost on the farm road that led to the river crossing, then eventually into town. Hugh insisted on pulling an all-nighter. While most found sentry duty monotonous and painfully boring, it was Hugh's happy place.

He stood outside the crude outpost, watching the rising sun illuminate the world with golden light. Heavy dew reflected off the low spring grass. Spiderwebs hung damp and heavy from tree branches, weeds, and fence posts. The dew collected on them glowed with brilliant light when the sun caught it. Birds sang and it was a soundtrack that would put a smile on the bitterest man's face. It was a world coming to life.

Hugh's mind wandered to how unaffected the world appeared to be by all that was happening. Inevitably, the world belonged to the animals, to nature, to the rivers, and to the sun. They set the pace, and continued on despite the ripples created by men. It was their world and man was merely living in it. Sometimes man borrowed it, mistaking in his naiveté that he had conquered and controlled it, but it was inevitably taken back by those creatures better prepared to inhabit it.

On one of his long shifts at the outpost, sometime last fall, Hugh had dug a pit in the ground so he could build a concealed fire. It was about the size of a five-gallon bucket. The old bushcrafter who'd taught him the technique referred to it as a Dakota fire hole. Though the smell of the wood smoke would carry for long distances, a hole in the ground concealed the flames. A tunnel coming off the side provided air. He kept a stash of tinder and kindling in the outpost so people could build a fire when they needed to warm up or cook. Once Hugh demonstrated it, Jim wished he'd known that trick when he and his friends were walking back from Richmond.

When he had a low fire going he laid a wire shelf from an old refrigerator across the pit, then set a scorched aluminum pot of water atop it. He would toss in some ground coffee, boil it to a strong brew, and drink it straight from the pot. As the coffee cooled, the grounds would settle. While at home he would have strained it through a bandana, he skipped that step in the field.

Hugh had learned a long time ago that when performing long, tedious tasks it was easy to ignore his basic needs. Being uncomfortable on guard duty made extended shifts seem longer and more brutal. One needed to move around, needed to stretch. For Hugh, it meant that he made coffee, cooked a meal when feasible, and drank plenty of water. He'd figured out that a big part of living comfortably with very little was to attend to basic needs and not let himself feel deprived. There were plenty of times suffering was unavoidable. This was not one of those times.

While the water heated, he glanced through his spotting scope in the direction of the river. He'd have preferred to own a twelve hundred dollar Leupold, though what he had was a thirty dollar Barska with a wobbly tripod. In the end, it pretty much did the same thing. He also knew that breaking the Leupold would hurt a whole lot worse than breaking the Barska.

As his eye adjusted to the view, he spotted movement. Four figures were coming in his direction. "You bastards," he mumbled.

The young men carried rifles and their pants were wet to their knees from crossing the river. Hugh knew in his gut there was probably only one reason these men were headed toward the valley, and that was to hunt Jim. At first glance they appeared to be hunters, but no one hunted the valley anymore except the people who lived there. Word had spread that the valley folk were tight-knit and didn't like outsiders. They'd blown up all roads into the valley which, in itself, kind of made a statement about how receptive they were to visitors.

He couldn't drop them in cold blood. There was no aggression and no clear indication they were there to harm his friends. If those intentions were expressed, he could engage them with no hard feelings. He decided to let them get a little closer. If they were inexperienced enough he could put the fear of God in them and send them packing.

Sometimes you got more mileage out of that. If he killed the men it was likely others would come looking for them. If he scared the absolute shit out of them and sent them back the way they'd come, it might deter others from trying to reach the valley. However, scaring away bounty hunters was a long shot. The reward promised by the flyer made a tempting offer. Starvation made for strong motivation.

Hugh was irritated that his morning coffee routine, the high point of his day, was being derailed. He used the toe of his boot to nudge the pot further from the heat, hoping this could be dealt with in a few minutes and he could go back to his coffee. He double-checked his rifle and confirmed it was ready to roll, took another glance through the spotting scope, and found the men where he expected them to be. They had not deviated from their course or their previous pace.

While they were far enough away that they wouldn't hear him, Hugh pulled his radio from its pouch and called Jim, who was still in bed after the late night. It took a minute to get him to answer.

"What is it?" Jim asked.

"I've got a couple of young punks approaching me on the road. They're armed but making no attempt to stay low-key. I'm getting ready to stop them."

"I'll be right there to back you up."

"I can probably take them," Hugh replied. "There're only four of them and I'm behind cover."

"We don't take chances," Jim said. *"I'm getting ready now. You hold them until I get there. Don't leave cover."*

Hugh reluctantly agreed, though he didn't know what all the fuss was about. He'd only wanted to let Jim know what was up in case it became necessary to shoot someone. He didn't want the shots flipping anyone out.

He moved to the position that offered the best vantage point while providing optimal protection against attack. He took a deep breath and relaxed, studying the men through his rifle scope. Neither their posture nor their manner of approach gave any indication these men had any training or skills he needed to be concerned about. They were casual and loose-limbed in their movements, chattering between themselves as easily as young men walking through a mall parking lot.

Hugh wondered if their presence here was the result of some scheme hatched over a night of drinking or smoking weed. Perhaps the chatter was an attempt to keep their nerve up as the effects of the alcohol waned. He let them reach a point about thirty-five yards away and flicked his safety off.

"You boys cooperate now," Hugh whispered. "I told Jim I wouldn't shoot anyone until he got here. Don't make a liar out of me."

A little closer and he could hear their voices. It was time.

"Don't you fucking move!" he bellowed.

The boys froze in their tracks. Experience told Hugh they were weighing their options, deciding whether to fight or to run. The key was to take control of the situation before they had time to arrive at a plan.

"Drop those guns! I will open fire and I will *not* miss. Unless you want to die, drop those weapons now."

When they didn't respond fast enough, he started counting backward. "Three! Two!"

Their rifles clattered to the ground.

"Turn away from me!" Hugh demanded. "Do it now! Do not look at me!"

The men hesitated to take action.

"NOW!" he barked.

They complied, slowly rotating in place until each man was facing away from him.

Hugh stepped from cover, his rifle at high ready and sweeping the line of young men. No one wore a web belt or holster but that didn't mean they didn't have deadly goodies stashed away somewhere.

"We're—" one of the men began.

"No talking," Hugh cut in. "You're going to keep your mouths shut until I tell you to talk."

Hugh approached the line of men. When he was about fifteen yards from them he stopped. "Starting on my right, the guy in the blue hoodie, lower your left hand and drop your pants to your ankles."

"What?" the young man asked, starting to turn.

"Do *not* turn around!" Hugh bellowed. "You do what I tell you or you die now."

He did as he was told, lowering his left hand and unfastening his pants. Once that was done, the weight of the gear in pockets pulled them the rest of the way down. Hugh worked his way down the line, having each man do the same thing. Besides effectively hobbling the men so they couldn't run, this reduced the chances of anyone pulling a surprise from their belt or pockets.

They were standing this way, lined up with their hands folded behind their head, fingers interlaced, pants around their ankles, when Jim rode up. He found it to be a somewhat appalling sight to ride up upon, like walking in on some bizarre cult performing a ritual.

"About time you got here," Hugh said. "You run into town for breakfast on your way?"

With his rifle at the ready, Jim moved alongside his friend. "This is a disturbing sight, Hugh."

"Had I realized that some of these men had dispensed with the practice of wearing underwear, I might have chosen a different approach. My intention wasn't just for my safety, but to add insult to injury."

"It's my eyes being injured," Jim remarked.

"I haven't questioned them and I haven't allowed them to say anything. I was waiting on you. I'm not sure if this is a serious attempt at a breach or merely one of those 'hold my beer' moments."

"Explain yourself, boys," Jim demanded. "Whose harebrained scheme was this?"

Whispers were exchanged and then one man spoke up. "Brady. It was all Brady's idea."

Jim moved his rifle from man to man. "Which one you assholes is Brady?"

Suddenly, there was an eruption of gunfire in the distance. Jim cocked his head and tried to locate the origin. With a sickening realization, he came to the conclusion that it was not coming from town. It was coming from his valley. Someone was shooting at his people.

"That's Brady," said the spokesman for the group, turning around to reveal a broad grin.

Jim erased that smile with a single 5.56 round to the spokesman's chest. He jerked and toppled. His companions twisted to stare at Jim in shock.

"You'd better run," Jim said to the rest of them.

One bent, yanked up his pants, and started running. The other two stepped out of their pants and left them behind, scrambling booted and bare-assed toward the river.

"Hide those weapons!" Jim yelled at Hugh. "Stash them then come on. It sounds like we might need all hands."

Hugh checked the progress of the fleeing men and decided they weren't running fast enough. He sent a couple of judicious rounds in their direction and they picked up the pace accordingly.

Jim was trying to mount his horse. It skittered away, startled by his rapid movements and sensitive to his heightened anxiety. Jim finally got a hand on the saddle horn and pulled himself up. Then he was off and running, hoping like hell he didn't fall off.

20

Before the young men showed up at Hugh's observation post, a larger force was entering the valley by another route. Their goal was to find Jim and take him prisoner, then hold him for the reward. Their strategy was to launch a diversion against the known observation post on the valley side of the river, then use stealth to bypass a second known observation post on the main road into the valley. They knew exactly where they were going and their strategy was sound. In fact, Lloyd might not have even noticed them if not for the Wimmers' dog.

"Shut the hell up, dog," Lloyd mumbled. "You're throwing off my timing."

He was trying to learn a new song on the banjo and the dog's irregular barking ran counter to Lloyd's internal metronome, throwing him off. Eventually Lloyd noticed that it didn't seem to be barking at another dog's distant bark; it sounded different. It was that urgent, persistent bark a dog uses when something is out of place.

Halfway suspecting that he'd find a bear crossing the pasture, which was a common enough sight, Lloyd threw a glance in that direction and froze. A distant line of men were moving across the field. They were in the open pasture behind the Wimmers' house, not far from where the sheriff was living. On that side of the road there were hundreds of yards of pasture that gradually increased in steepness as it ramped up the shoulder of Clinch Mountain. Where the land became too steep to mow for hay, forest took over. A little more than halfway between the houses and the tree line, the procession of men looked like a team of ants urgently working their way across the sidewalk.

Lloyd took up the cheesy pair of binoculars Jim left hanging in the observation post. Even through the low-quality glass he counted ten men carrying rifles and moving rapidly across the field. Some had on camouflage hunting clothing but others wore earth tones, trying to blend into their surroundings. Lloyd picked his radio up from the pile of gear on the dirt floor.

"Jim! Jim! I've got ten armed men coming into the valley behind the Wimmers' house. They're not moving like hunters. I think we're being attacked!"

Lloyd waited for a long moment and there was no reply.

"Jim! Someone answer me. I need some help up here!"

No reply.

"Dammit!" Lloyd shoved the radio into a back pocket and started frantically pulling on his gear. He checked his rifle and confirmed there was a round in the chamber. Jim made him carry one of those fancy AR-15s because of the capacity and range but he'd have been much more comfortable with a double-barrel shotgun, a traditional hillbilly weapon. These fancy black guns were too complicated. Too many moving knobs and moving parts.

After finally remembering how to pull back the charging handle and confirm the glint of brass, Lloyd slumped back against the thick poplar logs that made up the back wall. He was sweating and his heart was racing, his breath erupting in frantic gasps. He decided to try the radio one more time before dealing with this on his own.

"Gary! Randi! *Anybody*! This is Lloyd. I've got armed men running across the field behind the Wimmers' house. I can't get Jim on the radio. I'm going to try to intercept them and slow them down but I don't know if I can do it by myself. If anyone gets this message, I could probably use some help."

Lloyd shoved the radio into a pocket on the tactical vest he'd been given. Jim said it was a "battlefield pickup" and Lloyd hoped he fared better than the previous user. He ducked through the low door of the observation post and set an intercept path toward the group of men. He couldn't even believe he was doing it. He was never the type to run toward danger. It was going against every survival instinct he had.

Although he had no training of any kind, he used his common sense to keep himself concealed. He ran along the fence line, then used the terrain and foliage to block him from the other group of men. When he found a location that offered a vantage point, he checked his bearings to make sure he was headed in the right direction.

Lloyd didn't do much running and this whole endeavor was taking way more effort than he'd imagined. He couldn't remember the last time he'd run more than a few steps. Maybe it was that day he'd lost a few fingers in the woods behind Jim's house, or perhaps it was the day Buddy died.

He thought of all the times in his life that he'd joked about homemade liquor keeping him from getting worms. While that may be the case, one thing that it did *not* do was properly hydrate the body for extended running. Lloyd's muscles cramped and spasmed, eventually slowing him to a stilted, awkward stagger. He was limping and cursing when the radio in his pocket chirped.

"Lloyd, this is Randi, what the hell is going on?"

Lloyd fumbled to get the radio from his pocket. He raked the back of a forearm across his face to mop up the rivulets of sweat stinging his eyes. He wanted to sit down but was afraid he wouldn't be able to get back up. "Men," he gasped. "Counted...ten. They went around me. Headed into the valley. I'm trying...to catch them...but I suck."

"They might be headed for Jim's place."

Lloyd started limping on again. "I tried to get him but he doesn't answer."

"Ellen! Pops! Pete! Charlie!" Randi said. *"Is anyone receiving this?"*

"I tried," Lloyd moaned.

"I better head over to his place. You keep an eye on those guys but don't bite off more than you can chew. Got it?"

"You go ahead," Lloyd groaned. "If I can pin these guys down, hopefully I can hold them until help comes."

"Lloyd," came a voice. *"It's Gary."*

"Gary, Lloyd has armed men coming into the valley on his end," Randi cut in. *"Where are you?"*

"I'm at my house," Gary replied. *"Do I need to come back you up, Lloyd?"*

"Yes!" Lloyd said. "Please."

"No!" Randi countered. *"What if we're being attacked on all fronts? Men could be coming in on Gary's end of the valley too. He might need to stay down there and keep an eye on things."*

"Fine, I got this," Lloyd said. He didn't mean it. When he got killed, he hoped they lost some sleep over it. It would serve them right. He nearly had the radio back into its pouch when yet another voice entered the conversation.

"You say these men are high on the shoulder of the mountain, behind the Wimmer place?" It was Mack Bird.

"Yeah," Lloyd said. "Headed into the valley, halfway up to the tree line."

"That means they'll be approaching my place soon," Bird replied. *"I'll be ready for them. I'll engage from the front. When I start shooting, you hit them from the back. Just don't fire toward my house. Got it?"*

"Got it," Lloyd replied, relieved to not be carrying the weight of this whole effort.

After a minute or two of walking, the cramps began to subside and he picked up the pace, loping through the damp grass. One foot landed in a fresh green pile of fragrant cow manure and Lloyd slipped, nearly going down. He didn't fall but the awkward maneuver twisted his knee and added a new pain to the bitter fruit salad of aches plaguing him.

Had he been behind these men and trying to catch up with them, there was no way he'd had ever gotten within range. However, having a reasonable idea of where they were headed and setting an intercept course allowed him to gradually close the distance. As Lloyd gained ground on them, he hid himself in the narrow draws etched into the mountain by millions of years of runoff. Moving up the draw provided both concealment and cover for the moment he intercepted his target.

He bobbed up occasionally, like a gopher from its hole, peering over the lip of the draw to get his bearings. When he was within a hundred yards of the men a smile curled the corners of his mouth. He could do this. He didn't need any help. He could halve the distance, then halve it again. When they were trapped in the open with nowhere to go, he would open fire.

Yet it was not to be.

Lloyd made it perhaps twenty-five more feet when a painful spasm seized his entire body. He had no idea what was happening. The pain was so blinding and all-encompassing he feared he was having a heart attack or a stroke. He made it two more steps before pitching over into the damp grass.

He tried to push against the pain crushing his body like a vise, trying to curl him like plastic melting in a fire. The spasm stretched from his calf, up his thigh, through his abdomen, and along his back. His fingers curled and he could not straighten them. He could barely breathe. He could not recall ever having been in so much physical pain. Was this it? Was he going to die? If he did, these men were going to run unimpeded toward his friend's home.

If dying was going to take some time, he decided those minutes should be well-spent. He rolled to his belly and dragged himself through the wet grass, pulling himself up the gentle slope of the draw. He crawled to the edge and peered over. Sweat soaked his body and tears filled his eyes. The men were a good distance away and getting further with each second. If he was going to die, he could at least take a few of them with him.

He raised the rifle and rested it on a forearm to keep the magazine from hitting the ground. The low magnification scope had hit the ground when he fell. A clump of mud and damp grass seeds packed the end of it.

"Shit!"

He pulled the rifle to him and used a damp shirttail to scrub the lens clean. It wasn't perfect but it was going to have to do. He put the crosshairs on the cluster of men and tried to relax his body but it was a lost cause. The spasm had not subsided but the pain ebbed and flowed. If he could time the pain right and if the scope hadn't lost zero in the fall, he might be able to hit something.

Lloyd flipped the safety off, centered the crosshair on the back of the closest man, and started pulling the trigger as fast as he could. For a moment, Lloyd flashed back on his grandfather and his stories of being in the Pacific in World War II. He felt like he was in a machine gun nest trying to hold off Japanese soldiers determined to take his position.

When the mag ran dry, he awkwardly tugged it from the rifle, threw it over his back, and switched to another. He wasn't proficient at this and had to smack it several times with his hand to seat it securely. Then it took him a moment to recall how to close the bolt on the fancy modern rifle. He'd expected to take fire during the reloading pause but they were probably having trouble figuring out where to shoot. He was pretty well-hidden.

When he got his eye back on the optic, he found the men squatted down, trying both to care for their wounded and desperately trying to figure out where the gunfire was coming from. Lloyd was hit with another wave of pain and it took his breath. When he recovered, he targeted one of the crouched men and started to squeeze the trigger. Before he could fire, there was a massive *BOOM* and a new rifle entered the fight.

"You were supposed to wait on my fire!" Bird said into the radio.

Lloyd didn't answer him, not wanting to spare the effort required to retrieve his radio. He watched the men scramble, trying to find cover in the middle of a vast, empty cattle pasture. There was none. When it was merely Lloyd's rifle, the men seemed to think there remained a path forward. Taking fire from the front, they were less certain where to go. Mack Bird's rifle cracked again and another man disappeared.

Lloyd had heard before that Mack Bird was a proficient shooter. He used to compete in shooting competitions and was raising his children to do the same. The two little girls, armed with pink .22 caliber rifles, had no trouble dropping squirrels or rabbits with head shots. Lloyd didn't know what Bird was using but the report was as loud as a cannon, and with each shot a misty red cloud sprayed into the air.

Knowing that he was not the dead-eye shooter Bird was, Lloyd realized his best path was to impede the invaders' retreat and pin them down for Bird to surgically take out. When it seemed like the men were rallying for a coordinated retreat, Lloyd positioned his crosshair in the center of the cluster of men and started dumping rounds three at a time. He was never a good shot, more a student of the "spray and pray" school of marksmanship, but it served its purpose, making retreat no safer an option than advancing.

Soon, only two men remained in the group of attackers, both hunkered down against a jutting chunk of limestone that pushed from the core of the mountain like exposed bone from a desiccated corpse. Every time one of the men tried to shoot back, they were pinned down either by Bird's precision fire or the haphazard pounding laid down by Lloyd.

Aware that they were at a standoff, the attackers accepted that the only remaining course of action was for them to surrender or to bolt for the woods higher up the mountain. They wasted no time. They broke and ran like the devil was handing out kisses.

The runners must have thought that by launching their retreat as a pair it gave them a fifty-fifty chance of making it, apparently expecting Lloyd and Bird would be torn between which target to take, thereby increasing their chances of reaching the woods. That might have been true if Lloyd was the only shooter but he wasn't. Bird had no problem with those odds. It was no more difficult than a double when shooting skeet.

The lead runner must have already been hit once. He was

running with his body at an odd angle that threw off Bird's point of impact. Rather than hitting center mass or a headshot, whatever massive projectile Bird was sending caught the first runner in the side of his body between the waist and the ribs. For a moment it reminded Lloyd of the old comedian who used to smash watermelons with a sledgehammer. Blood and gore sprayed for twenty feet.

The invader continued trying to run, holding in his guts as they poured forth, streaming behind him like an uncooperative water hose. Soon the blood loss and trauma took its toll and he dropped. Bird had been confident enough of this eventuality that he didn't waste a second round on him.

The second man kicked it into a higher gear. He began weaving back and forth as if that might make him harder to hit. It could have worked if his motions were erratic but they were not. He swung with the consistency of a pendulum, going ten feet to one side and then back ten feet to the other. All Bird had to do was wait for him in the center of his path. When the fleeing man crossed back from one extremity of his range to the other, Bird gave him the appropriate lead and sent another round.

Even Lloyd, who had seen a lot of ugly shit in the last year, flinched at the result. The round center punched the body and for a brief moment Lloyd was certain he could see light shining through his middle like he was a sheet of dough and someone had just cut out a biscuit.

Lloyd dropped his rifle and dug frantically for the radio. He brought it to his mouth, holding it with both hands. "Bird! Bird! We got them!"

A second later Bird piped in. *"I think you're right. They're all down. I want to check the bodies but let's wait for backup first. We need to do this right."*

Jim and Hugh were at that very moment tearing across fields and farms, riding beyond their abilities to find where the gunshots originated. They'd missed all the previous radio traffic, the hills laying in such a way that they could communicate with Jim's home but not with people more distant. They didn't know what was taking place with Lloyd, Mack, and the rest of their people.

"Ellen, I'm coming by the house," Jim said as he neared his own property. "I want Pete to take a radio and get to his old outpost. No shooting. There're too many people running around. Just keep an eye on things."

"I'm here," came a response.

"Randi?" Jim asked.

"Yeah. Men slipped by Lloyd. The gunfire is him and Mack Bird dealing with it. I figured they were headed for your house so I came this way in case anyone got past them."

"Thank you!" Jim said. "We're going to go down the valley then, toward Bird's place."

"Be careful," Randi cautioned. *"I'm with Ellen and we got this."*

The distant gunfire became more sporadic, with multiple rifles involved now. Jim could hear what sounded like 5.56 interspersed with the massive boom of something high caliber.

Then he heard Lloyd's voice on the radio. He was talking to Bird and sounded certain that they had neutralized the threat.

"What's the fuck is going on?" Jim barked into his radio.

"Nearly a dozen men," Lloyd said. *"Caught them coming around me."*

"Why didn't you call for us on the radio?" Jim asked.

"I did, dammit!" Lloyd snapped. *"Several times."*

"I'm sorry," Jim said. "I guess I was out of range."

"How convenient. Leaving the heavy work to me."

"Just tell me where you are, Lloyd."

Lloyd gave their location and then Bird came on the radio.

"We haven't checked all the bodies. We'll wait on you guys. I want some cover while we make sure they're dead."

21

None of the attackers were alive by the time Mack, Jim, and Hugh approached. They checked and double-checked to make sure no one had any fight left in them. With no prisoners to deal with, they set about recovering any usable weapons and gear from the dead.

There was nothing special about the attackers' gear. They had a mixture of rifles from all over the spectrum—different calibers, different makes. There were low-end ARs and high-end hunting rifles. The couple of handguns they found ranged from decent to junk. There was no extraordinary quantity of ammunition. Each man carried enough to defend himself but not to fight a protracted battle.

With the chips falling as they had, the extra ammunition hadn't helped the men at all. It wasn't their supplies that let them down, but their planning. Had they chosen a better route, one less visible, they might have succeeded in reaching Jim's house unnoticed. With no survivors, folks in the valley would never know why they did things the way they did.

While nothing about the men's gear merited extraordinary attention, a hand-drawn map Hugh found in one man's pocket set Jim reeling. After Jim had a moment to study it, he began stomping around and muttering, making threats against any and all who would enter their valley unbidden.

"This would take them right to my house," Jim spat, waving the map around.

The crude map had enough significant landmarks to get someone from town into the valley, and just like with a treasure map, the final destination was marked with an X. That X was Jim's house.

"It has to be that bastard Fred Wimmer," Jim growled. "He's pissed at me over what happened at that meeting. He's ratting us all out. He's going to get someone killed unless I get to him first."

"I don't particularly like the guy either," Bird said, "but that doesn't necessarily mean he's behind this. Anyone could have gotten this information from tax maps at the courthouse. They could have got it from the power company. Hell, they could have got it from a newspaper delivery guy, a meter reader, or some old man who happens to know where you live. Like I said, I got nothing for the guy but if you zoom in too close on him you may miss something else important."

Bird was right. Jim was prone to holding a grudge and it could influence his judgment. He definitely didn't need to be wearing blinders and miss something important because he was pissed off at Fred Wimmer. He needed to keep an open mind.

Hugh stared at the line of dead men and shook his head. "They shouldn't have gotten this far. We need to rework this whole system of observation posts. Right after the disaster people stuck to the roads because that's what they knew. They're adapting. They're changing their tactics and realizing the roads are too exposed. We need to put people at clear vantage points where they can see more of the valley, not just down the road ahead of them."

"Like Outpost Pete," Jim said. "The boy had the right idea while I was gone. Get up high where you can see everything."

"You doing okay over there, Lloyd?" Bird asked.

"I thought you had medical on the way," Lloyd groaned. "Any longer and I'm more likely to need an undertaker."

Jim couldn't tell if the distress in Lloyd's voice was real or just his regular drama. "We got Randi on the way. She's old and it takes her a while."

"I'll make sure and pass that on," Lloyd said. "It would be a shame for you to survive this attack only to be killed by your own medic because you couldn't stop running that mouth."

For a brief, terrifying moment they thought Lloyd might've been hit by one of the few rounds that the attackers managed to get off in his direction. When Jim and Hugh arrived, they converged on the bodies with Bird, taking a moment to confirm there were no survivors. They'd expected Lloyd to join them there but he didn't show up. They put out a call on the radio and he responded. He wouldn't, or couldn't, tell them anything about his condition but confirmed he needed help. They ran to him while Bird continued to search the bodies.

It turned out that when the gunfight was over Lloyd released his weapon from his cramping fingers and laid his head down in the grass. Unable to keep himself positioned at the lip of the draw, he slid a few feet downhill in the damp grass, racked with pain and scared to move. When his friends arrived at his side, they made a quick search for any blood or wounds. They found neither.

"I wasn't hit," Lloyd protested. "I don't know what happened. I think it's a stroke or a heart attack."

Hugh probed Lloyd's muscles with the tips of his fingers and did indeed find them contracted. "Stick out your tongue."

"What?"

"Stick out your tongue, Lloyd," Hugh repeated. "One of the signs of stroke is that your tongue may deviate to the side when extended."

Lloyd did as he was told, an apprehensive look on his face. "Hair does it rook?" Lloyd asked, finding it difficult to speak with his tongue jutting out.

"Pickled by liquor but otherwise normal," Jim said. "Kind of reminds me of the worm at the bottom of a bottle of Mezcal."

Hugh and Jim assisted Lloyd to where the bodies lay stretched out. Hugh spread a poncho on the ground and Lloyd laid on it while they finished searching the bodies. While the men proceeded with the morbid work, Lloyd distracted himself by taking jabs at his old friend.

"Do I have to do everything myself? I tried to get you on the radio several times and you completely ignored me. I can tell you how much regard you have for your oldest friend that you sent him out alone to defend your valley. You ain't that likeable a person. You'd do well to better protect the friends you have."

"I was helping Hugh," Jim said.

"You weren't alone, Lloyd," Bird added. "I was helping you."

"I'm sure you were probably stretched out on a hammock somewhere, taking a leisurely nap. Maybe you were out there dipping your lily while I was in a life or death struggle for the fate of this valley."

"I was not stretched out in a hammock and I don't even know what the hell 'dipping your lily' means. You know I manned this outpost until after midnight when you came and took over for me. I was in bed this morning when Hugh called me on the radio and said he had men approaching his observation post."

That there had been visitors at Hugh's position was news to both Lloyd and Bird, whose locations prevented them from receiving Hugh's earlier radio transmissions.

"So what happened there?" Bird asked. "I heard shots but I assumed they were part of this attack."

"I got the drop on them," Hugh said. "They never got a shot off. I held them until Jim got there. When you guys started shooting they admitted they were a diversionary force, distracting us to improve the odds of this team."

"They sounded a little too pleased about it too," Jim groused.

"Any casualties down there?" Bird asked.

Hugh chuckled. "You know that old expression about not killing the messenger?"

Bird nodded.

"Jim kills the messenger," Hugh said.

"Good to know," Bird replied. "If I've got bad news, I'm sending Lloyd."

"Way to ease the spirits of a dying man," Lloyd groused. "I thought those present at the deathbed of an expiring warrior were supposed to tell them how brave they were and assure them they would rise to fight again."

"You're not going to die," Jim said.

"Unless you give Jim bad news," Bird stated. "Remember, he *kills* the messenger."

"YOU'RE NOT GOING TO DIE," Randi pronounced over Lloyd's moans.

He insisted on holding Randi's hand. "I don't want to die alone."

"It's a cramp, Lloyd."

"But it's *everything.* Feet to neck. It has to be a stroke."

"It's a full body cramp," Randi explained. "They're not uncommon in certain situations."

"What kinds of situations?" Jim asked.

"Like when an out-of-shape, middle-aged man who prefers liquor over water tries to perform a strenuous physical activity."

Lloyd sputtered, offended. "I'm in fine form."

"Sure," said Jim, "if your form is a loaf of soggy French bread."

"Fuck you," Lloyd spat. He tried to give Jim the finger but the hand curled in a spasm and he couldn't extend the finger. He looked at Randi in desperation. "What can I do?"

"Let's get some water in you for now," Randi said. "Then, if you can get on a horse, I'll let you ride double with me to my house. We'll make you an electrolyte solution and try to get your chemistry back where it should be."

Hugh and Jim helped get Lloyd on a horse and Randi rode off toward her house.

"What do we do with these bodies?" Bird asked.

"I've got too much on my plate to dig ten graves," Jim said. "I suggest we drag them to a shallow sinkhole and shovel dirt over them."

Bird shook his head. "I don't like it."

"Got a better option?"

"No, but I don't like it."

"I have a hard time showing proper respect to men who were on their way to attack my house," Jim said. "If it was just me, I'd leave them for the buzzards. They'd be gone in a week."

They used a horse and rope to drag each man to a nearby sink-hole. The valley was full of them, ranging from those large enough to conceal a mobile home to others no bigger than earthen hot tubs. Once they had the men stacked neatly, Bird left to fetch shovels from his place.

Hugh and Jim waited nearby, not wanting to sit in the presence of the bodies.

"What's your plan, Jim?"

"I've got a million ideas flying through my brain and no idea what to do with any of them," Jim answered. "It's two weeks from the 4th of July. Is this what every day is going to be like? Am I going to be fighting for my life on a daily basis?"

"Not just *your* life," Hugh said. "Everyone in your group is at risk."

"Thanks a lot, Hugh. As if I didn't feel guilty enough."

Hugh shrugged. "Not trying to make you feel guilty, man. Just stating facts. Anyone who gets between you and the men who want you is in danger."

"We're going to have to tighten shit up. I never planned on having to bug out but it's entirely possible I could be driven from my home. We all could."

"We're well armed but there could be thousands of people contending for this bounty," Hugh noted. "Though we've only seen folks from town, if they distributed the flyers regionally there could be other groups on their way here."

Jim stared off at his beautiful valley. He'd never seen it from this particular vantage point before. "That makes me sick, Hugh. How do I fix this? How does it end?"

"No idea, brother."

"I would pick my family up and move right now if I had a way to do so. We can't take all our supplies though, and we can't just wander around. Being nomadic is not sustainable."

"All we can do is increase our defenses and, like you said, make provisions for bugging out if it comes to that. It's going to make it hard to raise crops though. Everything is coming up now. People are already eating squash and peas. The whole business of preserving food hasn't even begun yet. I don't know how we're going to do it all. Raising food takes labor, guarding the valley takes labor, and we only have so many people."

"Have you heard anything from Scott yet?"

Hugh shook his head. "I've sent some messages but haven't received an answer. He might be working in the field somewhere, out on an operation."

"How are you sending messages?"

"Basically a secure text message through radio frequencies."

"I hope he's got some information."

"I'll check again when I head up the mountain."

"Meanwhile, I'll head back home and start caching some supplies in case we have to bug out. My family is *not* going to like the idea of that."

22

It was barely midday when Jim got home but he was physically and emotionally exhausted. He hadn't slept well the night before and had been jolted from his sleep to help Hugh at the observation post. Then, after all the adrenaline surges of the morning, he'd spent the last two hours burying a stack of bodies. This was not what he wanted his life to be. It wasn't what he wanted his family's life to be.

Ellen and Pops were waiting for him on the porch when he got home. Nana and Ariel were painting signs for the gardens that told what each crop was and had a picture on them. Jim wasn't certain if the task was more for Nana's benefit or for Ariel's. Neither liked to be idle.

"So what happened?" Ellen asked. She and Pops were desperate for news. They'd heard shooting all morning though had no idea what was going on, other than that Jim had been rushing around desperately with a gun.

"I'm thirsty," Jim said. "Let me get a drink first."

"You're drenched in sweat," Ellen said. "Sit down. What do you want?"

"Tea."

"Sweet?"

"No, strong and bitter, like your husband."

Ellen smiled. "Let me get some from the dairy. I've got some in the spring box and it will be nice and cold."

She returned with a plastic Gatorade bottle filled with sun tea. The cold bottle was already gathering condensation on the warm morning. Jim held it against his forehead and relished the cold. He was going to miss air-conditioning later this summer. And cold beer. He needed to derail that sad train. Once he starting thinking about the things he missed it was a no win situation.

He launched into his story and explained what happened from the minute he got the call from Hugh until he got home. He talked about the need to change up the observation posts and watch more than the roads, about Hugh trying to reach Scott from power restoration authority to see if he had any information on whether the bounty on Jim was legitimate or a rogue effort. Finally, reluctantly, he told them that the attackers had been carrying a map to the house—the very house where he sat this moment enjoying his cold bottle of tea.

Jim looked at Ellen's face as he made that final statement. She was terrified.

"They know where we live?" she asked.

Jim nodded.

"How?"

"I want to blame Fred Wimmer but the others have suggested that they could have found out any number of ways. There are people out there who know where our house is. Hell, they could have talked to the UPS man or something. We'll never know."

"That makes me sick, Jim. How are we ever going to have a moment's peace?"

Jim didn't have an answer. He didn't know what they were going to do but they had to figure something out fast, before it happened again.

"Nana will want to leave," Pops said. "She misses our home

anyway. This may seal the deal. You think you all should pack up and go with us?"

"Not happening," Jim insisted. "We'd never get all the things we need to survive moved that far. Plus people would notice and they'd get curious. They'd start talking. Pretty soon they'd put together the pieces and come searching for us at your house. Besides, we have people willing to fight alongside us here in the valley. If we go to town, we're back in the position of not having enough people to defend ourselves."

"We might not need people keeping watch in town," Pops said.

"You'll need people keeping watch wherever you are," Jim said. "And what about food? We've got crops in the ground now that might keep us going another year. We've got too much invested here."

"If we can keep it," Ellen said. "These people won't give up. They're just going to keep coming." There was desperation in her voice, a resignation that this was the new state of things and it was even worse than things already were. That possibility would have been hard to imagine a few days ago.

"How many people are you prepared to kill?" Pops asked.

"All of them," Jim replied. "As many as it takes."

Pops shook his head at that. It was not an expression of doubt but of a general distaste for the whole situation. This was not the world he wanted to live in. It wasn't for any of them. No one would have chosen this world over the old, this *life* over their previous one, but no choice was being offered. No one got to start over because things got tough.

"What do we need to do?" Ellen asked, practicality rising to the surface now that the surge of emotion was subsiding.

"Too much of our survival is tied to this house and it's compromised," Jim said. "Some of our gear is still in the cave from when you guys moved there while I was gone. We need to stash more there. I'm going to create more caches out of those blue barrels I've got. Instead of just keeping food in them, I'm going to paint them camo and set each one up to be independent. I'll store a weapon, ammo, food, and survival gear in each one and stash them in the woods. That way if we lose the house, we have options."

"Lose the house," Ellen repeated, her voice low and her eyes distant, as if she were trying to comprehend that possibility.

"We have to accept that could happen," Jim stated. "This is the one thing I've figured out this morning. This *family* is the people that make it up, not the house. We have emotional attachments to this place but we can't let that hold us back. We can't let the emotional bonds to this house affect our decision making. We can't put the important parts of this family at risk for something that's not really important at all. This house is replaceable but it's the *only* part of this family that can be replaced."

"You're right," Pops said. "That's the decision we ultimately had to make in leaving our own home. Nana continued to struggle with it. We built that house together and it's a monument to our lives and our family. That's not an easy thing to put behind you."

Jim could tell Ellen was trying to convince herself Pops was right but he could also see some of Nana's struggle within her. This would not be easy for him either. This farm was not just the house. It was all the extras he'd personally added to prepare for an event such as this. It was the cave, the gravity-fed water system, the solar backup, and the hundreds of other little touches. Without access to online shopping, he'd never be able to build something like this again. If they had to abandon the house, he'd never be able to replace it.

Never again in his lifetime would he be able to set up another house so perfectly for living without power and modern conveniences. Not only would the national recovery take too long, he didn't have the time or energy remaining in his life to do it. It had taken him twenty years. The next twenty years of his life would be harder. His energy and strength would diminish. He would not be building self-sufficient homesteads. It was a tough pill to swallow. If he was forced to give his place up he'd never, ever have anything like it again.

He pulled himself out of that spiral. It was leading nowhere but down that negative emotional path that he was trying to avoid. The house wasn't family; it was a resource. One he wanted to protect, yes, though it was secondary to protecting his family. He had to keep reminding himself of that.

"We restock the cave, cache stuff in the woods, disperse everything," Jim said, as much to himself as to Ellen and Pops. "Any gear that's redundant or a backup, I'm going to get out of the house and store somewhere else. As hard as it is to say this, I want the house to be disposable. It needs to be a shell we can jettison if the situation requires that. We have to start thinking that way."

Ellen got to her feet. "Then you come up with a plan for that. The next thing on my list this morning was weeding the garden. I'm going to get started on that. When I'm done, you point me toward the next thing you need me to do."

She started off the porch.

"Ellen?" Jim called. She paused at the bottom of the steps. "Rifle and handgun at all times now. And for God's sake make sure you have a radio with you."

Ellen backed up the steps and went inside without a word. He understood how she felt. Sick. Stunned. In shock. That was how he felt too.

23

Joint Base Anacostia-Bolling (JBAB)

WHILE HIS HUNDREDS of thousands of flyers worked their magic in southwest Virginia, Boss gave no indication that he was not fully onboard with his role on Owen's team. To anyone working with him, he appeared fully engaged, running missions and dealing with the numerous threats to the new national agenda. His broad experience and natural acumen made him excel at the job. Several times Owen commented that he was glad Boss had put any thoughts of vengeance behind him.

"This is where we need you. This is your future," Owen said.

In Owen's mind those words were merely a statement of the obvious. He felt as if he was complimenting Boss on how he'd risen to the occasion, but when Boss left the war room on a late June day those words stung him to the core. They replayed over and over in his head. They were a bitter rebuke of everything he stood for. Boss had always preferred being the tip of the spear. He was the guy who got things done. That was not what he felt like now. He felt emasculated–neutered–and it was a bitter pill.

One byproduct of his new job was that he had his finger on the pulse of nearly every operation underway on the East Coast, giving him the ability to monitor the comings and goings of aircraft. Not only choppers coming in and out of JBAB, but throughout what remained of the DC Metro and Northern Virginia area. By means of that resource, he'd figured out that his favorite chopper crew was on-base right now, staying overnight for routine maintenance before heading out again in twenty-four hours. He needed to track them down. They needed to talk.

After some asking around and some less than routine menacing glares, Boss discovered that Gordon was rendezvousing with several other crew chiefs on the fringes of the base. He'd returned from his latest mission with a couple of growlers of beer from a brewery in Tennessee that continued to operate despite the current hardships. Under recent conditions, drunkenness was not tolerated and there were no places for a man to legally buy a drink. The policy was only loosely enforced and command tolerated recreational drinking as long as no one got stupid.

After an hour of walking around in circles, Boss found the men outside a battered shipping container loaded with spare chopper parts. The group was sitting around on rusty chairs and upturned five-gallon buckets drinking dark beer from clear plastic cups. When Boss appeared, an unfamiliar face interrupting their party, there was a flicker of concern until Gordon spoke up.

"No, he's cool," said Gordon. "We've got some business."

A comment like that would raise no concern among the other crew chiefs. As the only men who got outside the walls on a routine basis, the chopper crews were the primary conduit feeding the black market. In fact, of the growlers Gordon returned with, most were being sold to a cook running a speakeasy from a similar shipping container located elsewhere on base.

Boss addressed the men. "You mind if I borrow Gordon for a

second?" It wasn't really a question. He was speaking with Gordon regardless.

Gordon drained his beer and set the empty cup on a rusty drum of hydraulic fluid. "Save me some, boys." After they were standing a few containers away, Gordon asked, "What's up?"

"I need a real favor this time," Boss said.

Gordon's brow furrowed. Distributing all of those flyers had been a pain in the ass. Of course, he'd been well-compensated for it so he had no room to complain. "What kind of *real* favor?"

"I've got an operation going down on the evening of the 4th of July. I need chopper transport to Southwest Virginia."

Awareness dawned on Gordon. "This is about those flyers, isn't it?"

Boss didn't answer, which was all the answer Gordon needed. The big man's look said it all.

"Listen, Captain Ballou, I will go wherever you need us to go as long as we got fuel and orders. My crew and I will do what we have to do. You got that part about orders though, right? There's a flight crew and ground personnel involved. I can't just fly off on a personal jaunt with no orders."

"I can cover that end of things," Boss said. "I've already laid the groundwork. I've got you guys up on a mission that'll fly you right over my destination on the day I need this to happen. I made a special request of your crew. No one will question that. It's customary and within my authority."

"I can promise you *my* assistance. You and I have an understanding. But I've got two pilots that have to be onboard with this. I can't make promises for them, especially if there's going to be flak when we get home."

Boss dug into a shirt pocket and extracted three Krugerrands. He handed them over to Gordon, who examined them in the palm of his hand. "Did these ease the minds of your pilots last time?"

Gordon stared at the dull glow of the coins in his palm. He hefted them, impressed at the weight.

"Consider that a down payment. One for each of you to show I'm serious. Tell them that each of you will get two more after liftoff on mission day."

Gordon's eyes widened. "Two more? That's a lot of money. Are we going to have to do anything shady?"

"Not you guys. If all goes as planned, you won't have to do anything but deliver me to the correct football field, let me pick up the package, and get me back in the air."

Gordon began to look nervous. The package wasn't a pallet of booze or a duffel bag of tobacco leaves. It was a person. He pulled a cigarette from his pocket and lit it, took a deep draw, visibly considered something, then came out with it. "I read your flyers. I didn't know how you felt about me doing that so I tried not to, but how could I help it when I had to scatter the damn things out all over the countryside? This operation is about those hillbillies, isn't it?"

"This is about insurgents," Boss stated. "It's about people delaying the national recovery effort by destroying public infrastructure."

Gordon inhaled and carefully blew the smoke away from Boss. "Yeah, I get that's the public story, and I'm no stranger to going on operations where I don't ask questions. I've been on ops where I was told to not even turn my head toward the back of the chopper. This is different. Before I put my career at risk, before I put my guys' lives at risk, I would like to know the real deal. I'm not a fucking idiot. If this was a legitimate operation you wouldn't be paying us to keep quiet."

Boss could have handled the situation with physical threats and intimidation to get what he wanted, but would play this differently. He liked Gordon and respected him. He'd risked his life to bring Boss home. Sure, it was his job, but he could have easily said there were no survivors, that they hadn't seen any signs of life at that dark, flooded power plant, and left Boss to die. No one would have ever known the difference.

Boss raised his right hand in front of Gordon's face. The stump was fitted with the carbon fiber gauntlet and the stylus attachment. "It's about this," he growled. "This is personal."

Gordon looked from the attachment to Boss's eyes and then away. He understood. That was indeed personal.

"If you read the flyers then you know I'm offering a bounty for the insurgent pictured in the photograph. I know he didn't pull off that attack alone. He's part of an organized effort. If I find him and locate his base, I can find the rest of his people and erase any future threat they may present. And, of course, I hope to find the person responsible for my hand. I remember exactly what he looks like. You don't forget someone like that."

"You're really offering a bounty? I mean, you're seriously going to deliver on that part of the bargain?"

"Definitely. I requisitioned a pallet of forty-eight buckets of survival food. I've got the ammo I promised set aside and ready to go. This isn't nearly as heavy a load as all those flyers you delivered. Like the flyer says, we search for a signal fire or smoke on that day. Then we land and hopefully exchange the reward for the prisoner. I take him into custody and we lift back off."

"Then we bring him back here for questioning or are you just going to shove him off the chopper at altitude?" Gordon's tongue had been loosened a bit by the alcohol, and he regretted his own words once he'd said them. Sometimes there were questions you didn't want to know the answer to.

Thankfully, Boss didn't take offense. "Neither," he replied. "You're dropping us off outside of town. I need some quality alone time with the prisoner. Hopefully that will lead me to the rest of his group and I can do what needs to be done."

"How are you going to coordinate a pickup? Or is this a one-way mission?"

"I'm hoping I only need a week. I'll have a radio and tracking beacon. You'll be able to find me using radio frequencies but this beacon will stay off the satellites. That makes it our little secret."

"I don't control my own schedule, man," Gordon said. "I can't guarantee I'll be back in a week."

"It doesn't have to be a week exactly. You just swing over the area when you're down this way. I'll give you a radio frequency. If I don't respond, try again when you're back this way."

"What if you never respond? What are we supposed to do then?"

“Then you go on about your life. No one in command knows about this mission or about your crew’s involvement. To be honest, I'd rather die out in the field than spend another five years in that office coaching the quarterbacks who are out there doing the real work. I’m not cut out for a desk job.”

Gordon sucked in a deep lungful of smoke and exhaled through his nose. "I appreciate you being straight with me. I need to talk to my guys but I'm fairly sure they’ll be in agreement with me. They tend to trust my gut.”

"What’s your gut telling you?"

Gordon flipped the smoldering butt into the gravels. "My gut says we can take care of what you’re asking of us. As far as your end of the mission, that’s all on you." He gestured back to where the rest of his buddies were. "Can I offer you beer? If those assholes haven’t drained it, it’s pretty good."

Boss shook his head. "No thanks. I appreciate it but I've got four more hours in the gym ahead of me. I'm going to need everything I’ve got."

24

"Get some shoes on that you can wear in the garden," Ellen told Ariel.

"I'm painting," Ariel said. "Can't I keep painting? I don't want to garden."

Ellen was upset, angry and frustrated over everything that had happened. Over the flyer, the attack on her valley, and over having to be scared again.

"No, you can't keep painting. I need help in the garden. Everyone has a job to do and this is one of yours."

"Why can't my job be painting?"

"Because we need gardeners more than we need painters right now."

Ariel gave a dramatic sigh and wilted, as if death by gardening was imminent. She slogged off to her room to search for shoes.

"And you better not take too long," Ellen warned, shouldering her rifle and heading out the door.

By the time the screen door clacked shut she was already at the bottom of the steps and headed for the garden at a determined pace. She normally enjoyed gardening–it was her happy place. Today, however, there were no happy places anywhere. She was angry at the world. For reasons she couldn't fully explain, she was also angry at Jim.

This wasn't his fault. He'd done nothing but try to keep them safe and comfortable at a time when those things were at a premium. If anything, she should be trying to support him, especially since he was the one in the crosshairs. That was part of what made her mad though. By putting himself in the crosshairs, his family was forced to be there also.

But *had* he put himself there?

He had indeed. The whole mission to destroy the power plant hadn't been necessary. It was revenge for the government stealing power from local people. It was a statement against forcing people to disarm to receive aid. How had Jim gotten to the point of doing something like that? How had he gone from being a hermit who simply wanted to be left alone to being someone taking action against the government on behalf of his community?

She had the sudden realization that if she was angry with him over this, she needed to be angry at herself. She was partly to blame. She was the one who'd pushed him to accept the mantle of leadership that he kept dodging. If left to his own devices, he'd probably have continued acting under his isolationist strategy. He'd only done what he did because he thought he was responsible for everyone and she was part of the reason he felt that way.

It made her want to cry. She was partly to blame for everything that had happened and everything that was yet to happen.

"What do you want me to do?" Ariel asked, startling her mother.

"Take this hoe and clear the weeds around those tomatoes," Ellen said, distracted and thinking about her role in everything. Should she have just left him alone to make his own decisions?

"You didn't say please," Ariel said. "That's the magic word." She skipped away, giggling.

Ellen took another hoe and was preparing to take up the weeds around the potato hills. Noise at the house drew her attention and she saw Jim setting a blue plastic barrel on the porch before returning to the barn to get another. She decided she couldn't offer him any more advice ever again. It carried too much of a burden. Too much responsibility.

The familiarity of those words took her back to previous conversations she and Jim had, particularly the conversations about him not wanting to take care of the other people in the valley. He didn't want the responsibility, didn't want the burden. When every action potentially carried drastic and irreversible consequences, what did one do? Hide out and avoid it? Pass the buck? Or did one try to make the best decision they could under the circumstances, accepting that they would have to live with the consequences?

That was the road Jim had taken and she'd been partly responsible for him going that route. If she felt strongly enough that it was the right course, then she had to accept that it was probably the right course. He'd done what he thought was right. She couldn't fault him for it. Maybe in the end they'd fail to save the valley and the people in it. Perhaps they'd all have to go their own separate ways and concede this valley to scavengers, rogues, and wildlife. If that was what it took to save her family, she'd have to do it, even if it meant losing the house and the elaborate preparations Jim had made.

"Mommy, I see something," Ariel said.

Ellen snapped to attention. "Where?"

Ariel pointed but Ellen saw nothing. She went to the garden fence and traded her hoe for the rifle. She raised the scope to her eye and scanned the woods where Ariel had pointed but saw nothing.

"It could have been a deer," Ellen said.

"I think it was a Bigfoot," Ariel said, excited.

Ellen returned to the fence, ready to trade the rifle for the hoe, and paused. She glanced back to the dense forest that Ariel had pointed to. It was a maze of hardwoods with a few cedars interspersed. It was a jumble of tall standing timber and fallen trees, with a mix of brightly lit pockets and regions of deep black shadow. Unless you caught something moving there was no way you'd find anything there.

Ariel had grown up here; she didn't imagine things. Was something out there? Were they being watched? Was there somebody ready to shoot them or take them prisoner to manipulate Jim into surrendering? They were in the open. Someone with a scoped rifle could be watching them right now.

Ellen watched her daughter. Her snarky, smart-aleck, intelligent, sweet daughter had gone back to work chopping at weeds with her hoe. Occasionally, she cut a sideways glance back at the woods. She had seen something, or at least thought she had. It wasn't an act, nor a diversion to get out of work.

Ellen slung her rifle back over her shoulder and waved to Ariel. "We can do that later, honey. Let's go back to the house now and get your dad to check the woods."

Ariel propped her hoe against the fence and ran past her mother, through the gate, and toward the house. She made no comments about how she hadn't wanted to work in the garden anyway. Jim always said you had to trust your gut and this was one of those cases. Ellen's gut said it was better to play it safe.

She backed out of the garden and shut the gate, keeping her eyes on the woods, watching for movement as she headed toward the house. Her heart was racing. She'd never experienced an anxiety attack in her life but she thought that was what was happening. She was short of breath and felt lightheaded.

Nearly at the house, still backing up, she tripped over the raised root of a flowering cherry tree and sat down hard.

"Are you okay, Mommy?" Ariel asked, running toward her mother.

"Ellen!" Jim was between the barn and the house with another blue barrel on his shoulder. He set it down and ran toward his wife.

"I'm fine," she said, getting to her feet and brushing her pants off.

"Mommy fell, Daddy," Ariel said.

"I saw that," Jim said, taking Ellen's arm. "Are you sure you're okay?"

"Yes," Ellen said, though her eyes told a different story.

"You don't seem okay," Jim said. He could see the fear, the panic that threatened to overwhelm her at any moment.

"Ariel saw some movement in the woods," Ellen said, her voice quavering. "It could have been a deer. We don't know."

Jim looked toward the woods. "Let's get you inside and then I'll go check it out."

She pulled away from him. "I'm fine. You go check it out. Ariel and I will wait for you on the porch."

"Okay." Jim was as concerned about Ellen at that moment as he was about anything in the woods. He'd never seen her like that, so consumed with fear. He went to the porch and picked up his rifle, chambering a round. He was already wearing his tac vest and sidearm. "I'll be back in a minute. You guys lock the door and keep an eye out."

Ellen nodded but said nothing.

"We will, Daddy," Ariel said, tugging at her mother's arm.

25

"Pete! It's Dad. Can you hear me?" Jim said into his radio.

"I got you, Dad. What's up?"

"Your sister thinks she saw something in the woods. It's probably nothing but I'm going to check it out. Your mom is a little freaked out."

"Got it. Charlie's up here with me. We'll keep an eye on you."

"Thanks. I appreciate that."

"No prob, Dad," Pete replied.

Jim tucked the radio back in its pocket on his vest and started jogging. He was already past the garden but it was a good distance to the woods. He stopped to go through a gate, closed it behind him, then started jogging. The pasture was covered in low, lush grass with occasional bright green tufts the cattle had somehow missed. At the small creek he stopped to cross a log bridge. He could have jumped the entire creek but last time he tried his feet slipped out from under him and he went down hard. No use taking risks when he couldn't run into town for an X-ray.

Beyond the creek Jim crossed a flat spot that had been used as a landing for a logging operation in the months before the world changed. It was where the skidders dragged the logs and piled them until the trucks showed up with their knuckle-boom loaders. The area was littered with stumps, culled logs, and piles of sawdust. There was a pile containing the ends of logs that had been cut off to get them down to marketable size. That pile had provided a lot of firewood for Jim's family.

He crossed the rutted expanse, the ground baked into a brown brick of mud and sawdust. He slowed to step over a dead electric fence, then continued walking up a rutted logging road. He watched for snakes, a lifelong habit, though he'd never run across anything on his farm but harmless varieties.

He paused to get his bearings. He was starting up a series of isolated hills that were not part of the larger mountain range. They were surrounded on all sides by farmland. It was a pocket of woods about seventy to eighty acres in size. Deer and turkey were plentiful there, as were the squirrels that the boys brought in from their snares nearly every day.

To his left was the area where Ariel indicated she'd seen movement. It was on a steep, wooded slope with no cross trails. He decided that he'd rather follow the easier route of the logging road and approach the area in question from above. Then he could cut straight down through it, confirm nothing was amiss, and exit into the pasture at the bottom of the woods. He pulled his radio from his pocket.

"Pete, you got eyes on me?"

"Roger, Dad."

"I'm going to follow this logging road to the top of the hill then come back down through the woods. You may lose sight of me after I get around the next bend. If you draw a line from the garden to the top of this hill, that's where I'll be coming back down. If you see someone, don't shoot, because it might be me. Got it?"

"Got it, Dad. Be careful."

"Be careful, Jim." It was Ellen. She sounded better now, her panic subsiding, though concerned for him.

The road got steeper. It had been carved into the mountain with a bulldozer. It was made for skidders with four wheel drive and massive five-foot tall tires weighing a thousand pounds each. It didn't observe the standards of roads designed for cars. It climbed sharply and Jim was soon chugging away like an engine, taking short, controlled breaths. He tried to look at his body as a machine, maximizing his stride and finding his most efficient pace. Move fast but don't bonk was the rule.

When the road leveled off near the peak of the hill, he stopped to listen. The mountain was littered with leaves, weeds, and branches. It was a hard place to navigate in total silence. He heard nothing but birds and a distant dog. It was exactly what he wanted to hear. He brought his rifle up to low ready and confirmed the glint of brass in the chamber. He flicked the safety off, that single sound louder than he expected.

He began to work on his own noise signature. He paused long enough to let his breathing slow, watching his steps to avoid rocks and branches. He dodged blackberry vines, aware that they generated their own sound as they ripped and tore at clothing. He took a step at a time, finding his next foot placement before he stepped again. He didn't expect to find anyone up there but caution was the rule anymore.

He searched for signs that others had been moving around there. Pete and Charlie had snares in these woods and he'd committed their boot prints to memory for just such occasions as this. If he saw those familiar prints, he could eliminate them.

Jim crept along, watching and listening. The crest of the hill was a tangled scrub of chest-high weeds and briars. Last year's logging had removed the tall hardwoods that sheltered the area and weeds were the first to stake their claim as nature retook the ground. The terrain was uneven. There were piles of spoils created by the dozer as it made roads and switchbacks, thick roots protruding from the dirt piles like outstretched arms, and slash piles of limbs. Occasionally there would be a complete tree that had been cut down before revealing a fatal flaw that destroyed its market value.

The terrain was a tactical nightmare. He couldn't see a thing. The same features that made moving around difficult also presented countless places for a person to hide. Jim keyed his microphone. "You there, Pete?"

"I got you, Dad."

"I'm on top of the hill. I'm going to circle around, then start down the hill directly toward our garden."

"Got it."

Thirty feet ahead of Jim was a pile of logs jumbled together, their butt ends jutting in all directions. It was culled and odd-lengths pushed into a pile with a dozer. When his eye roamed in that direction Jim thought he saw a flicker of movement in his peripheral vision.

He snapped his rifle from low ready to high. Wherever his eyes went, the rifle followed. He started at the top right corner of the pile and visually traced it in a grid pattern. He'd yet to find the source of the movement that had drawn his attention. He was about to write it off to being a bird or chipmunk when a figure in Realtree camo popped up from the base of a low log. He was on his knees, a rifle pointed in Jim's direction.

"Freeze!" he shouted.

When Jim's head jerked in the direction of the voice, his rifle came with him. The glowing red circle and dot reticle of his optic stopped on the man's chest. Jim didn't hesitate. Two quick flicks of the trigger sent the attacker sprawling backward.

Before he could even process what had taken place there was movement on several fronts. Jim was uncertain if the attack was launched off the man's command for him to freeze or if it was triggered by his own gunshots but it was on. Fifty yards to his right a man screamed like a banshee as he barreled through the underbrush. Jim swung toward him. If the yell was an attempt to intimidate him, it didn't work. All it did was give him advance warning of who needed to be killed next.

Jim was ready to oblige him when the running man ducked like a linebacker charging a line but continued to run, parting the weeds like a water buffalo in the tall grass of Africa. Jim couldn't see any part of him but aimed ahead of his wake and sent rounds flying.

The first two missed but the third brought a cry of pain and halted his progress. Jim didn't want to leave him alive—that was against his personal rules of engagement—but it was suicide to run into those weeds after him. He stood there frozen, trying to figure out his next move. His breathing was fast and shallow, his eyes scanning with a mechanical efficiency.

In the stillness, he noticed the chorus of voices on his radio. He'd turned the volume down earlier so it wouldn't give him away. He dropped a hand from his rifle and cranked it back up. There was Pete demanding to know if he was okay, the same from Ellen. There were other voices stepping on top of each other, people from elsewhere in the valley wanting to know where the shots were coming from.

Jim stood wide-eyed and terrified. He was in the open, alone, separated from any backup. Then he heard crackling; branches underfoot. Under several sets of feet. He jerked his head from one direction to the other, watching for whoever might be coming. Although there was no one visible the sound was growing louder.

Closer.

Heads popped up in the thick brush. They were several of them, forty to fifty yards away, branches snapping beneath their feet as they charged through the obstacle course of limbs, weeds, and logs. Part of Jim understood that these men had intended to take him alive at one point. Now that he'd shot two of them, he could no longer trust that was the case. Vengeance could overrule hunger. He turned and fled.

While his pursuers were slowed by the terrain and underbrush, Jim was on the cleared logging trail. He needed to put distance between him and these men before they reached the cleared trail. Clutching his rifle tightly in both hands he beat feet for all he was worth.

The men fired in his direction, their rounds whistling around him, snapping as they punched leaves and small branches. While nothing was close enough to indicate that their master plan of taking him alive had been abandoned he wasn't going to wait around and ask them.

Not wanting to run blindly, he flitted his eyes between the terrain at his feet and any potential threats ahead of him. Logging roads weren't exactly maintained like driveways. There were deep ruts and loose rocks the size of grapefruits. One misplaced step and he might go down in a tumble.

He didn't know if there were other pockets of men lying in wait for him. They could be hiding anywhere. They could be waiting to jump him or to put a bullet in his leg. The flyer hadn't said anything about the condition of the prisoner. They could both make him pay for the men he'd killed and leave him alive to collect the reward. He didn't want to think about that.

Jim hit a bend and started down a steep slope to more gunfire. He was running full tilt now. He had to be gaining distance but that only made him more terrified that a tumble was imminent. It hit him that he should be in visual range of Pete and Charlie. If the new guns in the fight belonged to those boys, he hoped like hell they knew who to shoot.

A scream of pain behind Jim let him know the boys were in the fight and had their range dialed in. He thought he recognized the sound of the rifle as his Ruger Mini-14. Whoever was behind the trigger had figured out the correct holdover for the distance and began dumping rounds as fast as they could pull the trigger. The heavy suppressive fire achieved the desired effect. There were more cries, shouts, and men barking instructions to each other. Their pursuit was falling apart.

At the base of the hill, Jim was nearly running out of control. He stumbled, his ankle almost twisting. "Dammit!" he gasped.

He reached the electric fence at the foot of the hill and vaulted it, expecting a foot to snag on it and send him rolling ass over teakettle. He made it though, and was soon at the log landing with its giant stumps and discarded logs. He dove behind a big stump and threw his rifle over it, leveling it on the trail and anyone who might be pursuing him. He fumbled to extract his radio, dropped it, then picked it up and keyed the mic.

"This is Jim!" he shouted. "I'm not hit but I've got bad guys on my ass. Some are down but I got no idea how many. Does anyone have eyes on?"

"There were five in pursuit of you. We hit every one of them. Two aren't moving. Two are down but moving. One is upright and limping back up the road, holding his arm. I'm sure I can hit him."

Jim adamantly keyed the mic. "No! You don't do that."

"Dad, you said yourself that we can't let these people get away. If we do, we just have to fight them again another time. We can drop the one trying to escape and finish the two still moving."

Jim's head sagged against his radio. He was pouring sweat and shaking, the adrenaline burning off with a vengeance. The idea of his son, his sweet boy, finishing off these men made him sick. He was aware Pete had been forced to kill before. There was no going back on that, no repairing the innocence that had been stripped from him. Yet he didn't want him to become so callous that he could take that action without thought.

"You boys put your safeties on and stand down," Jim said. "I'm going back up. Use your radios to guide me to each man and I'll deal with it. Let me know if you see anything concerning."

"Why is it okay for you to do it but not me?" Pete asked. *"What's the difference?"*

"The difference is..."

How did he explain to his son that he'd already let the blackness into his heart? That he would feel nothing when he killed these men?

"Because I said so," he finished.

26

It was nearly dark, mist rising from the ground and filling the lowlands, when Hugh came riding through the twilight like an apparition. Jim was sitting on the front porch wearing his full load-out and cradling his rifle. He looked out onto the world with resignation, a man fully expecting that death would attempt to claim him again before the day was out.

He was too paranoid at this point to go inside and relax with his family. Too much had happened. Pete and Charlie had been manning Outpost Pete most of the day. They said they were fine, alternating naps with each other, but Jim didn't want to leave them there any longer. It wasn't just for fear of the danger they were exposed to but for fear of Pete and Charlie becoming disconnected from family. From life. Jim knew what that was like. It was the dark place he found himself in most of the time anymore.

Randi had offered to man the outpost with one of her daughters but Jim didn't know what to do. He thanked her for the offer and told her he might take them up on it at a different time. He questioned the best way to guard the valley and his family. He'd been thinking about it all day and had reached no conclusions. That they were in greater danger with each passing minute was without question. The lure of the bounty on Jim was too great. People would keep trying and more people would die.

"Evening," Hugh said when he broached speaking distance. "Glad to see you're still on the sunny side of the dirt."

"I'm glad of it too. It was too close for comfort." Jim ran a hand through his hair. "You get any sleep? You've been on the go for over twenty-four hours straight."

"I took a siesta in the yard. Stretched out in a nice hammock under a tree and grabbed a couple of hours."

"That enough? You were up all night and most of the day."

"I'll be fine. Not sure I feel all that comfortable closing my eyes with so many unfriendly folks wandering inside the wire. Could you tell anything about that last group of attackers?"

Jim couldn't hide his disgust. It crept into his voice like blood spreading in water. "They had that same fucking map leading right to my house. I'd even venture it was drawn by the same hand."

"They may have been part of that wave that hit us in the morning. We just missed them and they laid low all day, waiting for the right opportunity."

"Yeah, I considered that. You learn anything on the radio?"

Hugh dismounted and tied his horse off to a flowering cherry tree. Jim noticed Hugh was loaded for bear, literally bristling with weapons. Knowing Hugh, Jim wondered how many were concealed. Hugh adhered to the philosophy that for every visible weapon there should be just as many invisible weapons. Jim listened to see if his friend rattled as he walked. No rattle, but there was a chorus of creaks from leather sheaths, holsters, and overladen web gear.

Hugh settled down on the steps and leaned back against a post. "I finally got a response. It was there when I woke up from my nap."

"You going to keep me in suspense?" Jim asked.

"Only if it provokes a reaction," Hugh said with a grin.

"Let's pretend it doesn't. It's been a rough day. At this point, my reactions are pretty over the top."

"In that case, in the interest of self-preservation, I'll just go ahead and tell you. Scott said he had to pick up a crew tomorrow night.

Their route will bring them in this general direction. He said he'd fly over the usual spot and if we want him to land we should mark an LZ with infrared beacons."

That wouldn't be a problem. Scott had left infrared beacons specifically for that purpose when he dropped some supplies off back in the winter. It always made Jim paranoid when he landed a chopper in their valley. He couldn't help but wonder if it was drawing attention to them. He supposed it didn't really matter. At this point, he didn't think the spotlight on his valley could be any brighter. The bounty would already have him and his valley on everyone's radar.

Besides, they needed any information Scott might be able to offer. They'd had some communication with him over the winter and spring but were pretty much operating in a vacuum. Jim hadn't minded that most of the time. He didn't want to know what was going on in the world. He wanted to be left alone, wanted to be able to shut out the world at large, but he couldn't wear blinders any longer. He needed information. There was a price on his head and he had to know who had put it there.

"Tomorrow," Jim said. "So I guess we just wait and hope we don't have to kill anyone else before then."

"I guess so," Hugh replied. "By the way, I'm sorry I wasn't down here when you got ambushed on that hill. What did I miss?"

Jim reeled off a description of the events that took place after Ariel spotted someone from the garden.

"That's awfully close," Hugh said. "That's practically in your front yard."

"Yep. Makes it hard for me to close my eyes. I'm sitting here waiting for the next attack."

"You think we should get an outpost on that hill where they jumped you? We could do it tomorrow. Call it Outpost Charlie. Then we'd control the only hills around your house."

"That's a good idea, Hugh."

"On that same topic, I was wondering if you might want me to take over Outpost Pete for the night."

"I've had Pete and Charlie out there all day. They like it, which worries me a bit. I don't want them to go native, as the expression goes. They need to be able come back from this one day, settle into a regular life and have families. I worry about them becoming too wild. Too used to killing."

"Call them in," Hugh said. "Let them come back and get some family time. You could probably use some too. I'm sure your family is pretty torn up about everything that happened today."

"Definitely. There's been a lot of tension around here this evening."

"All the gunfights today, all that shooting, has the sheriff shown up to ask you about any of it?"

"He's not said a word," Jim replied, the tone of his voice revealing his hostility at the sheriff's lack of intervention. "He had to have heard it. He might not want to know what's going on but burying his head in the sand isn't going to work forever. The bodies are piling up."

"I'm really surprised he hasn't checked in on you. Don't be too hard on him though. I was thinking about this last night. It's got to be tough. There's a lot more politics involved in being a sheriff than in other law enforcement positions. I'm sure he feels a burden over what the people in his county are going through. It's got to bother him. They're *his* people. They elected him."

"Sometimes I wonder if the killing should bother me more than it does," Jim said. "Every person I've killed bothers me a little less than the last one. I hate to say it but these folks I shot today didn't get a second thought. All their bodies meant to me was the inconvenience of having to roll them in a hole. I hate for my family to see shit like that."

"There is only so much you can let inside and continue to make the best decisions for your family. The sheepdog doesn't care for the wolf. It doesn't feel bad about killing it. Being a protector doesn't allow you to operate under the ideal of universal compassion toward your fellow man."

"But am I killing wolves?" Jim asked. "Or am I killing other sheep? Some days I don't know."

"The very fact that you worry about who you're killing tells me that your head is in the right place," Hugh said.

Jim sighed. "I didn't think it could happen but shit has gotten even more complicated than it was before. People I would have seen as good guys a week ago are now bad guys because they're coming after me with guns because of that stupid flyer. And because someone is waving food and supplies under their noses."

"That doesn't make you the bad guy," Hugh said. "That makes the person who put the bounty on you the bad guy, as well as anyone who decides to take up arms against you."

"That's what I keep telling myself."

"Things will level out, Jim. I really think so."

"Or things might go ape shit crazy and get way worse. That's where I'm putting my money."

Hugh pushed off the steps and got to his feet. "Stay positive. Either way, I'm with you, brother. Why don't you radio those boys to pack up their gear? Let them know I'm on the way."

"I'll do it," Jim said.

While Jim made the call on the radio, Hugh climbed on his horse and disappeared into the dark. While he was replacing his radio in its pouch, the front door opened and Ellen stepped out.

"I heard you telling Pete and Charlie to come in," she said. "That makes me feel better. I worry about them."

"There's a lot to worry about anymore," Jim said. Not only was he tired of worrying, he was getting tired of talking about worrying.

Ellen went to the porch and leaned over, resting her arms on the rail and listening to the night. "I've been thinking a lot today about whether we should just pull up stakes and leave. I can't imagine us ever being safe here again."

Jim was mentally exhausted, beyond the point of finding any new solutions. "I don't know as we could find anywhere to go or have any way to get there if we did know of a place. We might be able to scrape up enough fuel for a short truck ride but it would only be enough for a single trip. We'd be living off what we could fit in one load. I've considered the same thing but leaving most of our supplies behind would really reduce our odds of survival."

"The odds of our survival are impacted by staying here. They seem to drop every day. And assuming we make it past July 4th without you being kidnapped, what will they try next? You think they're just going to give up?"

"No," Jim said, defeat creeping into his voice. "It won't be over." His words were flat and soulless.

"We need a strategy. The reason we have all this survival gear, the reason we're doing so well now, is that you didn't accept things at face value. You wanted backup plans and contingencies. You still need to think that way. We need a plan. We need a backup location. I don't care what kind of hassles and inconveniences are involved. We need something in place so we're not caught flatfooted if we have to leave."

"I'm working on it," Jim said. "Scott from the power restoration authority is choppering in tomorrow night. Hugh reached out to him over this bounty on my head. He's going to see if he can find out anything and let us know tomorrow."

"That's something. I need to get back to Ariel before she comes looking for me. You coming in or you spending the night out here?"

"I'm going to wait on Pete and Charlie," Jim said. "When they get here I'll come in for the night. Hugh is out there watching over us. We'll be fine."

Ellen slipped back through the screen door. Solar lights were being illuminated in the house now and their yellow glow spilled out onto the porch. It gave the place a sense of warmth that pushed away the world, even if just for a moment. Jim listened to the sounds of his family inside. Nana was teasing Ariel over a game they were playing. Pops was telling Ellen a story about his great grandfather, a seven-foot tall captain in the Civil War. Something about that story jarred a memory loose in Jim's head.

He got up from his chair and went inside. He stood there a moment, blinking against the light.

"Everything okay?" Pops asked.

"You talking about the Civil War reminded me of a story," Jim said. "About Beartown Mountain."

Beartown was the looming giant of the local section of the Clinch Mountain range. It was the seventh highest peak in Virginia and one of the most inaccessible peaks in this part of the country. While there was no road or trail leading to the top of it, it dominated the view from Jim's backyard.

"There was a cave up there," Jim said. "In the Civil War, deserters from both sides supposedly hid up there because it was so remote no one would come for them. They stayed up there until the war was over. You ever hear about that?"

"I did," Pops said. "Not sure where it was located but it's supposedly a true story."

"What are you thinking?" Ellen asked.

Jim shook his head. "Nothing. Just thinking about that cave so high up on that remote mountain. It might be our last stand, if we could find it."

Nana frowned. "I've had enough of caves."

"Are we moving into a cave again?" Ariel asked.

Jim smiled. "No, sweetie. Daddy was just thinking out loud."

"Daddy needs to think quieter," Ariel said, bobbing her head in a snarky girl thing.

Jim couldn't help but laugh at her. "I thought you liked being Batgirl and living in the Batcave?"

Ariel looked at him like she didn't know what planet he'd come from. "No. I didn't."

"I'm going back to the porch," Jim said. "The boys should be back soon and we'll settle in for the night."

The expression Ellen gave him wasn't much better than those that Ariel and Nana had given him. She didn't want to live in a cave any more than they did. Jim hoped it didn't come to that.

27

Although the next day was calm, no one was relaxed. And while there were no attacks, everyone expected them, waiting for the next shot or the next wave of men to come rushing through the fields like the Mongol horde. There were no challenges at the outposts, and not even a glimpse of movement within the dark woods.

People went on about their daily lives, undertaking the tasks that piled up faster than they could be checked-off their lists. They collected firewood for cooking and in advance of the winter chill, tended gardens, cared for their livestock, performed repairs, and did laundry.

Early summer vegetables were being harvested and this new infusion into their diet was appreciated. Jim focused on caching supplies at various points, accepting the offers from folks who had volunteered to cover sentry duty so he could get it done. In between strenuous trips, rolling or carrying plastic drums, he stared at the imposing presence of Beartown Mountain. He could not help but revisit the idea that he might have to retreat there with his family to survive.

They were tough and resilient. He suspected they could do it if they had to, though it would not be easy. They would not have the conveniences they had now. He'd spent years putting in solar improvements, a dairy with a spring box, gravity fed water, and a million other things that would make their life easier in a dark world. They would lose all of that.

He decided to relegate that to the most distant of possibilities. It was his "scorched earth" plan, only to be undertaken if all else failed and they lost the valley. If there was any chance of keeping and protecting their farm, even if it meant living in the barn or his cave, that was what he needed to do. For now, he would continue establishing caches, making sure he had redundant stockpiles of gear, and that they did not have all their eggs in a single basket.

The cave was his bunker. Ever since he'd first visited this property, he knew that was what he was going to do with it. It would be the place they hid if the shit hit the fan at its hardest and most fragrant. It was designed for that, with its concrete entrance wall, steel door, wood stove, and fresh water. It was a prepper's dream.

Nana couldn't do it though. Her last experience there had almost been the end of her. If he proposed retreating back to the cave again, his parents would want to return to their own home. He understood their reasoning but it would be a death sentence. They would be overrun and robbed within days.

If things got so bad, the attacks unrelenting, perhaps they could move back in there short term. He thought Randi might be glad to take Nana and Pops in as guests. If he provided food for them, they could help out with her grandchildren. They would remain safe in the valley and not in the firing line of every hungry bounty hunter in southwest Virginia.

Charlie had been living with Randi since Alice died, except on those occasions that he and Pete stayed in the outpost. Charlie had always been fond of hunting and camping, and had no problem staying in the woods. On those occasions that he wanted a roof over his head, Randi's house was where he found it, and she seemed to enjoy having an extra set of hands around.

. . .

Over the course of the afternoon people began filtering onto Jim's property. He'd spread word through the families of his tribe that they would have a barbecue that evening. The event would serve multiple functions. Since several of them were going to be involved in the meeting with Scott's group that night, getting their families together in one place would, theoretically, make it easier to keep them safe. There had been an inordinate amount of stress on everyone and Jim felt the group would benefit from an opportunity to unwind. Realistically, he didn't really expect the adults to do much relaxing, yet they would benefit from seeing their children and grandchildren smiling. That worked its own kind of magic.

They'd slaughtered a young bull the day before and the meat had been divided between the families in their group. What couldn't be eaten immediately would be pressure canned or smoked into jerky, which was a staple for those working away from home all day. Jim saved back some ribs and other prime cuts for the barbecue.

He put together a large grill from cinderblocks and a thick wire grate. The cuts of meat were cubed and threaded onto skewers made of coat hangers that had been sanded to remove the finish. Besides the meat, there was grilled squash, onions, zucchini, and peas. Ellen put together a salad of fresh garden greens and homemade dressing.

Randi had been experimenting with making cheeses. She hollowed out some of the squash and stuffed them with homemade cheese, breadcrumbs, and morel mushrooms she found in the valley. Debra made cornbread. There were several apple pies made of pie filling canned the previous year.

The children played games together under the supervision of their parents and the older children. The Weathermans and the Birds attended but the Wimmers didn't respond to the invitation. Jim wasn't surprised, knowing that old Mrs. Wimmer probably felt she had to stay home out of respect for her son. Jim was okay with that, knowing that Fred Wimmer's mouth was responsible for a lot of his woes at the moment.

Jim was pleased to see that Charlotte had chosen to come. She was one of Gary's daughters and had lost her husband before Gary's family moved to the valley. He'd been killed in the attack that forced them to see they could no longer stay at their home. She hadn't adjusted well, having attempted suicide in the depression that followed the loss of her husband. Everyone expected they'd find her dead one day but she pulled herself out of it with some support from Randi. While Jim wasn't entirely certain how she'd done it, he expected that a practical dose of "tough love" was involved.

Pete and Charlie manned Outpost Pete, providing overwatch for the party. They were too old to play with the children and bored with the adults. They would rather be out there in the field than having to help with the party. Hugh, never comfortable with crowded situations, opted to take a sentry position on a high point between Mack Bird's house and the Wimmers.' He was within radio range if he needed backup and had a good vantage point of that part of the valley. He would come down when it was time to rendezvous with Scott's group.

The festive nature of the activities didn't mean there was no tension. A low hum of fear played constantly in the background, like static, keeping everyone on edge. The adults carried a sidearm at all times, and many had rifles. Those who weren't carrying them kept them nearby, like tactical party favors. If the enemy came rushing over the hill, no one wanted to lose time having to dig out their weapons. In fact, they'd already determined a course of action should that happen. One part of the group was to herd the children toward the cave while the rest laid down suppressing fire and engaged the attackers.

Despite the stress and undercurrent of worry the evening went well. Used to living off smaller rations than they'd been eating back in the regular world, the group dove into the feast. Lloyd played banjo and sang in between eating kabobs dunked in homemade barbecue sauce.

Around dusk it started to wind down. The Weathermans had animals to take care of and wanted to get home before dark. The Birds were in the same situation, needing to collect eggs and water horses.

The clear light of day turned to the orange of late evening. Long, narrow clouds, scratched into the sky by an angry God turned pink and drew everyone's attention. Despite everything, it was hard not to gawk. That there was even beauty in this world at all seemed an affront, the cruel joke of a bearded and spiteful storyteller. It was a reminder that the world continued, unhindered by the plight of these small and insignificant humans with their self-importance and faint flickers of awareness.

Jim threw back the tattered flap of his pack and checked the gear he planned on taking. He had a regular flashlight and headlamp, an infrared flashlight, and the infrared landing beacons he'd need to guide Scott in. He had the good night vision they'd gotten from the sheriff's department, and had several sets thanks to the late Deputy Ford. They also had the low-quality first-generation devices that both Gary and Jim bought several years ago.

They would be leaving their horses at home and walking the twenty minutes to the landing zone where they expected Scott to show up later tonight. Gary's family would stay at Jim's place until he returned so they could walk home together in the dark. Gary brought headlamps for everyone in his family and intended to make an entertaining field trip out of it. He wanted the girls to become comfortable with the night and with doing things that may be a bit scary for them. It was a good survival skill for their new way of life.

As Jim was zipping his pack shut, Randi came over to borrow a piece of duct tape. Some of the kids were playing Frisbee and didn't want to quit just because it was getting dark. Randi didn't want to have to treat a child with a broken nose or black eye because they failed to see the Frisbee coming. She wanted to tape a chemical lightstick to the bottom so it would glow like a UFO, making the game safer and way cooler.

"Are you guys comfortable with us being gone for a few?" Jim asked.

Randi frowned. "I don't know who you think you're talking to. The day I need a man to take care of me is the day I end it all."

"I wasn't talking so much about gender as about numbers," Jim said, trying to backtrack and quite possibly save his own life. "There're a lot of kids to keep up with and shit's been hairy recently."

"I know how things have been lately. Every woman here knows how to shoot. Every woman here has taken a life. You don't have to be concerned that we'll swoon, drop our guns, and run off."

"Uh, sorry I asked." Jim cocked his head, pretending to hear a voice. "Hey, those kids want their Frisbee back."

Randi gave him a death stare. "I know what you did, Jim Powell. You just want rid of me."

Jim flashed her his most charming smile, which was not very impressive at all. "Now why would I want rid of you, Randi, dear? I so enjoy your company."

She stalked off and Jim felt lucky she hadn't hit him. How a woman like her could be dating his friend Lloyd was nearly unimaginable to him. Lloyd had an early twentieth century mindset. He stated it loud and clear, accepting the blows that came along with his pronouncements. He offered no apology for thinking the old days were the best days. Somehow those two had struck a chord with each other in the midst of the chaos and violence around them.

More power to them, Jim thought.

He shouldered his pack and headed to the fire pit. The backyard was the hub of activity and where most people were hanging out. He approached Lloyd, then glanced around until he found who he was searching for and waved Will over.

"I had planned on leaving you guys behind at the party to keep an eye on things until I was informed that your services were not needed. Be that as it may, I want you on outpost duty while we're gone. Pete and Charlie have Outpost Pete covered, so I'll stick you at the new outpost up on the logged-out hill. We're calling it Outpost Charlie. I'll leave you Gary's gen one night vision. It's not the greatest but beats the hell out of a flashlight. Besides, anyone who tries to come in is probably going to be using flashlights to navigate. They'll be easy to spot."

"Don't you have some of the good night vision?" Lloyd asked.

"We do but I'm afraid we're going to need it."

"We'll be fine," Will said. "We've got it covered."

"You sure you want us both up there?" Lloyd asked.

"I do," Jim said. "Nearly everybody is here at this one house and the two outposts have a good view of everything. We'll radio you before we come back so make sure you guys have a working radio. It will probably reach us at the landing zone because there're no major hills in the way. You can use it to call us if you see something suspicious."

The men nodded that they understood and had no questions. Will went to grab his gear while Lloyd stashed his banjo in the house. On the way back, Lloyd stopped by the grill to pick up a few kebabs for the road. Jim was disgusted to see Lloyd shove them in his pocket.

"Can't keep watch on the empty fuel tank," Lloyd said defensively when he saw Jim's face.

"That's revolting. I've seen the kind of crap you put in that pocket. It's full of lint, dirt, and God knows what else."

"I just look at it as breading," Lloyd said. "You judgy bastard."

Jim joined Gary by the fire pit. Hugh had joined the group and was working to start a campfire for those remaining behind.

"I'm going to tell stories when everyone settles down," Pops said.

"Nothing scary," Jim warned. "If these kids can't sleep tonight, you're going to have some angry mothers to deal with."

Once he got the fire going, Hugh stood up and dusted off. He grabbed his gear from a folding chair and started loading up.

"You ready?" Jim asked.

"Almost."

Jim looked at Gary. "You?"

"I've got everything."

The three men checked for the glint of brass in the chambers of their rifles, double-checked that their mags were well-seated, and then did the same for their sidearms. They walked around the house to the side that faced up the valley. Putting the house between them and the group instantly muffled the sound and the valley lay incredibly still before them. Jim didn't know if it had the same effect on the other men as it had on him but he couldn't help being taken aback by the peaceful calm of it all.

As the world cooled, the mist rose and all things that sang in the night were tuning up. Cattle ambled in the gloaming, the sound of their chewing a subtle grinding that carried across the pastures. At once the country was as it should be, yet completely alien. Jim understood that the strangeness of things was in his own mind. If asked, the cows could not have noticed much difference between this summer and last, aside from there being fewer lights.

They set out across the side yard to a new gate Jim had recently added. He found it funny how transitioning to foot and horse traffic affected the layout of their various farms. Anything built since the advent of the modern automobile was laid out differently, built around road gates that were sized for vehicles. Everything was designed to allow trucks and tractors to get where they needed to go.

It was a narrow gauge world now. The primary means of travel was by foot and a single line of horses. The really old farms, the seventeenth and eighteenth century farms in the valley, reflected that in the bits of original infrastructure that remained. Jim was adapting his own place to accommodate their new life. Everywhere he had to climb a fence more than a few times he added a gate. Once he started doing that, he learned just how few walk gates were available in the valley. It wasn't something people tended to buy or use anymore. Nearly everything he found was eight, ten, twelve, or sixteen feet wide so he ended up building a lot of gates.

They walked in silence, each man revisiting his own persistent concerns, his own troubles. Each worried about the same and different things alike. In a global sense, each worried for the safety of the folks in the valley, and worried to some extent about their own personal fate. To a greater extent, each man found himself worrying about the future of those young folks among them who had no idea what the world held for them. What was their future to be?

Jim found himself harboring a degree of hope that tonight's visit would give him some options he didn't currently have. He didn't have a lot of hope anymore. Hoping for things had been disappointing so it wasn't something he resorted to often. It was a lot to ask for but he needed an infusion of positivity.

One of the benchmarks of a quiet country life, at least among men, was that he be able to pee off his own porch without neighbors to be concerned with. Jim didn't have any neighbors on top of him but he was quickly reaching the point where he didn't feel safe standing on his own porch. Every time he did so he imagined a sniper's bullet burning its way into his chest or an assassin's blade raking across his throat. The front porch was the rural American's window onto the world and someone was trying to take that from him. It would end badly. The only question was as to whether the unfortunate ending would befall the attacker attempting to take Jim's peace or whether it would befall Jim himself.

They travelled the fields, preferring them over the more exposed paved road. There was no trail in the direction they moved so they cut straight across tall grass that would have been mowed for hay during better times. When seeing became difficult, they went to night vision and kept going, though there was a learning curve there. Everyone had experience with it but no one was well-adapted to the practice.

"This is the spot," Jim announced.

While there was nothing about it that gave away the fact they'd used it as a landing zone before, Jim knew his valley. He took off his pack and unbuckled the top, removing four infrared landing beacons which would show Scott's chopper pilot where to set down in the moonless night. Jim had a variety of infrared gear in his preparations but he never expected there to be a need for something like this. They walked off the distances, turned the devices on, and placed them in the grass. Their night vision allowed them to see that the devices were all working correctly.

"Now we wait," Gary said.

The men retreated a good distance back from the landing zone. They found an exposed boulder the size of a Volkswagen Beetle that provided decent seating. Even as the night air cooled around them and the dew settled, the rock held warmth from the sunny day. A coyote called in the distance and more joined in quickly. It was a chilling, primal sound.

“Pete and Charlie haven’t got them all,” Hugh observed.

“They’re making a dent,” Jim countered.

The boys had been using organs from game they snared to bait coyote traps. They’d had some success, killing one every week or so.

"Listen,” Hugh whispered.

Jim was expecting more coyote calls but soon heard the low vibration of a chopper somewhere in the distance.

"I hear it," Gary said.

"Hugh, do we have a way to communicate with them?" Jim asked.

"No. The only radios I have that operate on their bands are not portable."

Jim began to feel the thrum of the rotors. They were closing in, but without lights it was difficult to judge how far out they were. Then his ears told him that the chopper was no longer approaching but slightly above him. The pitch of the engines changed and he was able to pick it out of the night sky with his night vision. The chopper hovered for a moment then settled precisely into the box they'd created with the infrared beacons.

Jim wasn't sure exactly how this was supposed to go down. Was the pilot going to drop them off and leave for a while? Was this going to be a short meeting where he sat there with the engine running? His question was answered when the chopper began to power down. That was fine with Jim. The whine of those engines drew too much attention. The sound carried a long way when folks weren’t sitting in their living rooms watching television at night.

He impatiently waited for the passengers to disembark. It occurred to him that this might not even be Scott. What if their messages had been intercepted? Had some random chopper seen the beacons, deciding to land and see what was up? It didn’t seem likely but this had been a year of unlikely shit. He’d stay put until he saw a familiar face.

While the rotors wound down, the door slid open. Men clustered in the opening, scanning the night. Jim gave two flashes from an infrared spotlight to let Scott's team know where they were. Three people exited the chopper and headed in their direction at a quick walk. They carried rifles but didn't wear web gear. They wore high-visibility green jackets with a patch on the chest. Even though it was too far off to read, Jim knew it identified them as being from the East Coast Power Recovery Commission.

When Jim turned his night vision off and flipped it out of the way, Hugh and Gary followed suit. Jim pulled a red chemlight stick from his vest, cracked it, and tossed it on the ground. The red would provide enough ambient light for a meeting without affecting their ability to see in the dark. Scott approached, stuck out his hand, and the two men shook. Jim could now see that Scott's companions were a man and a woman.

"This is Adams and Jodie," Scott said.

Jim introduced Hugh and Gary to the new folks.

"How's it been?" Scott asked.

Jim snorted. Under the circumstances, the attempt at small talk almost seemed laughable.

"Ugly and dangerous on all fronts," Jim replied. "And getting worse by the day."

"You got a copy of the flyer you were talking about?" Scott asked.

Jim let his rifle hang from the sling while he dug into a pocket of his vest. He found the flyer and handed it across to Scott, who clicked on a tiny flashlight with a red lens and began reading. Jodie and Adams leaned in and read over his shoulders.

"Shit," Scott muttered when he finished. "You sure stepped in it."

"Kind of feels that way," Jim replied. "Any clue what that's about?"

"I couldn't find anything out about this particular flyer or a bounty on anyone. If it's official, no one's talking about it. It has an unofficial feel to me, though. If it was legit, the people coming for you would make more of a show of it. They would want this to be a very public thing. They might even hold a show trial in town and hang you to send a message to the other insurgents."

"*Insurgents*?" Hugh echoed. "They're seriously labeling this as insurgent activity?"

Scott flicked off his flashlight and stowed it in a pocket. He extended the flyer back to Jim, who demurred with a raised hand.

“Keep it. I have plenty.”

"They’re definitely calling it insurgent activity. There are pockets of resistance scattered all over the affected areas of the country, although I don’t know how significant they are. A lot of people feel the same way about the comfort camps as you do. They don’t like the whole business of having to disarm to receive aid. The powers controlling most of government are choosing to ignore that for now. They’re concentrating their efforts on the people that want aid and are willing to play ball to get it. Any place dominated by resistance is being passed over and put on a list to deal with later. They’re not making any effort to help those folks. That's why I suspect that flyer is unofficial, and they may go after figureheads of resistance later. I doubt they’re prepared to do it yet."

“Figureheads of resistance,” Jim repeated with animosity. "So am I right in assuming that if it’s *unofficial* it could be *personal*? I'm not sure how I managed to piss somebody off so bad that they decided to take it this far. This is a pretty big effort to find one guy."

"Especially when there were no survivors," Gary added. “They’re clearly singling you out because they managed to get that picture of you from their security cameras. Why would someone care that much? This is like someone wants revenge, and I can’t picture some impartial department head in Washington taking our actions that personally.”

"How do you know there weren’t survivors?" Scott asked.

"After we got home from the operation, we became concerned about that exact thing,” Jim said. “We got Hugh back there the next day. All he saw was bodies.”

"There was a survivor," Scott said.

Jim, Hugh, and Gary were floored.

“How?” Jim asked.

"Someone set off an emergency beacon immediately following the attack. It was a high priority signal because the powers that be were scrambling to find a chopper crew close enough to check it out.

They had somebody on scene that night, probably before you even returned there, but I have no idea what they found."

Jim was shocked. This detail was critical. It could completely explain why someone was going to such lengths to find him. For a survivor of the attack, this might be *very* personal.

"So there could have been a survivor," Gary said. "There could be somebody out there with a big chip on their shoulder."

"I tend to agree with you, Gary," Scott said. "This is likely something personal arranged by a survivor. And people are really acting on this?"

Jim shook his head in disgust. "The fucking things are turning up everywhere. We've had attempts on us every day since we found out about it. Sometimes more than once a day. We haven't lost anyone yet but it's probably going to happen."

"It says they want you alive," Jodie pointed out.

"They want *me* alive. That's the only specification. How many are they willing to kill to take me alive? That worries me."

"You have any suggestions for us?" Hugh asked. "It's getting hairy. We've had to kill a lot of people. That only increases local animosity. Even if no one collects the bounty we stand a risk of becoming so reviled in our community that people will continue to want to kill us."

Scott rubbed his chin in thought. "I can't think of anything offhand, though I've got a lot of sharp minds working for me. I can ask around when we get back to our headquarters."

"Please let us know if you think of anything," Jim said. "I expect if no one captures me by the 4th of July, whoever sent this will offer a bigger bounty. People already know where to find us and word will continue to spread."

"Have you considered getting out of here?" Scott asked.

"Last resort, man. I'd have to leave a lot behind."

Scott understood that. "I did bring you guys some goodies. Got a couple of cases of ammo and some MREs. It's not a lot but it's what I was able to spare."

"How are things in the cesspool?" asked Hugh.

"It's getting worse," Adams said. "The fragmentation of government is several times worse than it was even a few months ago. Military bases that don't like their orders are acting independently and affiliating with whoever the commanding officer trusts. It's that way with everybody. Hell, if the Department of Education had the weaponry they would be trying to militarize schoolteachers and carry out their agenda too. It's what everybody's doing."

Gary snorted. "So basically it's business as usual?"

"Yeah, kinda." Scott chuckled. "Except it's more like the collapse of the Soviet Union. Everybody is fighting to gain a foothold in power. Stockpiles of weapons are disappearing or falling under the control of charismatic officers within the military. When this all shakes out, there are going to be new faces wielding power in government. People we've never seen before."

They were heading to the chopper to retrieve Scott's gift when Jim's radio chirped. He halted to retrieve it while the rest of the men continued to the chopper.

"This is Jim. Can you repeat that?"

"Get back here, man," Lloyd implored. *"Something is happening."*

More terrifying than the news was the tone of Lloyd's voice. He was in a state of sheer panic.

28

The scene around the campfire was relaxed. It was like the aftermath of an old-world cookout, when friends and family might stick around for a bonfire. The only obvious difference was the lack of marshmallows. There had been some discussion of the matter between those who enjoyed cooking. While no one could remember ever seeing a recipe for marshmallows, the consensus was that they couldn't be difficult to make. Yet it wasn't a time for experimenting with recipes. Anything wasted could not be replaced, and marshmallows were so nutritionally lacking that it wouldn't be worth the effort. That was sad news to some.

Pops was telling stories about the old days to those willing to sit and listen. The younger children were tired, slouched in camping chairs or reclining lazily on the laps of anyone who would hold them. Gary's older grandchildren and one of Randi's daughters, Carla, were catching lightning bugs in the yard. Between the bonfire and some solar landscaping lights there was enough illumination for them to see their way around.

"Granny, come see!" one of the children, Kayla, yelled to Debra, holding up a plastic soda bottle lit by fireflies.

Debra passed off the sleepy child in her arms to Charlotte and got to her feet. She stretched. Sitting on a wooden bench, unable to move because she was holding a child, had made her body stiff. She began walking toward her grandchild, her smile meeting Kayla's, her eyes meeting Kayla's eyes. Kayla held the bottle against her face, the yellow glow of the insects giving it an eerie cast. It made Debra laugh.

The rest happened in slow motion.

From out of nowhere came a figure dressed entirely in black, wearing a hoodie, his face smudged with soot. He was running. He stiff-armed Carla like a charging linebacker and knocked her off her feet. His other arm dropped in a hook and snagged Kayla around the waist. The bottle of fireflies went flying through the air, tumbling to a stop in front of the other stunned children. Carla screamed and Kayla was gone even before the smile had faded from Debra's face.

Without hesitation, Debra launched herself across the yard in pursuit. Her eyes were not adjusted to the darkness, having sat in front of a roaring bonfire for the last hour. She was blindly pursuing the sobs of a child snatched away in the dark. It was the magnet that pulled her through the darkness. There was no thought, no logic, no rationality, only the unadulterated pull of a grandmother acting out of instinct.

29

Chaos erupted around the fire, much of it a reaction to Carla's scream. It was so fast, no one else had even seen what happened.

"Someone took Kayla!" Carla screamed, sitting up in the grass and cradling her arm.

Randi ran to the back porch and snatched up her rifle and pack. She slung her pack on her back and took off running. Charlotte, Kayla's mom, handed the child in her lap off to Sara and bolted after Randi.

Ellen grabbed two rifles from the porch, handing one to Pops. "We need to get to the cave. There could be more of them. Make sure you have everyone."

She didn't have to ask twice. There was more screaming and sobs. The children were panicking.

"Do I need to help them get her back?" Carla asked. "What should I do?" Her face was red, tears pouring.

Ellen shook her head. "No, there are enough people out there now. There could be more attackers. Help us get these kids to the cave."

Pops lit a flashlight and played the beam around in the darkness, unsure of what he would find. "Follow me!"

Ellen found her radio and keyed the mic. "Pete! Charlie! I need you guys down here now. One of the kids has been taken. I'm sending everyone to the cave. Can you see flashlights headed in that direction?"

"I see them!" Pete replied.

"You and Charlie make sure they get to the cave safely. Stay with them no matter what."

"Do you need one of us to come to you, Mom?"

"Just do what I say!" Ellen barked, her voice revealing her panic and desperation.

"What's going on?" It was Will on the radio now.

"Someone took Kayla," said Ellen. "They're out there in the dark somewhere. Your mom, Charlotte, and Randi are trying to chase them down so don't shoot at anything unless you're sure what you're shooting at."

Ellen asked him another question but when there was no reply she understood Will was charging into the night at this very moment. He'd heard all he needed to hear.

"Jim?" she called into her radio.

There was no response. Surely he'd heard all this chatter.

"Jim?" she repeated.

There was no response. She had no way of knowing that the sound of the chopper engines winding down was drowning out any radio transmissions.

"Ellen, it's Lloyd. What's going on?"

"Did you hear what I told Will?"

"No. He was talking on the radio and then he threw it down and ran off."

"One of the children was taken. One of his nieces. I've got everyone else headed to the cave."

"What do you need me to do?"

"I'm going to stay at the house. Can you come down and keep watch with me?"

"I'll be there in a few."

"Announce yourself on the radio," Ellen warned. "I'm nervous right now."

"Got it."

While Pops led the group into the field, Carla was gathering up some of the packs, flashlights, and some rifles from the yard. "You coming?" she asked Ellen.

"No, I'm keeping an eye on the house. Pete and Charlie are coming with you. They know how to work the lights and secure the door. You'll be safe."

"Okay," Carla said. She extended something to Ellen.

"What is it?"

"He threw this down when he snatched Kayla."

It was a piece of paper. Ellen held it up in the firelight where she could read it.

IF YOU WANT TO SEE THE CHILD ALIVE
JIM POWELL MUST SURRENDER HIMSELF
TO US AT NOON TOMORROW IN FRONT
OF THE COUNTY COURTHOUSE

Ellen groaned and sat down, her legs going weak. "Did you read this?"

"I did."

"Please don't say a word to anyone else right now, okay? We don't know what's going to happen tonight."

"Okay," Carla said, struggling to keep three rifles slung over one shoulder.

"Go on. Catch up with those guys."

30

Debra charged through the night like a heat-seeking missile. She ran blindly, all of her senses desperately grasping for noises made by the child that would steer her in the right direction. Debra didn't make a single sound, other than her feet pounding through the grass. She didn't call after the kidnapper who'd abducted her grandchild, she didn't beg, and she didn't demand he turn the child loose. In fact, she didn't want to give him any clue that he was being pursued at all. If he thought he was getting away he might slow down, perhaps even turn a flashlight on. Either of those things would improve her odds and make it easier to close the distance.

However, she was not closing distance. The figure was putting ground between them. She did not know exactly how far ahead he was but the diminishing volume of Kayla's cries told her it could be half a football field or more. Debra was in better shape than she'd been in a long time due to the constant physical work over the winter, but she'd never been a runner. It didn't matter though. In a situation like this, one became what was required of them. She would be a runner if she had to. She would gladly become a fighter, and hopefully a rescuer. If not, she would die trying.

Debra became aware of footsteps behind her and whirled around, hoping it was one of her own group. It was Randi. Debra recognized her voice when the woman hissed, "I'm here."

Debra could only grunt in response. She was afraid speaking would make her lose her breath. Her concentration might falter and cause her to trip. Something bad would certainly happen if she allowed herself to lose focus for even a second. She couldn't allow it.

Then there was another sound behind her. It was the faster pounding of approaching feet and rapid breathing but it was different than hers and Randi's. It sounded like the rhythmic chugging of a train. There was no gasping or struggle in that breathing. It was the ultra-efficient processing of breath into fury.

Into hate.

The runner gained on them, then passed without a word or even acknowledging them.

"Was that...?" Randi gasped.

Then Debra uttered her first words since Kayla had been snatched and mouthed her daughter's name.

Charlotte.

31

Charlotte ran with her mother's intensity multiplied tenfold. It was the demonic rage of a woman who'd lost her husband, who'd lost her previous life to this disaster, and had nearly lost her mind along with it. She would not lose anything else. She would not lose Kayla.

She'd run track in school but perhaps that wouldn't have made a difference at the moment. She was fueled by everything that had happened to her in the last year. Fury, hate, and a mother's love powered her like an injection of nitrous into a car engine. Her eyes began to adjust but there was not enough moon for that to be helpful. She stumbled numerous times and twice ran into fences at full throttle, her body tossed backward like a deer charging a net. She was back on her feet without pause each time, charging again into the dark night.

Unlike her mother, and unlike Randi, she was gaining on the abductor. Her daughter wailed inconsolably and the sound got louder with each passing moment. Her kidnapper was probably slowing. He would see that there were no lights behind him, would not hear shouts and threats of pursuers, and would think he was getting away.

He would be wrong.

Charlotte did not know how much ground she'd covered when they crossed a small creek and entered the woods. She was pretty certain she'd never strayed in this direction during her time in the valley. She couldn't anticipate where they were going but that didn't matter. She would go where she had to go, even if it was all the way into town.

Eventually he must have reached a point where he thought he was safe because she saw a flicker of light. He'd turned on a headlamp. Charlotte nearly smiled. He was still moving but slower now. He looked down and in the harsh glare of his headlamp she saw her daughter's precious head. He chugged to a stop and dropped Kayla to the ground at his feet.

Charlotte heard him hiss a warning to her daughter. He was hunched over now, his hands resting on his knees as he fought to get his breathing under control. Beneath him, Kayla cowered on the ground in the severe light of his headlamp. Her vulnerability was heartbreaking to Charlotte but that was the last tender thought she would allow herself. She had managed to close the distance. All she had room for now was a murderous hate that poured from her like an overflowing bathtub.

His loud, gasping breath masked Charlotte's approach until she was nearly on him. He jerked his head in her direction and the white glare of his light caught her mid-charge. At first he was not even certain it was a woman attacking him. He saw a dark shape and the reflection of intense eyes. He thought it could be the charge of a wild animal, uncoiling from the dense blackness of the night to spring upon him not as an avenger, but as a predator intent on killing him. He was almost too startled to move, too terrified to react to the viciousness of her attack.

In the seconds before she went airborne, Charlotte dropped a hand to her belt and came back with the razor-sharp dagger that she carried with her always, the very knife she had once contemplated killing herself with. She wielded it like an extension of herself, a single razor-sharp talon. She dove toward the petrified man, exactly like the attacking beast he imagined her to be.

He screamed and tried to jump to the side but he was not fast enough. Charlotte's face collided with his head. She felt her nose burst and the warmth of her own blood running across her mouth and down her throat. It didn't matter because she was where she wanted to be. She threw her left arm around his neck as they tumbled and pulled him to her as tight as she'd ever hugged someone she loved, keeping him from pulling away to fight back. She held him close enough that she could plunge the knife into his back over and over again.

His cry of surprise at having been overtaken turned into shrieks of pain. He got a hand to her hair and gave it a brutal pull, yanking her far enough away from him that he could get an arm between them. He put his hand to her throat and she sliced down the length of his arm, flaying his bicep from the bone. The flap of meat fell across his face, splattering it with blood. He let go of her neck, his scream now a constant, unending drone.

They rolled and she landed astride him, placing her left hand on his face. She clawed into his flesh to gain purchase on the blood-spattered skin. His good arm ineffectively punched at her head but the one she'd cut was too damaged to be of assistance. The muscles didn't work any longer. He could not stop her. His head twisted suddenly, yielding, the muscles of his neck surrendering.

He'd failed to see her intentions, not realizing that her ultimate goal was to expose his vulnerable neck. By the time he understood his mistake, it was too late. His eyes twisted in their sockets, screwing in her direction, and he saw the bloody knife in the glow above him. He felt a solid, stinging punch to his neck.

There was grating inside his body, the steel blade crunching and scraping against the vertebra of his neck. He tried to cry out again and found he could no longer scream. His windpipe was severed and air whistled through his neck in an unfamiliar manner. He gave a wet, choking cough and blood sprayed from the hole in his throat, a pink mist in the harsh light.

Charlotte's taste for blood and revenge was not sated. She raised her hand again, ready to deliver one more blow, until her daughter's whimper penetrated her bloodlust. She glanced to the side and saw that his tilted head placed the beam of his spotlight directly on Kayla. Her terrified daughter stared at her in paralyzed horror.

Charlotte opened her arms to her daughter but Kayla was too terrified to move. Charlotte could hardly blame her. She could only imagine how she must look. She thought about the things Kayla had just seen her do. Staring at her daughter, trying to decide what to do next, she noticed movement in the trees behind Kayla.

She assumed it to be her mother and Randi, the pair having finally caught up with her, but it was not. Three horrified faces stared at the scene. Three bearded men. Men who must have been waiting on the kidnapper to reach them with his victim. Two of them she'd never seen before. One she knew.

Fred Wimmer.

Charlotte had not come this far to lose now. The knife upraised in her hand, she brought it down on the dying man's headlamp, crushing it and throwing the scene into darkness. She threw herself to the side, across her daughter, as gunshots began whistling through the air above her.

Already raising their weapons, the men chose to shoot before turning their lights on, thinking the memory of the scene before them would guide their aim. They got off several shots before one finally raised a hand to his headlamp and clicked it on. All they found was their dead friend. The two girls were gone.

Charlotte, safely behind a tree with Kayla, would not flee these men. As far as she knew, they were as complicit in the kidnapping of her daughter as the one she'd already killed. She drew her handgun and aimed around the tree. Fred Wimmer would die first. She pulled off a shot and hit him. He dropped and screamed, clutching his stomach.

One of the remaining men scrambled for cover, while the second dropped to Fred Wimmer's side, grabbed the back of his shirt, and tried to drag him away. Charlotte sent rounds in his direction but didn't connect. A barrage of new gunfire lit up the night and some of those rounds found their targets. Help had arrived.

Randi and Debra had come upon the scene in time to see Charlotte shoot one of the attackers. They flattened themselves against the ground and opened up, Randi with her rifle, Debra with her handgun. The man trying to drag Fred Wimmer away began flinching and jerking like he'd disturbed a hornets' nest. A 5.56 round caught him in the side of the head and he dropped like a ragdoll.

The remaining uninjured man was lit by his own headlamp. Although he'd placed a tree between him and Charlotte, it didn't block him from the new arrivals. He hadn't seen them arrive and made a fatal mistake in the positioning of his body. Randi put a red dot on the right side of his chest and pulled the trigger twice. Two rounds pierced his lungs and he was down.

Debra tried to get to her feet but Randi held her back.

"That one hollering is still alive. He might be armed," Randi said.

"Are you okay, Charlotte?" Debra called out, desperate to put eyes on her daughter.

"Yes," Charlotte replied.

As Debra and Randi lay there trying to get an angle on the injured, screaming man, Charlotte took matters in her own hands. In the bubble of light created by Fred Wimmer's headlamp, Charlotte appeared like an actor in the spotlight, gun raised. She stepped on Fred's right hand and stood there, her pistol pointed at his face.

"Why did you try to take my daughter?" she demanded.

Fred coughed and spoke, his voice wet, weak. "We thought we could trade her for Jim. He's brought nothing but grief to this valley."

Charlotte was gripping her pistol so tightly that her arm trembled. Her jaw was clenched, barely releasing enough for her to form words. "You would steal a child to get rid of Jim?"

He met her eyes, his expression sincere. "Without a second thought."

The boom of the pistol sounded so much louder than any of the other shots, isolated as it was from the chaos of battle. Debra broke from cover and ran to find her granddaughter. Randi got to her feet and approached Charlotte, who was standing over Wimmer, gun aimed at his face as if he might repair himself and attack anew.

"It's okay," Randi said, her hands extended in a comforting gesture. "Put the gun up."

The crackling of footsteps drew everyone's attention and they whirled around to find a light bobbing toward them through the woods. All guns leveled on Will as he ran into the clearing. He froze in his tracks, a hair away from dying.

"It's me!" he said.

They lowered their guns, not wanting to think how close they'd come to killing one of their own. Everyone knew to be certain of their target first but their adrenaline was up, and everyone was in fight mode.

"Will," Randi said firmly, "I need you to keep watch while I try to clean Charlotte up."

She dropped her pack, digging through it for alcohol wipes. In the background, Debra was soothing Kayla, talking to her in low, soothing tones as the girl wept. Charlotte was silent, somewhere else in her head. Still in a violent place. Still in warrior mode. Randi talked to her while she cleaned the blood off her face, the tone of her voice similar to that Debra was using with her granddaughter.

"You did well," Randi said. "You got her back. It's okay now."

Charlotte's eyes flickered and met Randi's for a second, then pulled away.

"She needs you, Charlotte. This is like before, when you wanted to die," Randi whispered. "You found your way back then and you can do it now."

Charlotte's eyes met Randi's and stayed there this time. Her wall crumbled and she burst into tears. She was a morbid visage in the unforgiving glare of Randi's headlamp, her tears streaking the bloody gore on her face. Randi took her in her arms and let her weep.

It occurred to Randi for the first time how similar Charlotte and Jim were. Each struggled to find their way back from the world of violence and death. Each seemed as if there might be a day when the single strand they followed back from that dark place, their love of family, may no longer be enough to get them home.

32

Will and Randi searched the bodies, taking any weapons and ammunition, then the group headed back toward Jim's house. They had to travel a fair distance before they were able to communicate by radio with the rest of their group.

"We got her back," Randi reported immediately, certain everyone was desperate for that single piece of information.

There was a barrage of questions from everyone with a radio but Randi said they'd be at Jim's place in a few minutes and could talk then. She'd learned from Jim not to speak too openly on these cheap radios. When they reached Jim's house, he, Gary, and Hugh were there, along with Scott. Lloyd was there as well, having waited nervously with Ellen until everyone returned.

Gary took Kayla in his arms and immediately broke down into tears. Debra and Charlotte did the same and he wrapped them into the embrace. Gary stroked Kayla's hair, hardly able to believe what had transpired in his absence. He had come so close to losing his granddaughter.

Pete and Charlie escorted the group from the cave back to the house and everyone gathered in Jim's backyard once more, and wood was thrown onto the fire. They established a secure perimeter using the good night vision, no one wanting a repeat of what had transpired earlier. Concerned about the shooting, Mack Bird checked in by radio. When he offered to come down, Jim assured him it was probably better he stay with his own family in case there was more trouble. Carla took all of the children inside and occupied them with a movie so everyone could speak outside the range of sensitive ears.

"There has been a lot of trafficking," Scott said. "Selling women and children as slaves. Some people have even sold themselves into slavery just to get regular meals."

"This wasn't about anything like that," Charlotte said.

"How can you be so sure?" Scott asked.

Randi, Debra, and Ellen exchanged glances. They all knew what this was about but no one had spoken of it yet.

"This wasn't about Kayla. It was to bargain for his surrender," Charlotte said, pointing accusingly at Jim.

"What?" Jim looked around the room, unable to believe what was being said. He was waiting on someone to protest that the idea was preposterous but no one did. When he caught Ellen's face, the way she was looking at him, he understood it was true.

Her eyes on Jim's, Ellen unfolded the ransom note from her pocket. "Carla found this in the yard. The man who snatched Kayla threw it down. It basically says they would have given her back if you surrendered to them. One of the men was Fred Wimmer. The other two were from outside the valley. I didn't recognize them."

Jim's mouth gaped in shock. He took the note from his wife's hand and sat down unsteadily. He had an expression of revulsion on his face as he read the note, the unpleasant realization that this was all his fault. A child had been taken because of him. The fact she'd been rescued was immaterial. What if she hadn't been?

"Can I see that?" Scott asked.

Jim stood and handed it over. "This is exactly what we're dealing with here, Scott. This is why I reached out to you guys. I'm at a loss here." He looked around at his tribe. "I'm sorry. I apologize to you all. I never intended for this to happen. I can't take a chance on anyone else getting hurt."

Before he could continue, Randi spoke up. "I know what you're thinking but leaving won't help," she said. "They'll just keep coming for you. They may even kidnap someone else to see if they'll reveal where you are. We have to find some way to end this once and for all."

"I'm not thinking about leaving," Jim said. "I see no other solution but to turn myself in to them."

Ellen shot to her feet. "The *hell* you are!" Her eyes were wild, both angry and terrified.

Jim appeared defeated. "I don't see that I have a choice here. What am I supposed to do? I can't have children being kidnapped on my conscience. I don't want anyone here to die because of me. I know I'm a bastard but I actually care about the people here."

"But you're willing to condemn your own family to death?" Ellen demanded. "How do you think we're going to get by without you? You don't know what it was like when you were on the road and we were waiting for you to get home. You have no fucking idea!"

Her use of profanity silenced the group. No one had ever seen her this angry.

"We'll talk about it later," Jim said. "I'm not sure this is the time or place."

"We'll talk about it *now*," Ellen replied with venom. "If you're making this decision because of other people, then they can damn well listen. There might even be some here that secretly feel relieved you would turn yourself in but there's nothing honorable about this decision. It means my family will die. Your wife and your children will die. Our things will be stolen and we will suffer for this. Is that what you want?"

"You know I don't," Jim said.

Ellen turned on the rest of the tribe, imploring. "Is this how you repay the things he's done for you? Is this how you repay Jim for bringing you to the valley and finding homes for you? For helping get Gary and Randi home? For all of the things he's done for each and every one of you?" Tears of rage welled and filled her eyes.

"Ellen," Jim said, his voice low, trying to calm her.

"NO!" she roared. "It's not going to happen. I cannot do this by myself. I will not. If you're going to turn yourself in, you might as well go ahead and kill us now because that's that will happen eventually. We'll. All. Die!"

Ellen glared around the fire circle, glaring at every silent face, then stalked off. She climbed the back steps, went inside the house, and slammed the door behind her. Jim sat focused on the fire. He didn't know what to do or say. Judging by the silence, neither did anyone else.

"I might have an idea," Scott ventured.

Everyone turned to him but not all expressions were receptive. He was an outsider inserting himself into an emotionally charged situation.

"You don't necessarily have to turn yourself in, Jim. The townspeople just have to *think* you turned yourself in," Scott said.

Jim shrugged doubtfully. "I'm sure it's going to be a public spectacle on the 4th of July. If I don't show up, I doubt people are just going to accept a rumor that I've already turned myself in. They're going to want to see proof."

Scott shook his head. "I'm talking about a group of men escorting you into town in cuffs. I'm talking about a chopper dropping out of the sky to take you away."

"It would be hard to keep you safe walking through town," Gary said. "You'd be walking a gauntlet. I can't imagine people just letting you waltz through town. One group would likely be trying to steal you from the other up until the second the chopper landed."

"We could counteract some of that with diversions," Hugh suggested.

"If people are gathered at the football field," Scott said, "we could land somewhere else first. It might draw them off, thinking they had the wrong location."

"When I say 'diversion,' I mean explosions," Hugh said. "We could blow some shit up. If people think the town is under attack, some of them might decide they don't want to stick around for the show."

"So we reduce the number of people who might try to take him, but it sounds like we can't eliminate all the risk," Gary clarified. "There will always be an element of danger."

"That's probably true," Scott said. "I don't know that taking all of the danger out of it is a possibility."

Hugh held up a finger in a *eureka* moment. "Scott, you don't land somewhere else. What you do is shove out two pallets on cargo chutes. If the people gathered at the field think they have a chance of intercepting the reward without even having contributed to the capture, they'll clear the benches and race after those chutes. It'll be like kids chasing an ice cream truck."

Scott grinned. "That's genius."

"I don't care how dangerous it is. I'm agreeable to trying it if we can stay alive for a few more days," Jim said. "It's going to take some planning."

"I can leave Hugh a radio that will allow him to speak to the chopper," Scott offered. "We'll plan on heading back this way early on the 4th of July. When we get close, Hugh can update us on your position so we minimize how much time you're exposed to danger."

"We take a low profile route into town," Hugh said. "Set off some decoy explosions. By the time people figure out what's going on, we have you at the football field, pop some smoke grenades to draw the chopper, and wait to hand you off. There'll be a lot of confusion and people won't know what's going on."

"What then?" Jim asked. "I go into the witness protection program?"

"No," said Scott. "We drop you back in this valley and you don't show your face for a good long time."

Jim glanced around the fire circle. "Is everyone agreeable to trying this? It's risky and I'm going to need some help to pull it off."

"Everything is risky," Randi said. "I don't see this as being any more risky than anything else we do every damn day."

"Thanks," Jim said.

"And for the record," Randi went on, "I am not agreeable to you turning yourself in for real and just giving up. I owe you. Several of the folks here owe you. I'll always have your back."

"Agreed," Hugh said.

Randi looked at Gary expectantly.

"I agree too," he said. "I assumed it was understood."

Some folks did not express an opinion either way. Jim understood that.

"Well, I need to go in and talk to my wife," he said.

"Hugh," said Scott, "if you'll get me back to my chopper, I'll give you the radio and we'll coordinate logistics for next week."

Hugh nodded. "Gary, if you all want to come with us, I'll follow you home."

"I appreciate that, Hugh."

Jim rose and disappeared into the house. Ariel was in the living room playing with the other children. Carla was watching them.

"We're done," Jim said. "People are getting ready to pack up and head home. I'm going to go speak to my wife a second. You might want to get the children ready to leave."

"Yeah, you better get in there and talk to her," Carla said, a warning expression on her face.

Jim hugged Ariel. "I'll be back out here in a second, sweetie."

"If Mommy doesn't kill you," Ariel mumbled. "You're in bad trouble."

33

One of Jim Powell's favorite movies was *The Godfather,* in particular a scene in the movie where the competing mob families have gone to war. Things get hairy so the families decide to "go to the mattresses," an expression meaning that they all hole up together with armed men sleeping on mattresses on the floor. The expression didn't originate with the movie but it was where the phrase became part of Jim's vocabulary. It was basically the same as circling the wagons in one of those old Western movies and it was an apt description for the state of the valley in those days leading up to the Fourth of July.

For the few remaining days until his appointment with destiny, Jim and his tribe decided it was best they "go to the mattresses" too. Some of the homes, like Mack Bird's, Jim's, and Randi's, were not too far apart. Gary and the Weathermans were the most distant, living toward the head of the valley. Lloyd, living in Buddy's old house not far from the Wimmers and the sheriff, were on the end of the valley closest to town.

Despite Jim's invitation, the Birds felt comfortable remaining where they were. They were close enough to maintain radio contact with folks if there was an emergency. The Weathermans were distant enough that radio communication was hit or miss from their place but they didn't give a damn. They weren't interested in packing in with a bunch of other families and leaving their home to be ransacked. Jim completely understood that sentiment.

Hugh chose to remain on the mountain, feeling that his place was far enough off the beaten path that no one would come up there even if they were aware of his presence. Besides, it took some serious walking to climb that mountain. The primary reason he stayed home was to monitor his radios. If Scott turned up new information or had to change the plan, he needed to be there to receive that message.

It took a bit of effort to get a group this size situated. They split everyone between Jim's house and Randi's. Jim was ready for this. When he built his shop and the storage buildings on his property he intentionally designed the wall-mounted plywood shelving to be the same size as a bunkbed. Every shelf was wide enough, long enough, and had enough headroom for a man in a sleeping bag to stay there indefinitely. Jim had never mentioned this design feature to anyone, even his wife. He just thought there might be a time when he could have to take folks in so he'd planned for it.

Pete and Charlie were becoming more serious about hardening their outdoor skills. While Jim harbored concerns about them going native, he was impressed at how they adapted. The pair split their time between Outpost Pete and the barn. Although Ellen worried about them, the boys seemed happy.

The rest of the children enjoyed it in the same way that children always enjoy the newness of a sleepover. It was less enjoyable for the adults. It reminded Jim of those family gatherings he'd gone to when he was a kid where you'd have forty people in a tiny house with one bathroom. This was not nearly so festive.

There was a significant amount of tension in the air. While people tried not to talk about it, the upcoming operation in town seemed to be weighing on everyone. The group maintained a heavy state of security. They continued to tend animals and maintain their gardens with the hopes that they would be around to harvest them but everything was done with armed security. Children were only allowed to play inside the homes or in the immediate backyard, under the watchful gaze of heavily armed parents. It was an oppressive and joyless existence.

When Jim's watch confirmed it was the third of July he wondered if the others in his community continued to be able to track dates with any accuracy. Were there people showing up in town today because they had the date wrong? Would some people be showing up in two days because they had missed the fourth?

For Jim, this day was for meeting with his team and finalizing their plans. He wanted to make sure the people escorting him to town knew exactly what they were supposed to do, regardless of what they ran into. He didn't want anyone to get hurt. Neither him nor anyone else.

Besides a few farm chores, meeting with his people was the main thing he had to do that day but it was not the only thing. Before that meeting he had a visit he needed to make, the results of which might impact the success of his team. As much as he didn't want to make that visit, he felt he had no choice. He geared up in the house, sliding on his vest and strapping on his gun belt.

Ellen heard the firm snap of a magazine locking into his rifle and glanced at him. "Where are you going?"

Jim explained it to her.

"You need to take someone with you, Jim."

"Not this time," Jim said. "I'd rather keep my shooters here."

"I'm not happy about it."

"There's nothing for you to be happy about. It is what it is."

"Then go on and get it over with." Ellen hugged him hard and sent him on his way.

Outside, Jim got on the radio and let his people know he was going off the farm but that he should be back in two hours.

Randi demanded to know where he was going.

"You sound like my wife," Jim said.

"Smart and good-looking?"

"I was leaning more toward bossy."

"If you'd learn your place we'd have less to be bossy about. Now where are you going?"

"I'm not ready to say," Jim replied.

"Bullshit. You wouldn't let any of us by with an excuse like that."

"Randi, I'm pretty sure it's against FCC regulations to use the word 'shit' on the radio."

"Oh, so Mr. Fuck The Rules is all about following the rules now? How convenient."

Jim keyed the mic and sighed loudly, trying to make a point. "Hell, I could have been there and back in the time I've wasted arguing with you. Since you're so damn insistent, I have to run up to the sheriff's place for a few minutes. I have something I need to talk to him about."

"You sure you don't need some company?" Randi asked. *"Some backup? I don't think he likes you very much."*

"Nope. Don't need backup. It should be a cakewalk. And I'm used to dealing with people who don't like me."

"Yeah, you should be," Randi said.

Jim pocketed his radio and started down his gravel driveway. The condition of it irritated him. Had this been normal times, he would scrape this driveway with his tractor once every week or so and keep the sides of the road mowed. Now there were weeds all over the place. Gradually, the two gravel tracks that led in and out of his home were fading, being swallowed by the Earth. He had to wonder what the place would look like in a year. He hoped he lived long enough to see it.

He exited the gate, the chain that fastened it making that familiar clank as it bounced against the tube gate. Once he was through, he closed it and started up the road, lost in his thoughts, though not so lost that he was being careless. Anymore, a state of vigilance was the norm. It was ingrained into their behavior. Accustomed to always watching for threats, he wondered how one could turn that off. He didn't imagine anyone ever could.

Even if things went back to normal in his lifetime, would he be sitting at the gas station with a gun in his lap waiting for someone to try to steal his fuel? Would he hold his breath in crowds, waiting for the moment that chaos erupted? Would he forever be ready to draw and shoot, afraid that giving someone the benefit of the doubt would get him killed?

He had friends who'd gone to war and come home different. They tried to explain this feeling to him and he'd never understood it until that moment in his driveway. It was the realization that there was no going back to normal once you'd lived that way. It wasn't fear exactly. Just the understanding that any situation could go totally apeshit in the blink of an eye. One moment you were laughing with a friend. A second later, you were plastered to the ground, eating dirt, and hoping to God that today wasn't your last day.

How did one reconcile that? How did a person push it back down within oneself?

34

Jim called from the gate but no one answered. No one gave him the finger, threw rocks, or otherwise discouraged him either, so he went through the gate and climbed the driveway. He found the sheriff in the backyard trying unsuccessfully to get his beans to climb a series of strings stretched between posts. He had that hopeful appearance of a man trying to train a dog to do a trick. Like a dog, the beans had a mind of their own and sprawled in every direction except the one which the sheriff intended.

"I called from the road but no one answered," Jim said.

The sheriff didn't look up. "And you didn't take that as a hint?"

"I'm not easily deterred."

The sheriff made a grunt of some sort. Jim wasn't fully certain what it meant but he assumed it to be a dig of some sort. "How are things going?"

"I guess I should be asking you that." The sheriff successfully managed to hook another tendril of a bean vine over the string. It stayed several seconds before springing back to the ground.

"Things have been sporty," Jim said. "I expected to hear from you. Thought you might at least be curious what all the fuss was about."

"I assume you're referring to all the shooting?" The sheriff straightened and stretched his back. "I got no taste for hearing what your body count is up to now. Every time I hear a gunshot it makes me sick. I know more folks are dying."

"It's not just *us* doing the shooting," Jim remarked. "My people are being fired on too."

The sheriff raised a skeptical eyebrow. "And just how many have you lost?"

"Well, none."

The sheriff gave Jim a smug expression, as if the answer validated his point.

"So I should feel bad about keeping my people alive? You think I should sacrifice a few for the sake of equality? So my enemies feel better?"

"No, I don't think that," the sheriff replied. "It ain't right no matter who's doing the dying."

"I can almost agree with you there," Jim said. "If given a choice, however, I'd much rather bury those folks than bury mine."

"I got no doubt about that. You've more than demonstrated it."

Jim's attempt at a friendly conversation was failing. Trading jabs with the sheriff wasn't accomplishing anything. He needed to get to the meat of it. "I'd like to ask a favor."

"Well, you're a froggy bastard, aren't you? I've made it pretty clear I don't approve of your techniques and you still got the nerve to ask me for something."

Jim handed the flyer over to the sheriff and waited patiently while he read it. When he was done the sheriff let out a low whistle.

"You're practically a Picasso of pissing people off."

"I had good intentions."

"And hence you've paved the road to Hell."

Restating the obvious accomplished nothing. Yes, Jim was an asshole. Yes, he'd screwed up in his attempt to make a stand for his people. "Will you at least hear me out?"

The sheriff refolded the flyer and handed it back to Jim. "Go ahead. Shoot," the sheriff replied. Then in a moment of mock panic he threw his arms up in surrender. “Oh, I’m sorry. Probably a bad choice of words to use ‘shoot’ in your presence."

"Are you done yet?"

"Yeah. Go ahead."

Jim launched into an explanation of all the events that had taken place recently, resulting in the gunshots the sheriff had heard. He explained Scott's plan and how they hoped it would bring an end to the bounty hunters launching attacks on the valley.

"What exactly would my role be?" the sheriff asked.

"I'd like you to be one of the team escorting me through town. It would lend an official atmosphere to the operation and cut down on the likelihood of people shooting at us."

"Wasn't that your reason for bringing me to this valley in the first place?”

“It was.”

“How did that work for you?"

Jim opened his mouth, ready to launch into an explanation of the complexities, the emotions, and all of the reasons his plan didn’t work. He didn’t have an opportunity. The sheriff cut him off with a single word.

"No."

Jim was shocked. “No? Seriously?”

"You heard me right. I'm not doing it. I lost my job, my friends, and I lost my mother. I pretty much lost my county, and who knows how many citizens I lost? I'm not putting myself at any more risk for you. When you asked me to come out here, I could see a benefit in keeping the peace. I thought it would help keep people alive. It didn’t work. Now, I don’t see any more value in helping you out. I know this sounds harsh but the longer you live, the more people are going to die."

Jim was stunned. He felt a surge of anger and let it pass before he spoke. "I’m sorry you feel that way. I hope you understand that this is kind of a turning point in our relationship. I’ve always respected you, but I’m going to have a hard time helping a man who thinks the world is better off without me in it."

The sheriff knelt back down in his garden and started working on the beans again. "I won't be your problem much longer, Jim. We'll be moving back to my family farm soon. I'm holding on to squeeze what I can out of this garden and then we're gone."

"I hate that it's come to this."

The sheriff shook his head indifferently. "It's probably for the best. Eventually this would have come to a head. One of us would end up dead and that wouldn't help anyone."

Jim searched his mind for anything else left to be said. There was nothing. They'd already talked out everything that needed talking, and anything else was just pollution. Jim had struck out. He could almost understand it, could almost see why the sheriff was done believing in him. He wondered if the rest of his tribe was reaching that same point.

Jim left without a goodbye. He trudged down the driveway, sweat trickling down his back as the sun beat down on him. It was going to be a hot day.

35

Jim's team met at his house at 2:30 AM on the 4th of July. No one had slept well, if they even slept at all. Although Jim's family tried to maintain their composure as they said goodbye, everyone had a sick feeling in the pit of their stomach about this operation. Even the people who agreed to escort Jim—Randi, Gary, Lloyd, and Hugh—knew their safety was not guaranteed. Anything could happen. They'd been through some shit but this was as dangerous an operation as any they'd undertaken. They would be walking into town, likely in front of a mob, and hoping they could hold them at bay. It was maximum vulnerability.

Jim led his team out. Familiar with the route, he rode in the lead and used night vision to see his path. The rest didn't use anything, their horses understanding to follow behind Jim's and go where he went. As they exited the farm they exchanged low greetings over the radio with the folks on sentry duty. They were being entrusted with the safety of all the loved ones until this operation was over. The way things had been going lately, there was no promise it would be any easier than the trip into town.

Those riding behind Jim could see very little of the terrain around them. There was barely a sliver of moon and it was just enough to reveal the profile of the Clinch Range against the night sky.

"I'm taking you into town by a route we've never travelled before," Jim quietly explained. There was a large cattle farm way down the valley, close to Lloyd's parents' home. The farm stretched from the valley road nearly to town.

The landowner did not live on it. It was just a place to graze cattle, cut hay, and relax. There were no farmhands or rental homes, only a decrepit old house that had once belonged to a previous owner. The two-story home had been stately and ornate in its day but was now completely uninhabitable, with boards instead of windows and doors hanging open to the elements. In the frugal manner of farmers everywhere, the owner used the house for storing square bales of hay. It was not built as a barn but it was dry and available. At times cattle found their way in and were discovered standing in the living room by a collapsed piano, gently tugging hay from a compacted bail.

Jim only knew of this place because he'd grown up with the owner's children. As a kid, he rode dirt bikes all over this property and fished in the farm pond. When he was older, he'd camped on the property while school was out for the summer. It felt like a lifetime ago and took him down that dark track of wondering what had happened to those childhood friends. Were they alive? If so, how were they faring?

It took nearly two hours for Jim's group to arrive at the dark shape of the old house. Jim turned his headlamp on. "I think we're safe to use lights now. This house is down in a hole and you can't see it from anywhere. It's in too bad a condition for anyone to live in it over the winter."

"Why?" Gary asked.

"Can't heat it," Jim replied. "Most of the windows are gone. There are definitely better options around. We can leave the horses inside there. There's probably enough hay on the floors to keep them occupied."

While the others were processing his suggestion to leave the horses *inside* the house, Jim walked his mount across the front porch and through the front door.

"This feels weird, leading a horse into a house," Randi muttered. “Where does he come up with that shit?”

"I guess it just depends on how you grew up," Lloyd said.

"You didn’t grow up with a horse in the house," Jim said, overhearing the comment. "Your mother never would've allowed that."

"Yeah, but I had a big dog,” Lloyd said defensively. “It’s practically the same thing.”

"And you’re practically the same as an idiot," Randi quipped.

They got the horses settled in the large living room and shut them in by closing the simple oak paneled doors.

All of the gear they’d removed from their horses was piled in the dusty entry foyer on its hay-strewn floor. By the light of their headlamps they strapped on their heavy gear. They had the body armor that had come from the sheriff's department, heavy plate carriers covered with an assortment of pouches. They’d added more pouches of their own and jammed every one with spare magazines until the plate carriers were difficult to lift and brutal to wear. No one knew what the day would bring, and running out of ammo could make a bad day even worse.

They also had their Go Bags since they didn't know if they might have to spend the night in town or not. The day could go in any direction. Every member of Jim’s escort team carried multiple weapons and several backups. Jim wouldn’t be carrying a Go Bag but he did wear a plate carrier. Knowing he was public enemy number one, it was reasonable that he might wear one to keep from getting shot.

He carried a weapon for now but he would have to turn it over to one of the others when they made their final walk through town. His hands would be cuffed and he was supposed to look like he was a prisoner. Because he didn't need to carry a Go Bag, Jim carried a pack with extra party favors for the day. He had loaded magazines for his team which would be stashed with the horses. Regardless of what happened in town, the abandoned house would be the rally point they would all return to. If things went sideways and they burned up all their ammo, they could collect more when they retrieved their horses.

Just because Jim would be cuffed and not carrying a rifle did not mean he was going into the situation unarmed. He had no idea what the day might hold for him. Ideally, he would put on a good show, board a chopper, and be dropped off close to home, but things tended to go the other way where he was concerned.

If the worst happened, he had his faithful Ruger LCP that he'd allowed Randi to carry on the way home from Richmond. It was stashed in an ankle holster. He carried three different knives in several places on his body and had a North American Arms .22 caliber mini revolver shoved in his pocket. He would feel vulnerable, practically naked, walking through town in such a state, but what choice did he have? Right now there was only Scott's plan.

All he had to do was remind himself Kayla had been snatched because of him and things couldn't continue as they were. She could have been killed. It could have been Ariel and she could have been killed. Fred Wimmer was an ignorant piece of trash and Jim was glad he was dead, but he was going to have to face Mrs. Wimmer at some point. He would have to tell her what happened. He would tell her what her son had done and how he paid for it.

Everyone was geared up and ready to hit the road. They were too nervous, too amped up, to just stand around. The next stage of the operation was to get as far into town as they could before the sun came up. Jim had several potential hiding spots planned out. They would just have to see which presented the best opportunity and wasn't occupied by squatters.

As with many rural towns in the middle of farming country, the terrain was simply pasture until it wasn't anymore. One minute it was cows, the next it was backyards, trampolines, and rows of small houses. For Jim's team, the type of threat they were facing changed with the terrain. The open country of pastures and the valley required a certain type of vigilance. Neighborhoods and towns required another. The concentration of people, coupled with their general state of unpreparedness, made for bad juju. They'd crossed the line where desperation went up a notch.

They entered a gate and landed on the paved road of an average American neighborhood. This particular one was composed of around thirty small ranch houses with a few Victorians scattered in closer to Main Street. The road was paved but they stayed to the shoulder to avoid scuffing gravel that might catch the attention of someone huddled in one of the dark homes. Jim kept the lead. It was his town and he was familiar with the overall layout, the shortcuts, and the narrow back streets.

They reached the hospital and gave it a wide berth, assuming the dark, hulking building was probably occupied. They passed the church Jim's parents had attended and in the distance the Confederate statue marked the crossroads of Main Street. They continued down a back alley behind the town's oldest street and were soon behind a tall row of nineteenth-century brick buildings. One was the town's old movie theater.

Jim gestured toward it. "That's where I saw *Apocalypse Now* and *Roller Boogie*. The last time we came through town I stuck my head in there and it was empty. The bottom is wrecked but the top might give us a good view of Main Street."

"I'd like to catch some sleep," Lloyd said, fighting back a yawn.

Randi looked incredulous. "You could sleep? Now?"

"I could try," Lloyd replied. "In fact, the more you talk, the sleepier I get."

Randi shot him a warning glare.

"That's not a bad idea," Hugh said. "One of you could take watch and the rest try to get some rest. This may be your last opportunity for a long time."

"I notice you didn't include yourself in that," Jim said.

"I have those charges to plant. This is the optimal time to do it. Most of the town is asleep."

"Help us clear the building first," Jim said. "You're good at this shit."

The back door to the theater, the emergency exit, stood open, barely visible in the pre-dawn gray. Hugh took the lead. Once inside the back door, each clicked on their light. They found a vast trash pile in the auditorium of what had once been the Russell Theater. It had undergone several renovations and several grand openings but none had ever taken hold. Bigger towns offered better movies and it became difficult to compete.

Someone had spray-painted a crude pornographic cartoon on the dingy screen. Elaborate cast-iron sconces hung crooked, their globes shattered. The seats had been torn from the floor and rearranged. Much of the wooden flooring was gone, likely to fuel heating fires over the long cold winter. The room had once featured a wide center seating area with an aisle to either side. Now there were no aisles, just meandering routes between the piles of trash and wreckage.

Everyone had guns raised and lights playing methodically over every inch of the room. Hugh caught Jim's attention, gestured to the projection booth, and made his way up there to check it. In the lobby they found the doors to the street wide open. Jim carefully closed them and shoved a mop through the handles to keep them shut.

Gary and Randi checked the balcony and found it empty, though there was plenty of indication that people had been there at some point. Stained mattresses, discarded rags, and old cans opened with a knife told the story.

The last place they needed to check was the point that interested them most. They entered a small door off the lobby that led to an upstairs apartment. Jim knew of its existence but wasn't sure if it was intended as an apartment for a theatre employee in the old days or if it was an attic storeroom that had been converted to an apartment. It had a low ceiling, perhaps six and a half feet, and faced out onto the street through old windows with heavily painted trim. One of them was broken out and a trail of blood revealed that the building had taken vengeance on the vandal.

A thorough search of the apartment revealed it to be empty. It had been looted and all of the furniture broken but it was generally in better shape than the theater downstairs. Maybe people hadn't noticed it, or perhaps there had been an occupant until recently.

Jim strode to the windows, the stained oak floors creaking underfoot. He looked out the window onto the street and found they had a good vantage point of Main Street. It was exactly what they'd hoped for.

Lloyd leaned back against the wall and let his feet slowly slide out from under him until he was sitting on the ground. "I'm beat."

"I'm tired too," Randi said, tugging at her armor, trying to let some heat escape. The hike into town had been strenuous.

"You guys get some rest if you want," Jim said. "There's no way I'm sleeping. I'm going to find a chair, plant it in front of this window, and keep an eye on this town."

"If you're good with it, I may stretch out and rest," Gary said.

"Go for it," said Jim.

"I'm going to plant some good cheer around town," Hugh said. "When I get back, I'll knock on the door. I'd prefer that you check to see if it's me before you start shooting."

"I'll try to remember that," Jim said.

IT TOOK Hugh nearly two hours to return. When he did, his light tap on the apartment door jolted everyone to awareness. Those who had dozed off scrambled for weapons. Jim, who'd been watching the street the entire time, reminded them that it was probably just Hugh.

While the rest of his crew came to life, Jim descended the stairs and asked who it was.

"It's the plumber, I've come to fix the sink," Hugh deadpanned.

Jim unlocked the door, let Hugh in, and locked it behind him. "You really need to work on your jokes, Hugh. You'd think hanging with Randi and Lloyd would be rubbing off on you but it hasn't. Your material is dated."

"I'll move that to the top of my list. Should I put it above saving your ass or just below?"

"Point made," Jim replied. "Did you deliver your goodies?"

"I placed a few distractions in case we need them."

"You see anything interesting out there?"

Hugh shook his head. "There are pockets of people coming to life. I could smell meat cooking and saw a few fires. I was afraid to see what was roasting on the spit."

Jim understood that. He'd seen several unappetizing things grilled in the past year. Upstairs, he retook his seat in front of the window. Lloyd was sipping from the canteen and chewing on a cold biscuit while Randi hand-rolled a cigarette.

"Hey, you got Prince Albert in a can?" Lloyd asked her.

"No," Randi said, looking at him like he was an idiot. "Hugh found this in a barn."

Lloyd cracked a grin. "If you did, I was going to say you better let him out. He might suffocate."

Hugh shook his head at Jim. "What was that you said about *my* material sucking?"

"Yeah, sorry about that. He has his moments. This ain't one of them."

Hugh had found a barn over the winter hung full of curing tobacco. He and Randi now had jars of the stuff and could smoke with abandon, using rolling papers and even toilet paper to roll their own.

Hugh pulled the radio Scott had given him from his pack and turned it on. He'd said it was unlikely Hugh would receive any transmission from the chopper until it was right on top of town. According to their plan, from the time they made contact, Jim's group would have exactly ten minutes to get in place at the football field.

The whole operation was delicately balanced. There needed to be plenty of witnesses in order for word to spread that Jim Powell was gone from their community. Also, the whole operation needed to take place before the true issuer of the bounty arrived. They decided that noon was the optimal time. That was several hours off and they would have to wait. It was something none of them were good at.

36

J*oint Base Anacostia-Bolling (JBAB)*

TRUE TO HIS WORD, Boss was able to arrange orders for Gordon's crew to fly to southwest Virginia on the 4th of July. Their destination, at least on paper, was delivery of supplies to a remote team working to bring up a hydroelectric facility in the New River Valley area of Virginia. In reality, they were to deliver Boss, a pallet of freeze-dried food, and some ammo cans to a high school football field somewhere in the vicinity of the power plant where they'd found Boss.

Boss met them at mid-morning and supervised loading of the food and ammo.

The crew was doing pre-flight checks and going over their gear. They were surprised when Boss brought in a team to install an M240D for a door gunner.

"We haven't run operations with a door gunner on American soil," Gordon protested.

Boss led him away from where the gun was being installed and the ammo loaded. "I'm concerned about folks rushing us when we land. Word will have spread that we're bringing food. The sound of your chopper is going to be like a dinner bell. There could be a riot. I don't want them overrunning us."

Gordon gave a concerned nod.

"Don't worry about it," Boss said. "I won't tell you how to fly your chopper, you don't tell me how to run my op."

When the gun was mounted, everyone climbed aboard and slipped on their headsets.

"Got coordinates for me?" Davis asked.

"Not exactly," Boss replied. "I have a list of high school football fields in the area. We'll fly over each one and watch for signal fires. That's what my flyer told them to do."

Davis and Stanley exchanged a glance, wondering what they'd agreed to.

When the door was shut, Boss removed a pouch of Krugerrands from his pocket and handed two over to each member of the crew. "I know you men have concerns. I hope this helps alleviate some of them. Just do as I say and you'll be fine."

"So where to first?" Stanley asked.

"We'll start at the most distant school and work our way back. We're going to hit Wise County first, then Dickenson County. West to East."

"Got it," Stanley said.

In seconds, they were airborne and departing the JBAB. Boss knew he was going to have some explaining to do when he got back to the base. Owen would be pissed but it would be worth it. Although this might well be his final mission, he could live with that. When he got back, if Owen didn't lock him up, he'd run his missions, plan his ops, and do what he was told. For now, this was what he *had* to do, consequences be damned.

37

"*Big Bird for Oscar. Big Bird for Oscar. Do you read me? Over."*

Hugh shot a glance at Jim then grabbed for the radio. Scott's chopper was here. "Big Bird, this is Oscar. We got you."

"Oscar, lot of traffic on the roads today. We're seeing people walking toward town in big groups. Over."

"Big Bird, that's confirmed. We're seeing the same thing."

Jim's team had already noticed more people out on the streets than they'd seen since the onset of this disaster. In a world where there'd been no public events, no football, no county fair, no block parties, and no television for a year, people were desperate. Jim expected that some of them were people with a true sense of outrage at what he had done. They came in hopes they'd see him strung from the goalpost. Others were probably just there for the spectacle. Either way, it was turning into a circus.

"Oscar, if you can confirm you're in position, we will begin flyover and jettison our cargo. Over."

"That's affirmative, Big Bird. We're in position and ready to go. We shouldn't have any trouble reaching the target on schedule."

"Then ten minutes starts now. Three, two, one, mark. Over."

Hugh pushed a button on his watch, activating a ten minute timer. He got to his feet. "Showtime, kids. Let's do this."

Everyone got to their feet and tugged on the gear they'd removed. They stretched muscles sore from the hike in and took final drinks from their water bottles. They checked their weapons and made sure spare mags were ready to go. Jim reluctantly handed his rifle over to Hugh and then turned his back, extending his hands behind him.

This was the part he'd been dreading but they had to make it look good. It had to be convincing to sell it to the locals. He needed to appear to be a prisoner pulled into town against his will. The body armor they'd acquired from the sheriff's department had come with several sets of flex cuffs and they brought some with them. Hugh strapped them closed while Jim took a deep breath and let it out slowly. He had a touch of claustrophobia and this was going to be a challenge. For as much as he hated going out into town with no weapon, going out cuffed was a serious blow. It was the most vulnerable he recalled feeling in his entire life.

Before they left, Hugh went to the old fireplace with its oak mantle and tile surround. He rubbed his hand inside the flue until he'd covered his fingers in soot. He rubbed some on Jim's face and did his best to make it look like bruising. As a final touch, he removed a ketchup pack from his pocket and dabbed the thick red sauce in a stream from his hairline to beard.

"Those are kindergarten level special-effects," Lloyd said. "You think they'll fool anyone?"

"They will if we keep them at a distance," Hugh replied. "If someone is close enough to tell it's fake we're not doing our job."

"Yeah, keep them away from me," Jim reminded everyone.

"We got you," Randi said.

When he was done, Hugh glanced at his watch. "Nine minutes."

While seeing Jim cuffed reminded everyone of the seriousness of this, Hugh's reminder of the ticking clock pushed them into action. Everyone clambered down the steps and piled up at the front entrance. Hugh yanked the broom out of the door handles, glanced out the narrow window, raised a garage door opener, and pushed the first of a row of buttons.

BOOM!

There was a loud explosion to the east.

"What was that?" Jim asked. "Don't tell me it was something historical."

"Tacky brick building," Hugh said. "Nothing important."

Hugh and Gary threw back the doors and Randi burst out, leading the way. Lloyd followed, then Jim. Hugh and Gary brought up the rear. The explosion had the desired effect. Some of the folks on the street were running in the direction of the noise while others were running away from it, afraid they were under attack. Some stood still like it was the beginning of a fireworks display and they were waiting for the good stuff.

Everyone on the street was talking excitedly about what must have happened. It took several moments before anyone noticed the banged up man under armed escort. A hand raised and pointed at him. That one raised a hand, one pointed finger, spread like wildfire. Soon there were more raised hands and the murmur of voices. People knew what this was. Someone had brought in the wanted man and was going to collect the bounty from that flyer everyone had seen or heard about.

A group of women started in their direction. They appeared to be unarmed, likely wanting to ask a question or see the arch-villain up close. Hugh figured this was enough attention for now. They needed another diversion. The garage door opener hung around his neck and he raised it, hitting a second button. A block away and on the opposite side of the street, the twelve foot light-up pig that advertised the Piggly Wiggly grocery store exploded in a shower of pink plastic pieces.

There were screams and people running now. No one had been close enough to be injured, however, it was close enough that more people were wondering if they were under attack. No one appeared to connect that there was a relationship between the prisoner being escorted through town and the explosions taking place. The explosion had the desired effect. People were running and cleared a path for them.

Building on this success, Hugh pushed a third button. There was a loud *boom* and a majestic old maple on the high school campus splintered. Immense branches sagged to the ground on all sides. The deep pop of cracking wood filled the air as the tree toppled over.

"Shaped charge?" Jim asked.

"Bored a hole in it with an auger," Hugh said.

This third explosion further cleared the path for them but it also brought a dose of the unexpected. Jim's team hadn't anticipated that there were already people filling the bleachers around the football field, waiting to see if this would be the location where the prisoner showed up. At the sound of the explosions, folks streamed from the bleachers and came around front of the high school to see what was going on. There was now a larger crowd than they'd planned for. More of a crowd than they could handle despite their weapons and stockpile of ammo.

The team halted in their tracks.

"Why are all these people here?" Lloyd asked. "It could have been any football field in the area. How did they know to come to this one?"

"Because word got around that this was where Jim lived," Gary replied. "It's the only possible answer. Word travelled that the guy in the flyer lived outside this town. All these people must be waiting to see if it's true."

In the midst of the chaos, of people running in all directions, Jim's team stood out like a sore thumb. They were anchored to the ground, heavily armed, and circled around one man. They were like the boulder in the stream and people quickly noticed. Just as it had happened before, an arm was raised, a finger pointed, and a ripple spread to the crowd.

The problem was that this crowd was directly in the path of Jim's group. This was the route they'd planned to use to get from the theater to the football field and now it was blocked. A vast lawn, perhaps one hundred and fifty yards wide, separated them from the leading edge of the crowd. They needed a plan quick. They couldn't just stand there drawing attention.

"What do I do?" Randi hissed, her voice low and urgent. She was in the lead and had no idea where to go.

"I don't see any choice," Jim said. "If we try to go around them, try to pass around the other side of the building, they'll only follow us. I say we point guns at them, fire some shots, and hope they run."

"Of course that's your plan," Randi sneered.

"Are you freaking kidding me?" Lloyd exclaimed. "That's hundreds of people. This could turn into a slaughter."

"Any more tricks up your sleeve?" Jim asked Hugh.

"Just one," he said. "Last resort."

He pointed the garage remote at the front of the beautiful brick school. The building was built in the 1930s in the Greek revival style. There were massive columns with elaborate carved corbels supporting a roof over the front entrance. Hugh pushed a button and a shaped charge at the base of each column exploded simultaneously. The columns were sheared off their bases, teetered precariously, and then toppled over. Unsupported, the massive roof structure sagged and then failed, pulling parts of the front facade with it.

Terror spread through the crowd and people were running in all directions. Some screamed as they were pulled under and trampled. There were some injuries, people hit by splinters from the wooden columns, shrapnel, or flying bricks.

"Hugh!" Gary said. "That was too close. Innocent people are getting hurt."

"You have a better idea? If that group rushed us we wouldn't be able to stop them."

"Quit debating!" Jim yelled. "There's no time for this!"

"Five minutes and seventeen seconds," Hugh said. "We're cutting this close."

Randi gestured toward the side of the building where a gap had formed in the crowd. "There's a path. Let's go *now*."

The group rushed forward, moving as a unit, as if this was an executive protection detail and Jim was the VIP. He felt like anything *but* a VIP at the moment. Without his gun he felt ineffective and useless, like he was failing to carry his weight and letting his friends down. He desperately wanted to help but was in no position to do so.

They accelerated to a jogging pace, weapons at high ready, scanning all directions. This was like nothing anyone had ever trained for. It was impossible to assess the multitude of potential threats. They were everywhere—people in all directions, some with weapons, screams and yelling as people were trying to figure out what was going on.

The explosions apparently made some people rethink the idea of sticking around for the main event. The crowd was thinning and a few were leaving town at a run. Jim's team circled around the back of the high school. No one got close to them. Before them lay the football field with its chain-link fence and goalposts. They were taken aback at the sight of it. There were cattle grazing on the muddy field, working at the overgrown grass. It made sense yet appeared very out of place. The fencing around the field captured blowing trash and debris. The fancy electronic scoreboard sat dark and was riddled with bullet holes.

"That way," Jim said, nodding to the far side of the field. "The fieldhouse."

That was part of the plan. The fieldhouse was a simple block structure built for locker rooms and gear storage. The cinderblock walls would provide some ballistic protection while they were waiting for the chopper to arrive. They had to be down to just a couple of minutes left on the timer, but they would be very long minutes.

There were over a hundred people in small clusters in the bleachers and Jim's group moved with determination, trying to be discreet, yet understanding that was impossible. They were trapped in a narrow aisle of chain-link with a four foot fence on one side of them and an eight foot tall fence on the other. There was no concealment and everyone noticed them.

Jim chanced a look at the stands and saw those accusing fingers pointing again. People understood who the cuffed man was and why he was here. Even if they didn't know his name they knew that he was *the guy*. The face on the flyer.

They reached the fieldhouse and Randi rattled the door handle. It was locked. "Shit. What do we do now?"

"Back up!" Hugh said.

He withdrew a Ruger Redhawk .44 Magnum from a shoulder holster and took aim at the lock. Two shots and he'd sheared the mechanism connecting the handle to the strike. He drew back and kicked. The door flew open and bounced off the inside wall.

Hugh holstered the Redhawk and raised his M4. He pressed the pad switch on the vertical foregrip and his weapon-mounted light flared to life. He charged in and cleared the network of musty, dark rooms. Oddly enough, it appeared that no one had been in there since the attacks. It seemed like the room was ready for the football team to come in and prepare for a new season.

Hugh snapped a white chemlight and tossed it on the floor. The ambient glow was just enough to illuminate the windowless room. When everyone was safely inside, he returned to the front door and stood watch.

"Time?" Jim barked.

"Three minutes twenty-two seconds."

"Shit," Jim said. "This is killing me."

There was a sound from the radio. Hugh pulled it out and increased the volume.

"Big Bird for Oscar, Big Bird for Oscar. I'm over your town. I can't see the field. Pop smoke," came the command of the radio.

"Roger that, Big Bird," Hugh replied. "Gary, cover me."

Hugh bolted from the door and stopped at the chest high fence. He yanked the pin from a smoke grenade and heaved it toward the center of the field. There was a pop and hiss and red smoke streamed out in a dense cloud. Not satisfied, Hugh popped another and tossed it after the first.

It took a moment, but soon smoke spread throughout the tiny football stadium. Heading back toward the fieldhouse, Hugh paused when he spotted three young men approaching from the direction of the bleachers. He didn't have time for this. He levelled his weapon at them. "Another step and I kill you!"

"We just wanted to see the terrorist," one of them said.

Something in the way Hugh looked at them convinced them he was utterly serious. If they got closer they would die. They turned and ran. Once he was certain they were gone, he returned to the shelter of the fieldhouse doorway and raised the radio to his mouth.

"Oscar for Big Bird. That's two smokes. You seeing anything?"

It was a long, concerning pause before he received a reply. *"That's affirmative, Oscar. I'm seeing red smoke to the south. We'll get some altitude for maximum visibility, dump our cargo, and see you at the fifty yard line."*

"Roger that," Hugh said. "Let's get the show on the road."

Jim had been sitting on a bench but he couldn't take it anymore. The anxiety was wearing on him. He got to his feet and started pacing the room. He probably looked like a football player from years gone by trying to psych himself up for a big game. For him, this was a big game. In fact, it was the only game and he only had one play in his playbook. If he screwed it up, there wouldn't be a next season. It would be game over.

38

"I've got radio chatter," Davis said.

"What? Locals?" Boss asked. "Amateur radio shit?"

"I don't think so. It's one of our frequencies. It's got to be chopper traffic."

"Are you kidding me? I can't imagine there's another chopper in the area."

"We've seen them before," Gordon said. "Operating out of other bases, run by other agencies. We don't completely control the air."

"Somebody just said something about landing at the fifty yard line," Davis relayed.

"As in football field?" Boss asked, looking from the pilots to Gordon.

Gordon threw his hands up in a gesture of ignorance. "No clue."

"Find them," Boss ordered.

Frustrated with his own lack of a view from the back, Boss clipped into the tether system and threw open the door, scanning the surrounding skies for a chopper.

"I've got smoke," Stanley said.

"That's the signal!" Boss said. "Whoever collected my prisoner is supposed to bring him out on the field and signal with smoke."

Davis raised his visor and squinted to the south. "Is that a parachute?"

Boss raised a pair of binoculars to his eyes and scanned. "Got it. A couple of pallets with cargo chutes." Boss scanned the area around the drifting pallets and found the chopper. "There!"

Gordon looked in the direction of the chopper. "That's another Black Hawk. Not military though."

"Get them on the horn," Boss ordered. "And close the distance."

Davis maneuvered them closer while Stanley worked the radio, trying repeatedly to hail the chopper.

"They're not answering," he said.

"Keep trying," Boss said, glaring out the door of the aircraft. He had no idea who they were but they were not about to screw up his operation. He'd waited too long and worked too hard for this.

39

"The cargo is deployed," Hugh said. "I can see the chutes. It won't be long."

"Is this where we take Jim out?" Randi asked.

Hugh nodded seriously, then turned his eyes to Jim. "Are you ready? No turning back from this next step."

"Not sure I'm ready but it's now or never."

"We escort him to the goalpost as a group and I tie him off to it. We all retreat to the sidelines and circle up back to back, wait for the chopper to drop and pick him up. Once he's safely on the chopper, we get the hell out of this town and boogie back to the horses."

"We don't stick around for our reward?" Lloyd asked, trying and failing to defuse the tension.

"If you want the reward, it's at the end of those cargo chutes. You better start running now because you're going to have some competition," Hugh said.

They could hear the rotors now, the chopper not directly over them but close. They had to move. Hugh put a hand on the back of Jim's body armor. "This is it, my friend."

Jim swallowed. "If I don't make it—"

"We're not having that conversation!" Lloyd interjected. "Let's do this!"

Hugh held his rifle at low ready, steering Jim with his left hand. Gary, Randi, and Lloyd followed him in line. They went through the gate in the chain link fence that players used to access the field, then jogged toward the goalpost.

Jim tried to make it look good, playing up his injuries, making it appear as if he'd been roughed up. Hugh jerked him around as if reminding him that he needed to be cooperative or he'd get another beating, shoved him into the goalpost, and spun him around. The post was padded so it looked worse than it was. He held Jim in position while Lloyd hooked a long zip tie through the flex cuffs and fastened it around the goalpost

"You guys be extra careful," Jim said. "I better not get home to find one of you missing."

They all made eye contact with Jim but nobody had any words left. They were too scared to speak. They ran for the sidelines as a group, their hearts pounding as they watched the helicopter move into position over the center of the field where it just hovered.

Hugh stared in anticipation. "What the hell? Why aren't they landing?"

There was no answer. No one knew. They needed to descend while the football field was empty and get the show on the road. The longer they hovered there, the more attention they attracted. Soon people would be streaming back in from town. Those who hadn't pursued the cargo spiraling down on the parachutes might wander back in their direction wanting to see how this show ended.

Hugh heard something from his radio. He pulled it out and raised into his mouth. Whatever they'd said, he'd missed it over the sound of the chopper. "Scott, what's the problem?" he shouted into the mic. "Get down here and let's get this done."

He held the radio to his ear and maxed out the volume. What he heard was like an injection of ice water into his veins.

"Big Bird to Oscar, please stand by. We have a second chopper approaching."

The transmission was followed by another. It was no one Hugh had heard on the radio up until this point. *"Civilian aircraft, identify yourself and your mission. Please pull off and leave the area immediately."*

Hugh looked around at the group and his panicked expression terrified them.

"What's going on?" Gary asked.

"There's another chopper," Hugh said. "It has to be the people who threw out the flyers. These are the people who really want Jim."

"Then tell Scott to get down here now," Randi said. "He needs to land before they get here."

Hugh raised the radio to his mouth and keyed the mic. "Oscar to Big Bird, I don't give a damn who's up there. If you don't get down here and pick up the prisoner, it's over. We need to finish this."

"Roger that," came the reply from the chopper. *"Please stand by."*

Hugh, Randi, Gary, and Lloyd crouched there on the field, back to back. Their eyes flitted between Jim, the hovering chopper, and the people in the stands. They felt exposed and anxious. They'd thought this was going like clockwork, until suddenly it wasn't.

A banging sound caught their attention, audible even over the hovering chopper.

Randi jumped. "What the hell?"

They tried to locate the source.

"The press box," Gary said, pointing at the elevated booth from which announcers called the game.

All eyes turned in that direction and they saw two men beating the glass window with chairs. There was a crack, then the glass let loose from its frame and tipped out. One of the men inside threw his chair and the weight of it carried the glass downward. It tore loose from the frame and dropped thirty feet to the concrete bleachers and shattered, fragments flying in all directions.

Jim's team watched with concern, unsure of what was going on. Was this related to the second chopper? Was this someone after the bounty? They had their answer in a moment. The four men inside stuck rifles through the opening created by the missing glass and opened fire. They were not shooting at Jim, nor at the hovering chopper. The target was Jim's team.

Divots of grass erupted near the group, accompanied by the blasts of multiple rifles echoing off the concrete bleachers.

"*RUN*!" Hugh screamed, shoving the team in opposite directions.

These men were shooting semi-automatics. The rounds kept coming. Hugh returned fire, trying to force the men down, trying to stop the barrage of bullets, but there were too many shooters. Hoping he'd bought the team a head start toward cover, he ducked and ran.

He wasn't sure where the rest of his people had gone but instinct told him to return to the fieldhouse with its cinder block walls. He tore in that direction, weaving as he went. He considered leaping the chain link, however, was uncertain if he could do it with the burden of his gear. If he got snagged on the fence, he'd hang there like a sitting duck, a stationary target that no good shooter would miss.

The shooters had anticipated his obvious plan from the direction he was fleeing. At least one of them already had the crosshairs of his rifle on that gate opening. Hugh expected that possibility because it's what he would have done. Feet away from the opening, he hit the gas and crouched, trying to make himself a smaller target as he charged through.

There was a barrage of gunfire and Hugh felt rounds impact his back. The force of the rounds knocked him off his feet and he tumbled into the weeds.

40

"What are they saying?" Boss demanded.

"The ground team is requesting the chopper land to pick up the prisoner," Stanley replied. "The chopper is hovering over the field."

"Did you order them to stand down and get the hell out of here?" Boss asked.

"I did, sir. They are not responding to my transmissions."

Boss had no idea who these people were or what they were up to but there could only be one prisoner down there right now. They had to be talking about the man his bounty had brought in. He was *his* prisoner and he would not allow anyone else to take him.

Boss took a position at the M240D and charged the weapon. He was wearing the hook attachment which assisted with operation of the charging handle but it was awkward. He hadn't operated one of the weapons since losing his hand.

"What are you doing?"

Boss whipped his head around to find Gordon standing to his right. "Excuse me?"

"I asked what the fuck are you doing?" Gordon demanded. "You can't open fire on that chopper. We don't know who's in there."

"We've asked and they haven't responded," Boss stated calmly.

"That doesn't mean we can shoot them out of the sky."

Boss stared at Gordon coldly. "This is my operation. You'd do well to not interfere with it." He proceeded to aim the M240D toward the other chopper.

Gordon stepped in. "And this is my fucking chopper!"

Then Gordon made the fatal mistake. He put a hand on Boss's shoulder and attempted to pull him away from the weapon. He did not get a warning.

Boss shot his right hand past Gordon and then withdrew it with lightning speed. The hook caught Gordon in his calf like Boss was gaffing a large fish. He screamed as Boss yanked his leg from beneath him. Boss raised the heavy tactical gauntlet and slammed it down on the screaming man's face one, twice, three times, until the yelling stopped. Boss calmly unsnapped Gordon's tether and rolled him out the door of the aircraft. Gordon bounced once off the landing gear before spiraling to the ground.

Boss shot a look at the cockpit and found two terrified pilots staring at him. "Hold steady or you're next!" he barked.

They returned their gaze to the front and did as they were asked.

Boss swung the M240D back onto the hovering chopper and hit the trigger. The chopper was around two hundred feet off the ground and broadside to Boss's weapon. His first barrage was targeted at the engine compartment. The chopper jolted, then swung erratically, smoke pouring from it.

As the chopper banked and the cockpit swung toward him, Boss pressed the trigger again and the rattle of gunfire filled the cabin. His rounds chewed up the Plexiglas and anyone sitting behind it. The pitch of the engines changed and the chopper swung again, then began a rapid, uncontrolled descent.

The school itself prevented Boss from seeing the chopper crash and burn, but the plume of rising smoke told him he'd accomplished his mission. Now he just had to get on that field while his prisoner was still there.

"Put me down on that field!" Boss demanded. When the chopper didn't immediately move, he added, "If I have to ask twice, one of you dies."

The chopper banked and headed toward the plume of black smoke. Boss gave his weapons a quick check. He switched his hook attachment for the tactical knife, smiling at the fit and function of it. If only those machinists knew the field-testing it was about to get.

In seconds they were over the field. The other chopper was canted awkwardly on the concrete bleachers, a fuel fire spreading around it. There were bodies and screaming people. When they neared the field, Boss caught the flash of rifle fire from the press box.

"There are shooters in that press box!" Davis said.

"On it!" Boss replied. "Swing me toward them!"

Davis swung the chopper broadside, positioning it so Boss could light them up with the M240D. When they were in his sights, he pressed the trigger and sent a hail of bullets into the press box. He fired until he ran dry, sending shards of glass, drywall, plywood, and roofing materials in all directions. He reloaded but saw no more movement.

"I think I got 'em," Boss said. "Take me down."

The chopper swung to drop him mid-field and Boss got his first glance of the agitated figure tied to the goalpost. He was trying his best to yank his bonds loose but was having no luck. A rare smile creased Boss's face as he recalled the King Kong movies. The prisoner reminded him of the movie's heroine tied up outside the walls as an offering to Kong. This asshole would not fare nearly as well.

41

When the figure disembarked the chopper and started running in his direction, Jim felt like a minnow on a hook being born down on by a toothy pike. He couldn't believe this whole thing had gone so badly. He had no idea how his friends had fared. They'd scattered under the gunfire from the press box and he'd lost sight of them.

Worst of all, they'd gambled on their timing, thinking they'd beat the other chopper, and they'd lost. That cost Scott his life. The inferno that was the Black Hawk stood as a testament to that, one more reminder of how badly Jim hurt the people around him. Whatever this man had in mind for him, he probably deserved, but he could not go with him. If he got on that chopper he was a dead man. If he went, it would be kicking, screaming, or unconscious.

Jim tried to pull free of his bonds. Why the hell had they insisted on making it look this good? Why did they have to really tie him to the goalpost? He tried to shift his body to reach one of the knives hidden on him but they were all out of reach.

When he couldn't get free, he searched desperately for his friends. Were any of them still alive? Couldn't one of them squeeze off a few shots and drive his pursuer away? If not, he was going to be here any minute and it was going to be the beginning of the end for Jim Powell.

And worse, perhaps for his family too. Could they survive without him? They might have to. He fought to get free but could not pull loose. The cuffs were cutting into his wrists, burning, but they would not let go.

Then Boss was before him and they stared at each other. Jim didn't recognize him from the battle at the power plant, and wasn't certain that he'd ever seen him before. He was several inches taller than Jim and probably outweighed him by sixty pounds, all of it muscle. He had a bullpup rifle around his neck and was loaded with well-worn gear. This told Jim the guy did this often. He was a professional.

Jim was scared. He was fucked.

"You send out those flyers?" Jim asked.

Boss closed to within a few feet of him, stared Jim in the eye, and nodded.

"What did I ever do to you?"

Without a word, Boss raised his severed hand, the gauntlet, and the wicked knife extending from the end of it.

Jim stared at the amputated limb and the impressive weapon that protruded from it. "You've got me mixed up with someone else," he said. "I'd remember cutting someone's hand off. I've done some shit, but pretty sure that wasn't me."

Boss lashed out, stabbing the tactical blade straight for Jim's chest. Jim squeezed his eyes shut, then the knife hit the armor plate and stopped. When he opened his eyes, Boss was glaring cruelly at him.

"I thought you were wearing armor. Just wanted to make certain. Probably a good thing for you."

Jim couldn't speak. He'd thought he was a dead man. He probably was. He needed to keep this man talking, though, delay him. He might not know that Jim had a team on the ground with him. As far as this psycho knew, the men he'd killed in the press box *were* Jim's people. He needed to play that up.

Boss raised the knife blade in front of his face and saw that the tip broke off when it impacted Jim's armor. "You broke my knife."

"Sorry," Jim croaked, his voice tense with fear. He looked toward the press box. "You killed my people."

Boss pushed a button on the gauntlet and launched the knife into the air. "Those were your people? Guess we're even. You killed my people at the plant." Boss pulled the hook attachment from a pouch on his plate carrier and inserted it into the gauntlet. "We're getting on that chopper. We're going for a ride and you're going to tell me all about that attack at the plant. You're going to tell me who the other men were. Then I'm going to find them and kill them."

Jim stared at the sharp tip of the hook. It was as terrifying and wicked a weapon as he'd even seen. He could imagine a multitude of torturous things that could be done to him with it. He hoped he died before it came to that. Then he noticed the man's rank.

"Captain..." he muttered.

Boss paused and stared at him.

"Captain...Hook," Jim said with a grin.

Boss lashed out and struck Jim in the side of the head with the gauntlet. It was a powerful blow, like being hit in the head with a bat. Stunned, Jim sagged forward against his bonds. Boss moved around behind the post, the zip tie binding Jim to the goalpost was severed, and he staggered forward.

"Run!" screamed a familiar voice.

It was Hugh and Jim obeyed. Although disoriented by the blow to the head he ran blindly in the direction of the voice. There were gunshots from ahead of him and he hoped they were aimed at his attacker. Gunshots exploded behind him, and he knew his would-be captor was returning fire in Hugh's direction. Jim felt like he was slewing to one side, that he was running in sand. It had to be the blow to his head. He fought to stay upright.

Boss closed on him and lashed out with the hook, snagging Jim's plate carrier. Jim lurched to a stop and dropped. Boss had been trying to keep his prisoner between him and the shooter, banking on whoever it was not wanting to hit his prisoner. With Jim now on the ground, there was nothing blocking him from gunfire and Boss hit the ground, laying prone behind Jim.

Jim tried to crawl away. His hands were flex-cuffed and he couldn't use them. He moved like a caterpillar, arching and pushing, arching and pushing, then he felt a sharp pain in his calf. He saw that the captain had snagged him in the leg just above his boot. He yanked and Jim screamed in pain. He felt like his calf muscle was being torn loose from the bone.

Boss slithered on top of Jim's body, wrapping a powerful arm around his neck and jerking Jim's head back. The sharp point of the bloody hook touched his neck and Jim could only imagine it tearing into him in the same way it had his leg. He wondered if that might be more merciful than what this man had in store for him. Maybe he should just get it over with.

"We're getting to our feet and we're backing toward that chopper," Boss hissed in his ear. "If they shoot, you'll take the round, so you better pray they don't."

Boss rose to his feet, using his power to tug Jim up in front of him. He pulled Jim against him. No one would be able to shoot Boss without taking the risk of hitting Jim.

"I'm not sure I can walk," Jim said.

"You'll walk or I'll drag you with this hook!"

The pain in Jim's leg was excruciating but each step cleared his head. As they backed toward the chopper, Jim wondered about his other friends. Where were Lloyd, Gary, and Randi? Were they dead? Had they been hit by the shooters from the press box? He couldn't bear the thought of it.

A figure rose from the weeds near the fieldhouse and staggered toward them. Hugh. He was bloodstained and moving slowly, but he headed for the gate and onto the field.

Boss drew his handgun and levelled it over Jim's shoulder. Before he could pull the trigger, Jim pushed his shoulder up, throwing off the shot. At the sound, Hugh dropped and flattened himself on the ground.

"Son of a bitch!" Boss hissed. He dropped the hook to Jim's

shoulder and yanked, the point tearing through shirt and into muscle.

Jim screamed.

"You try something like that again and I'll pull you the entire way like that," Boss warned.

With every yard, they moved closer to the chopper. With every yard, Jim felt hope slipping away from him. He thought of everything he'd been through to get to this point. He recalled all of his preparations and his fight to get home. He thought of what his family had gone through and what they would continue to go through without his help. His children would get older and he wouldn't be there for them. He thought of his wife growing old without him. He would never live to see his grandchildren, never live to see his country rebuilt.

Then they were at the chopper, his thoughts pushed aside by the powerful roar of the engines and the buffeting of the blades. In the distance, he could see Hugh on his feet and moving steadily toward them. The captain didn't seem to be concerned about Hugh now. He ignored him and didn't attempt to fire on him. Jim assumed it was because they were at the chopper. This was over.

Jim made one last attempt to break loose and was clouted on the head for his effort. He nearly passed out, seeing flashing lights before his eyes. His stomach heaved and he vomited on himself. Another hit like that might cave in his skull.

Boss looped his hook into Jim's web gear to hold him in place as he climbed into the chopper. Once aboard, he grabbed the drag handle on Jim's plate carrier and hefted him aboard. Jim didn't know what to do. He had no idea what lay ahead of him but it could only be pain, torture, and misery.

He resolved at that moment that, once they were airborne, he would jump out to his death. It was all he had left. He couldn't take a chance he might disclose anything under torture and put his friends at further risk. At this realization, his eyes filled with tears. It was the last thing he wanted. He was a fighter, not a quitter.

"Take us up!" Boss yelled at the pilots.

He holstered his weapon and shoved Jim against the wall. He clipped a tether onto the front of his web gear. With Jim's hands cuffed behind him there would be no way for him to unfasten it.

"I said take us up!" Boss repeated when the chopper didn't move.

He spun toward the cockpit to repeat his order and found the helmeted pilots turned in their armored seats and staring at him. He immediately noticed that their clothing was wrong. These were not his pilots, and they had weapons leveled on him.

Boss let out the bellow of an injured bull and went to draw his weapon. Just as he'd feared, in the heat of combat he defaulted to the wrong hand, the missing hand. There was no holster and no hand to grab with it.

"Move!" one of the pilots barked.

It was Randi and she was screaming at Jim, afraid to take the shot with him so close. It was too late. He wasn't thinking clearly.

Boss corrected his bobble and drew with his left hand this time. He raised his handgun toward the pair of pilots and got off a shot, striking one of the helmeted figures. There was a cry and the figure twisted away, falling in front of the seat.

Jim had a flash of fear. Randi had been hit and it was his fault. He'd failed to move, failed to give her a shot. His hesitation had gotten her shot.

Before Boss could fire on the other figure in the cockpit, Jim lashed out with a powerful kick and struck Boss in the side of the knee. He folded and fell, his shot going wild and punching a hole in the windshield of the craft. He fired again, the shot clipping the edge of a pilot's seat. The second helmeted figure crouched in front of his armored seat, trying to escape certain death.

Boss was on his side, flat on the deck of the chopper, swinging his weapon for another shot at the pilot when Jim stomped viciously on his hand. He pinned it to the steel deck and put all his weight on it, trying to break the fingers wrapped around the pistol. The gun fired a wild shot, then jammed from the pressure of Jim's boot. Boss lashed out with his hook, burying it in Jim's leg and pulling it away.

Jim cried out with pain but got some satisfaction from the fact that he'd possibly broken a finger or two on his attacker's remaining hand. Boss had some trouble regaining his grip on the weapon. He struggled as he fought to clear the jammed weapon, then swung it toward Jim. Jim met his eye and knew that Boss was making a decision. Was Jim worth the trouble or should he kill him now?

Their locked gaze was broken by a mechanical ratcheting from the doorway. They both turned and found a bloody Hugh glaring at them over the barrel of the M240D. It was unfastened from the mount and aimed directly at Boss. He had a split second to process the face on the other side of the gun. It was the man who'd cut off his hand.

Jim threw his body as hard as he could toward the back of the aircraft.

Boss managed to get out a "NOOOOOO!" as he swung his handgun on Hugh but there was not enough time. Hugh pressed the trigger. Boss's body thrashed as the rounds ate him alive. When Hugh let up on the trigger, there was only the sound of the twin engines.

Jim's ears rang and smoke filled the cabin of the chopper. "Get me out here!" he yelled, his face red, bloody saliva strung from his mouth.

Gary popped up in the cockpit and flung the pilot's helmet from his head.

"Check Randi!" Jim yelled, unable to hear his own voice anymore.

Gary crouched over Randi. Jim felt a hand on him. He jerked, startled, and turned to find Hugh in front of him, a knife in his hand. He unfastened Jim from the tether and cut the flex-cuffs loose. Jim staggered to the cockpit and found Randi sitting up, conscious. Gary was pressing a bandage to her arm.

"How is she?" he asked.

When Gary answered, Jim couldn't hear the response. He pointed at his ears. Gary gave him a thumbs up and Randi did the same.

Jim was not thinking clearly. The blow to his head, his wounds, the noise... They were missing someone. He grabbed Hugh. "Lloyd? Is he okay?"

Hugh gave him a thumbs up and led him off the chopper. On the far side of the chopper, near the visitor's side bleachers, Lloyd stood behind two blindfolded and bound men, holding them at gunpoint. Their uniforms identified them as the pilots of the chopper.

Hugh leaned close and shouted into Jim's ear. "Our ride home!"

42

They stripped Boss of his gear and left him on the football field. As the chopper climbed and banked away, Jim thought he barely looked human. He was torn and ruined, sprawled like roadkill in the middle of an overgrown high school football field.

"This was personal, Jim," Hugh said. "I'm sure of it."

"How can you be so certain?"

"I recognize that guy. He's the one I fought with on the catwalk. I cut off his hand when he was fighting with your friend."

Jim gestured at his wounds, the blood, his banged up face. "All this should have been for you?"

Hugh grinned. "I wasn't careless enough to get my picture taken."

"Then maybe it is over."

Lloyd continued to hold a gun on the pilots while the rest tended to their wounds. Hugh had taken several rounds to his rear armor plate, leaving his back one solid bruise. Splatter from the rounds had lacerated his scalp on the back of his head. He'd also taken a through-and-through wound to the shoulder.

Randi had been caught in the front plate and the ricocheting round had sliced open her bicep. The wound would require stitches and antibiotics, but was not life threatening. Jim had several deep punctures and tears to the tissue of his muscles but most concerning was the wound to his head. He'd been hit hard several times and likely had a concussion.

They guided the pilots to the field in the valley where Scott usually landed. Hugh had them turn off the engines, and they directed the pilots outside where they had them kneel in the grass.

"Please don't kill us," Stanley asked.

"We can't let you bring other people here," Jim said. "If we let you go, this will just happen again."

"No, it won't," Davis said. "We were paid to perform this mission. The captain was acting outside his orders. No one knows he was here."

"How do we know you're telling the truth?" Hugh asked.

"He killed our crew chief and threw him out of the chopper. Our chief tried to stop him from firing on the other chopper," Stanley said. "We didn't know what we were signing up for. Can I show you something? Look inside my pocket."

Hugh went to him and stuck his fingers inside the shirt pocket. He came out with the Krugerrands and held them up for everyone to see.

"See? He paid us. This wasn't a sanctioned mission. He falsified orders to get us down here and paid us for silence. We can't go back and talk about this or we'll be locked up for participating. You have to believe us," Davis said.

"I'm inclined to think we just kill them and be done with it," Randi said.

"Then we have to get rid of the chopper," Gary said. "It will draw too much attention."

"Can't you fly it out of here?" Hugh asked.

"I can fly planes, but not a chopper. Whole different animal."

Hugh looked at Jim. "What do you think?"

Jim weighed his options. As he did, he noticed his family emerging over a nearby hill and starting down into the pasture. They were followed by the other members of their tribe. If they killed them now, it would be in front of everyone. Jim had seen enough killing. He'd spilled enough blood.

"Do you have your identification?" Jim asked.

The pilots looked at each other, then Davis replied, "Yeah."

"Give them to me," Jim said.

The men dug around and handed over the military IDs to Jim.

He held them up. "I know who you are now. If you come back with people, I'll hand these over with a good story about how you all have been providing supplies to assist us in our insurgent activities. I can't be sure it will do any good, but do you want to take that chance?"

Both men shook their heads.

"You can take the gold," Stanley said.

Jim shook his head. "I don't want your gold. If the money was to buy your silence, I hope it does the same coming from me. We're going to strip the chopper of anything we can use, and take that belt-fed weapon. Then you can leave."

Their families were calling to them and waving now. Although the joy of the reunion was derailed by the extent of everyone's injuries, they had all come home and they were all alive.

In five minutes they had everything they wanted from the chopper. The pilots thanked them repeatedly, vowing their silence. Jim hoped he was doing the right thing. They backed their families away from the chopper and everyone watched as it rose into the sky.

"Let's get you home," Ellen said.

"I'm not sure I can walk," Jim said.

Pete and Charlie had remained to watch the house. They radioed back and the boys came out with a string of horses for the injured. Jim felt odd riding while his family walked but he was glad to be sitting astride the horse and not strapped dead across its back.

43

While he healed, Jim stayed put in his valley. He shaved his head and grew his beard long, altering his appearance in the easiest way. He switched to a different style of hat, changing his cap for a wide-brimmed felt hat from Lloyd's collection. He worked the land and focused his efforts on the crops. With his wife, they grew, harvested, and preserved.

The residents continued to man observation posts throughout the valley but there were no more incursions. No one ventured into town to monitor the rumor mill but the valley folks assumed the ruse had worked. People thought Jim Powell was gone. Hopefully that meant they'd get their power back soon. The big bad man had been sacrificed on the altar.

Jim thought about mending fences with the Wimmer family, ultimately deciding to avoid them. He didn't want them knowing he was alive. He stuck to his part of the valley and did not cross paths with them. Everyone in his tribe knew to do the same. They needed the Wimmers thinking he was dead. No one wanted to go back to having to watch their backs all the time.

Jim worked every day on pushing the dark thoughts from his mind. He spent time with his children and did the things they used to do. They fished and played games. He read books with Ariel, trapped with Pete and Charlie. As his healing muscles allowed, he split firewood and thought. He stared off at Beartown Mountain in the distance.

When the calf muscle healed and he was able to walk better, he was going to try to get up there and see if he could find that cave where the Civil War deserters had hidden out. Things were calm now but it would be naïve to assume they'd stay that way. He needed that next step in his planning. The final option. The scorched earth plan. Besides, backpacking trips like that used to be important to him. He could take Pete and Charlie with him.

He tried to sit on the porch with his wife every day and reconnect. She needed to know she hadn't lost her husband entirely to the violence and darkness. Sitting there made him think of wine. It would be his winter project to make some from fruit harvested in the valley. In the meantime, they made do with a bottle of blackberry moonshine Lloyd had parted with. He made a great show of crying fake tears as Jim walked away with it. At least Jim assumed they were fake tears.

On a warm July evening, he sat on the porch swing with his wife and had a glass of the dark burgundy liquor. There was a mild breeze and they stared out at the tall corn waving in the garden.

"I'm sorry for what I've become," Jim said. "I know I've been distant. With the internet down, I guess you're stuck with me. There are no more dating websites."

"You've been what you had to be," Ellen said. "It's difficult sometimes but I don't blame you. I blame the world."

"I'll try to do better."

Jim knew it was all he could do. Society brushed a thin veneer over people but it wasn't real. You combed your hair, put on nice clothes, and behaved yourself to remain gainfully employed. You drove the speed limit and tried not to kill the people who pissed you off. You bit your tongue every day to keep from saying all the things you wanted to say. You got by.

The thing about veneer was that sometimes it chipped off, and when it did, you didn't always recognize what was beneath it. The people around you all thought the same thing, trying to figure out what happened to the nice, normal, sane person they used to know. Hard times could scrape you raw, like a glacier bulldozing the Earth flat. You couldn't plan for what might be revealed in that raw, pink wound.

Jim had lost his veneer and was adapting to that self he found beneath it. He only hoped the world could adapt with him.

BONUS CONTENT

Please enjoy this sample chapter from *The Mad Mick*, the first book in The Mad Mick Series

MEET THE MAD MICK

Conor Maguire felt the approach of colder weather in the morning air. He wore short sleeves but caught a slight chill on his front porch until the sunlight hit him and warmed his skin. He sipped coffee from a large mug, his favorite, embossed with *Coffee Makes Me Poop*. It had been a Father's Day present from his daughter Barb, who really knew how to pick a gift.

There had been no frost yet, but that would come soon. The previous night had probably gone as low as the upper forties, but if the recent weather pattern held they should see upper sixties to lower seventies by the end of the day. It kind of sucked to not have a goofy weatherman updating them each evening on what to expect. It sucked not having an app on his phone that would allow him to see a current weather radar. All that technology had disappeared with the nationwide collapse.

Goats and hair sheep wandered the fenced compound nibbling at clusters of grass poking through crumbling fissures in the asphalt, dry leaves crackling beneath their hooves. Chickens trailed the goats, searching for bugs, worms, or anything unfamiliar to eat. Crows cawed in the distance, making their plans for the day. Conor dreaded the winter. He dreaded the cold and the inevitable discomfort winter brought. He dreaded the misery and suffering. Not so much for himself, as he was well-provisioned and had wood heat, but studies both public and private had shown that the first winter with no power would result in a massive loss of life.

As a statistic, those lives meant little to him. He was a solitary person. But when you zoomed in on them, those lives were neighbors, they were kids he saw playing in the yards of homes he used to drive by; and elderly folks who waved to him from the porches of humble houses with white aluminum siding and cast iron eagles over the garage door. When spring came, when the crocuses pushed through the cool, damp earth, the world would be a changed place. Conor could not help but be very concerned about what stood between the world he looked at now and that future world he could not even imagine. Between those two bookends lay volumes of death, sickness, suffering, and unthinkable pain.

Conor's friends called him "the Mad Mick," and if you knew him long enough you would understand why. He walked to the beat of his own deranged and drunken drummer. He had his own code of morality with zero fucks given as to what others thought of it. He lived with his daughter Barb in what he referred to as a *homey cottage* on top of a mountain in Jewell Ridge, Virginia. His cottage had once been the headquarters of a now-defunct coal company. It was a massive, sprawling facility where there had once been both underground and longwall mines. Numerous buildings scattered around the property held repair shops and offices.

When Conor first looked at the property he thought it was absolutely ridiculous that a man might be so fortunate as to live there. It reminded him of the lair of some evil genius in an old James Bond movie. It was surrounded by an eight-foot high chain-link fence and topped with barbed wire. There was a helipad and more space than he could ever use. There was even an elevator that would take him to an underground shop the coal company had used to repair their mining equipment.

The ridiculous part was that the facility, which had cost the coal company millions of dollars to build out, was selling for just a fraction of that because it was in such a remote location no one wanted it. In the end Conor came to own the facility and it did not even cost him a penny. His grateful employer had purchased the property for him. It was not an entirely charitable gesture, though. Conor was a very specialized type of contractor and his employer would do nearly anything to keep him at their beck and call.

In an effort to make the place more like a home, Conor had taken one of the steel-skinned office buildings and built a long wooden porch on it, then added a wooden screen door in front of the heavy steel door. Going in and out now produced a satisfying *thwack* as the wooden door smacked shut.

Conor placed his coffee cup on a table made from an old cable spool and sat in a creaking wicker chair. Barb backed out the door with two plates.

"I hope you've been to the fecking Bojangles," Conor said. "I could use a biscuit and a big honking cup of sweet tea."

Barb frowned at him. "You're an Irishman, born in the old country no less, and you call that syrupy crap *tea*?"

"Bo knows biscuits. Bo knows sweet tea."

"Bo is why you had to take to wearing sweatpants all the time too," Barb said. "You couldn't squeeze that big old biscuit of yours into a pair of jeans anymore." She handed her dad a plate of onions and canned ham scrambled into a couple of fresh eggs.

Conor frowned at the insinuation but the frown turned to a smile as his eyes took in the sprinkling of goat cheese that topped off the breakfast. "Damn, that smells delicious."

"Barb knows eggs," his daughter quipped.

"Barb *does* know eggs," Conor agreed, shoveling a forkful into his mouth.

Conor was born in Ireland and came to the U.S. with his mom as a young man. Back in Ireland, the family business was bomb-making and the family business led to a lot of family enemies, especially among the police and the military. After his father and grandfather were arrested in *the troubles*, Conor's mom decided that changing countries might be the only way to keep what was left of her family alive. She didn't realize Conor had already learned the rudiments of the trade while watching the men of his family build bombs. Assuming Conor would one day be engaged to carry on the fight, the men of the family maintained a running narrative, explaining each detail of what they were doing. Conor learned later, in a dramatic and deadly fashion, that he was able to retain a surprising amount of those early childhood lessons.

He and his mother settled first in Boston, then in North Carolina where Conor attended school. In high school, Conor chose vocational school and went on to a technical school after graduation. He loved working with his hands to create precise mechanisms from raw materials, which led him to becoming a skilled machinist and fabricator.

Conor was well-behaved for most of his life, flying under the radar and avoiding any legal entanglements. Then he was married, and the highest and lowest points of his life quickly showed up at his doorstep. He and his wife had a baby girl. A year later a drunk driver killed his wife and nearly killed Barb too. Something snapped in Conor and the affable Irishman became weaponized. He combined his childhood bomb-making lessons with the machinist skills he'd obtained in technical school and sought vengeance.

How could he not? Justice had not been served. There was also something deep within Conor that told him you didn't just accept such things. You continued the fight. There was the law of books and there was the law of man. The law of man required Conor seek true justice for his dead wife.

When the drunk driver was released from jail in what the Mad Mick felt was a laughably short amount of time, the reformed drunk was given special court permission to drive to work. Conor took matters into his own hands. He obtained a duplicate of the headrest in the man's truck from a junkyard and built a bomb inside it. While the man was at his job, Conor switched out the headrest. A proximity switch in the bomb was triggered by a transmitter hidden along his route home. One moment he was singing along to Journey on the radio and enjoying his new freedom. The next, his head was vaporized to an aerosol mist by the exploding headrest.

No one was able to pin the death on Conor despite a lack of other suspects. He had a rock-solid alibi. The proximity trigger detonated the bomb because the man drove within its range. No manual detonation was required on Conor's part at all. After putting everything in place, Conor took his young daughter to the mall to get a few items. Dozens of security cameras picked up the widower and his daughter.

Oddly enough, his handiwork resulted in a job offer from an alphabet agency within the United States government. A team of men who made their living doing such things were impressed with Conor's technique. They recognized him as one of their own and wanted to give him a position among their very unique department. He would work as a contractor, he would be well paid, and he would be provided with a shop in which do to his work. There were no papers to sign but it was made quite clear that any discussion of his work with civilians would result in his death.

Conor knew a good opportunity when he saw it. He accepted the offer and, as he proved his worth, his employer decided it was worthwhile to set Conor up in his deep-cover facility in Jewell Ridge, Virginia. On the surface, Conor presented himself to the local community as a semi-retired machinist who'd moved to the mountains to get away from the city. Mostly as a hobby and to help establish his cover, he took in some machining and fabrication work from the local coal and natural gas industry. Behind that façade, Conor was *the guy* that certain agencies and contractors came to for explosives and unique custom weapons for specialized operations.

Over his career, Conor created pool cue rifles that were accurate to 250 yards with a 6.5 Creedmoor cartridge. A rifle scope was integrated into a second pool cue and the matched set was used for a wet work operation in Houston that never made any newspapers. He once made a music stand for a clarinetist turned assassin that transformed into a combat tomahawk. It was used for an especially brutal assassination in Eastern Europe.

He turned automotive airbags into shrapnel-filled claymore

mines that replaced standard air bags in most vehicles and could be triggered remotely or by a blow to the front bumper. For another job, he'd created a pickup truck that appeared to have standard dual exhausts from the rear. In reality, one exhaust pipe was normal while the other was a rear-facing 40mm grenade launcher.

He routinely created untraceable firearms, suppressors, and unique explosive devices. His explosives contained components sourced from around the world which made it difficult to ascertain the bomber's country of origin. It gave his employer plausible deniability. He had resources in every shadowy crevice of the world and they were always good to send Conor the odd bit of wire, circuitry, and foreign fasteners to include in his handiwork.

Like many bomb makers, Conor was fastidious in his level of organization and preparation. That carried over to his home life. His compound on the mountain had backup solar, available spring water, and food enough to last him for years. Even with those food stores, he maintained a little livestock just to freshen up the stew pot.

"What's on the agenda today, Barb?" he asked. "What do you have planned for yourself?"

"There's a girl at the bottom of the mountain, JoAnn, who I've become halfway acquainted with. It's just her and her dad. Kind of like us. I ran into her yesterday and she said she was going to be doing some late-season canning so I offered to help. She's canning things I've never done before, like French fries."

"Canned French fries. That sounds bloody magical," Conor said. "Plus I'm sure it would be nice to get some girl time, huh?"

Barb smiled back at her dad, a wee drop of mischievous venom in the expression, and yet another demonstration she'd been aptly named. "Actually, it would just be nice to be around somebody who's not telling the same old tired jokes and boring stories all day long. Somebody who doesn't think they're God's gift to humor and storytelling."

Conor faked offense. "I always thought you liked my stories. I thought they were part of our familial bonding. Those stories are your heritage."

"You need new stories, Dad. I don't know if you've noticed or not but, when you tell a story, I'm usually sitting there beside you mouthing the words along with you. I know exactly how they all go. But I guess sitting there making fun of you also counts as bonding."

Conor looked smugly at his daughter. "I had a new story for you when I went over to Damascus and helped that girl Grace and her family. You were on the edge of your seat."

"Yes, but as much as I'm tired of the old stories I don't want you putting yourself at risk just to bring home new material. Besides, you're getting too long in the tooth for those kinds of adventures. You're not an operator anymore. Your days would be better spent puttering around the garden in a cardigan, half-drunk on Guinness, cursing at the beetles and weeds."

"Don't be so quick to put your old dad out to pasture, Barb. I've got plenty of good years left in me. And plenty of good fights."

Barb raised her cup of tea toward him in a conciliatory toast. "Well, here's to hoping those fights die on the vine. I hope you never have to use them."

"I'll toast to that," Conor said, raising his coffee mug.

"So what's on *your* agenda today, dear father?"

"I spoke to a man the other day who lives down in the valley near the Buchanan County line. Since the shit hit the fan he's been taking in horses people could no longer feed. Now he's got more than he wants to take care of over the winter. I told him I might be willing to trade for a few so I'm going to go look at them."

"Ah, a horse would be nice. It could take me an hour to walk to JoAnn's house this morning. It would be half of that on a horse and a lot less effort."

"It will damn sure be easier to carry a load on a horse than on a bicycle," Conor added.

"So you've given up on your bicycles, have you? I'm shocked. I thought you were training for the Tour de Bojangles, twenty-one days of bicycles and biscuits?"

Conor shook his head. "I've not given up on bicycles but my tender arse has. It's become *delicate* in my golden years."

Barb smiled at that. Despite her banter with her father, she loved him dearly. It was just the two of them in the world and that was fine with her. One day she may have room for a husband and children but she was in no hurry. She would try to wait the world out and see if things got back to normal one day.

"An hour is still a long walk," Conor said. "Take your full load-out."

Barb rolled her eyes. "You know I don't go out without my gear."

"It doesn't hurt to remind you. We check and we double check. That's what we do and that's how we stay alive. Not just your rifle and your pistol, but your go bag and your radio."

She gave her dad a thumbs up. "Got it, Dad."

"You better," he warned. "Some things are joking and bullshit. This is not. This is life and death. Every single day."

"Roger that."

"Plates too," he insisted. "Plate carrier and armor plates."

Barb groaned. "It's too hot, and it's heavy."

Conor gave a conciliatory smile. "Well, if you're too weak to carry the weight..."

"I'll take them," Barb said, getting up from her seat. "You're driving me nuts with this." She went into the house to get her gear together. She had no intention of carrying those heavy plates. She would have to find a way to slip out without him seeing her.

This story continues in
The Mad Mick by Franklin Horton
Available on Amazon

Printed in Great Britain
by Amazon